George W. Samson

The Atonement Viewed as Assumed Divine Responsibility

traced as the fact attested in divine revelation - shown to be the truth uniting

Christian theories; and recognized as the grace realized in human experience

George W. Samson

The Atonement Viewed as Assumed Divine Responsibility
traced as the fact attested in divine revelation - shown to be the truth uniting Christian theories; and recognized as the grace realized in human experience

ISBN/EAN: 9783337368524

Printed in Europe, USA, Canada, Australia, Japan

Cover: Foto ©Andreas Hilbeck / pixelio.de

More available books at **www.hansebooks.com**

THE

ATONEMENT

VIEWED AS

ASSUMED DIVINE RESPONSIBILITY;

TRACED AS

THE FACT ATTESTED IN DIVINE REVELATION;

SHOWN TO BE

THE TRUTH UNITING CHRISTIAN THEORIES;

AND RECOGNIZED AS

THE GRACE REALIZED IN HUMAN EXPERIENCE.

BY

G. W. SAMSON,

FORMERLY OF WASHINGTON, D. C.; NOW OF NEW YORK.

———————

PHILADELPHIA:

J. B. LIPPINCOTT & CO.

1878.

The Writer to his Readers.

The idea of the central Gospel truth presented in this pamphlet, was conceived by the writer, in the study of his father, when, as his reader, from eight to thirteen years of age, the works of Fuller, Gill and Emmons, various sermons on the atonement, and the German translations issued at Andover, were read and discussed, and its realization in personal conversion, at twelve years of age, left an impression never eradicated. The suggestion, in college, of Prof. Hacket, that the Greek and Latin classics and the Hebrew and Greek Scriptures should be mastered without note, and the formation of a Club in the Theological Seminary to read the leading Calvinistic and Arminian authors in Latin, as well as the Greek and Latin notes in Giesoler's Church History, formed habits of Scriptural and of analytic study, which have matured throughout a long series of years. The suggestion of Dr. Wayland, in his College Bible Class ; life at Washington, D. C., for nearly thirty years, when men like Macon and Adams "read little but the Bible ;" the criticism, in Washington, D. C., of hearers like Amos Kendall, Wm. L. Marcy, Sam. Houston, Duff Green and Henry Dodge, and many others of kindred mind, most of whom, in old age, embraced and professed faith in Christ's atonement ; these influences gave clearness and force to the view which centres in Paul's epistle to the Romans. The study of the history of opinions elaborated by theologians and jurists, pursued for many years as instructor of Theological and Law Students, has confirmed the first impressions of earlier days, by enlarging the field of survey. Above all, the effort at comparison of religious experience, as developed in redeemed men of different ages and nations, embodied in Bible, Ecclesiastical and Missionary records, has given the force of demonstration to what is the manifest teaching of the Divine Spirit in His word and work.

THE ATONEMENT.

THE WORD ATONEMENT.

The English word "atonement" is frequent in the Old Testament; its import appearing in the Hebrew verb *kaphar*, to "cover," whose synonyms are found in leading Asiatic and European languages. The religious signification of this word, employed about one hundred and forty times by the inspired Hebrew writers from Moses to Daniel, is indicated by the English terms "pacify, reconcile, purge," and the like; and it always indicates man's effort to appease the Divine Being. The English word "atonement" is found only once in the New Testament, and there as the translation of the Greek *katallage*, a term only four times employed, and elsewhere rendered "reconciliation." The English translators seem to have selected the term "atone," because its literal, or etymological signification, " to set *at one*," involves the special moral idea implied in the technical or theological employ made of the word "atonement."

The Idea of Atonement.

The theological use of the word atonement, has grown out of a human conviction so universal that no people on earth, however obscure or rude, has yet been found, into whose language the New Testament could not be translated; a fact which demonstrates that the idea of atonement, and the words expressive of that idea, are as much a part of human instinct as the words for water and bread.

Every human being has a personal consciousness of failure in keeping the law of his being, and of fulfilling the rule of duty to his fellow-beings. Yet more, every human being has a conviction of coming short in positive love to his Creator, whose constant, sacrificing and forbearing fidelity as a Father deserves to be reciprocated by His children. This universal sense of personal unworthiness impresses the necessity of seeking some way to make expiation for the ill-desert, and to propitiate the aggrieved Deity. To effect this,

two resorts have been suggested : sacrifices in
expiation and offerings for propitiation ; both
of which, though moral in design, have been
expressed by material signs; while at the
same time these material substitutes have
tended to become the substance, instead of
the shadow, in supplying the moral need
thereby signified.

Sacrifices for expiation have assumed two
characters: penance, or the infliction of suffering as the penalty of guilt, on the person
of the guilty ; but, more universally, the infliction of death on an innocent victim,
animal or human, as a substitute for the penalty due to the guilty. Offerings for propitiation, too, have been of two kinds : gifts of
property, the material result of personal
effort, directly presented to the Divine Being ;
and services of devotion, the moral effort to
prove worthy in personal spirit and conduct,
and especially to do good to beings who may
be aided in their need. The first class of
both sacrifices and offerings have been in all
ages unsatisfactory, since they fall below the
moral idea of atonement; though as *signs* of
that idea, they have been naturally suggested.
The second class of both sacrifices and offerings, are the commemorative signs and ser-

8 THE ATONEMENT.

vices for God and man, universally recognized as meeting man's moral want; and
they enter therefore as fundamental into
the revealed and perfect atonement provided
through Jesus Christ, the Son of God.

FIGURATIVE TERMS AS MATERIAL ILLUS-
TRATIONS OF THE ATONEMENT.

The idea presented in the word "atonement," is in the New Testament further indicated by no less than seven select Greek
words. There is, first, the word *airo* and its
compounds, expressive of the simple act of
taking away; as in the announcement, "Be-
hold, the Lamb of God that taketh away the
sin of the world." There is, second, the
noun *paresis*, "over-looking," and *aphesis*,
"remission," which are figures drawn from
mercantile and judicial waiving or cancelling
an obligation. There is, third, the verb
agorazo, to purchase, and its compounds;
which add to the former the idea of a price
paid for the cancelling. There is, fourth, the
noun *lutron*, and its compound *antilutron*,
a "ransom," as an offset, calling special
attention to a sacrifice made by a mediating
and responsible party. There is, fifth, the
verb *aleipho*, "to blot out," indicating the

erasing of the record, after payment made, or satisfaction furnished. There is, sixth, the verb *katharizo*, "to purge," and its compound *ekkatharizo*, "to purge away," implying the moral clearing of the party implicated, in addition to the erasing of a record. There is, *seventh*, the masculine or concrete noun *ilasmos*, "propitiation," and its neuter or impersonal derivative *ilasterion*, "propitiatory sacrifice," giving the completer idea of a personal assumption by the ransomer or redeemer of the moral as well as material obligation.

THE SPECIAL MORAL TERM DESIGNATING THE ATONEMENT.

There is finally the leading and essential term; whose root *dike*, is rendered "judgment," whose adjective *dikaios*, is rendered "righteous," whose verb *dikaioō*, is rendered "justify," whose participial or concrete noun *dikaiōn*, is rendered "justifier," and whose three abstract nouns *dikaioma*, *dikaiosis* and *dikaiosyne*, are all rendered "righteousness" because the English language has no special words to distinguish the three ideas of the Greek terms. The meaning of these terms may be illustrated in the English root "act," adjective "active," verb "actuate," the con-

crete noun "actor," and the three abstract
nouns "action, activity and activeness." The
verb *dikaioō*, it should be noted, always means
"to make" or "cause to be righteous;" as
"actuate" means to "make" or "cause to be
active:" while the three abstract nouns imply
respectively; first, one completed act; second,
the spirit that is always repeating the act; and
the third, the fixed personal character thus
established. The special force of the first and
second of these two Greek nouns *dikaioma*
and *dikaiosis*, is illustrated in the two English
words, transferred in form from the Greek,
"poem" and "poesy;" the first of which is
one completed work of the poet, while the
second is his ever-working spirit. The
special import of the third term *dikaiosyne*,
is illustrated in the English word, transferred
from the Greek, *eleemosynary*; the Greek
term *eleemosyne*, rendered "alms" in the
New Testament, really indicating the *character* of the act, as does the English word now
in use.

Force of Moral Terms in Translations
of the Hebrew and Greek Scriptures.

In all translations it is found that the
essential idea in words can only be approx-

imately presented in the words of another language; because time and circumstances modify the meaning attached to words. This is especially to be noted in translations of the word just considered; which Christ and his apostles employed as presenting the essential idea in Atonement.

The words right and justice, righteous and just, are quite distinct as indications of moral character; the first being comprehensive, the other partial in meaning. Thus, before a human tribunal, men can have but three different characters: first, the good or innocent; second, the evil or guilty; and third, the evil for whose guilt there are mitigating circumstances, and who may be reclaimed to good. For the first, a *good* judge is requisite, for the second, a *just* judge, and for the third, a *merciful* judge. Each of these attributes in the judge is partial, and is perfect only when he has the class corresponding to his excellence to deal with. On the other hand, right, righteous and righteousness, are comprehensive attributes of character; for if a magistrate is righteous, always doing right, he is fitted to judge righteously alike the innocent, the guilty, and those who may be reclaimed. The glory of the divine character, as men without revelation have inferred, and as revelation declares, is that he is "righteous," answering fully the soul's earnest inquiry: "Shall not the Judge of all the earth *do right?*"

It is important to note that the old Greek word for natural right, *themis,* was early lost to use, and was only personified as a deity of the past; after Homer's day, the very idea of right, taught by man's conscience, being merged in the word just, *dikaios,* whose meaning was determined by human statutes; and this is the only word that could be used by the New Testament writers. So when the Latin translation, substantially that of Jerome, in the fifth century, was made, the the word "*fas,*" natural right, had been lost in *jus,* the term embodied, with its various derivatives, in Roman law; and hence, only this term could appear in the Latin translation of the New Testament Scriptures. The same may be said of the French language; whose word "*droit,*" though revived in modern times, was at the time when the Abbé de Sacy made his French translation of the New Testament, lost in the word "justice."

On the other hand, the German language,

at the time of Luther's translation, retained
the term *recht*, corresponding to the English
right, almost to the exclusion of the Latin
and law terms just and justice. In Luther's
translation we have, from the root *recht*, the
adjective *gerecht*, righteous, and the noun
Gerechtigkeit, for righteousness.

Here these peculiarities of the German
translation, as compared with the English,
are to be noted. *First*, the word *dikaiosyne*,
as used by Christ and Paul, is always rendered " righteousness " by the English translators; as it is rendered *Gerechtigkeit* in the
German. *Second*, the more general term
dikaioma, used ten times in the New Testament, is rendered in both the English and
German translations by terms of moral import, "judgment" and "righteousness," with
application to the Gospel system, (Rom. 1:
23; 2:26; 5:16, 18; 8:4; Rev. 15:4; 19:
8,) and by the English word "ordinances,"
and kindred German terms, when applied to
the Mosaic rites which were symbols of those
moral ideas. (Luke, 1:6; Heb. 9:1, 10.)
Third, the special term, *dikaiosis*, only twice
used, (Rom. 4:25; 5:18,) is rendered in
English by the special word "justification;"
by which English word, only three times used,

the word *dikaioma* (Rom. 5: 16,) is also once translated; while in the German translation of *dikaiosis* the general term *Gerechtigkeit* is used in the more general statement, (Rom. 4: 25,) and the specific term *Rechtfertigung*, equivalent to the English word "justification," in the special statement, (Rom. 5: 18).

TERMS BORROWED FROM COMMEMORATIVE RITES, AND FROM MORAL RELATIONS.

Among the Jews and Greeks alike, sacrifices, as commemorative rites illustrative of the atonement, were practiced. These began with Abel, in the first human family, and no nation has been found where tradition, or continued observance, does not record their existence. Hence both the Old and New Testaments employ, as a language universally recognized, terms borrowed from these sacrifices.

It is worthy of note, that the earliest ages present the simplest rites, and the most purely moral conceptions relating to atonement; a fact justifying the hint of Dr. Wm. R. Williams, that theories of comparative religion must begin with an instructed as well as a simple faith, just as true philosophy of human development begins with the

mature man Adam. To the first human
family, the truth in the forbidden tree and
in sacrifices must have been alike suggested
by direct revelation; for who can conceive
that Abel would not have regarded his sin
as aggravated, instead of expiated, by the
slaughter of an innocent lamb, unless it had
been divinely required? In the patriarchal
history, the moral expression of faith in
atonement is prominent; in the Mosaic civil
legislation, the moral element appears, though
less clearly; and in the age of David and of
the Prophets, the moral and ritual terms are
constantly blended. Again, in the Gospel
narratives, Matthew writing for Jews,
abounds in ritual illustrations used by Christ;
while the Sermon on the Mount is purely
moral. Mark, on the other hand, writing for
Romans, Luke for Greeks, and John in his
supplementary memoirs, successively use
more and more moral terms. Finally Paul,
the Apostle to the Gentiles, studs even his
epistle to the Hebrews with terms drawn
from the higher spiritual conception of men
like Abel, Enoch, Noah and Abraham; and
in his epistle to the Romans, he draws out
a logical statement of surpassing moral
grandeur.

TERMS FROM DOMESTIC AND CIVIL RELATIONS.

The terms drawn from moral relations illustrate the nature of atonement by representing the Divine Creator, now as a Monarch, and now as a Father. Both these relations, however, vary in the conceptions of different ages and nations. Rulers are despotic in Asia and Rome; but government is moral, rather than arbitrary, in the early Hebrew and the later Greek history. So the parental relation, in the patriarchal ages, changed gradually from a paternal to a regal authority; the father having the power to exact life-long obedience, to prefer any one son to his brothers, and even to make wife, children and servants slaves for life, or to condemn them to death ; though a very different ideal is inwrought into the New Testament statements, which has given gradually new conceptions of the relations of the " everlasting Father " to his earthly children.

As in all ages and nations, poets have gone back to the age of patriarchal government, the rule of a father over his children as the ideal of perfect government, and, as in the moral advance of society family rule has become so purely moral that the ideas of

punishment and of chastisement have seemed
relics of a past age, so the representations
of the relations of God as a Sovereign and a
Father are so framed in the Old and New
Testament as to meet the moral convictions
of any and of every age, whether more or less
advanced in moral refinement.

The true character of the Atonement made
by Christ will be utterly misconceived, if the
lower, instead of the higher moral conceptions, which struggled for human expression
on the tongue of Jesus and the pen of Paul,
be allowed to prevail in the Christian reader's
mind.

THE NECESSITY FOR GROUPING AND HAR-
MONIZING THE TERMS EXPRESSIVE
OF ATONEMENT.

These words thus viewed, each and all, presenting only partial and approximate conceptions of an infinite and divine reality, as
inadequate as the words " eye " and " ear " in
expressing the idea of the Divine Omniscience,
require from a three-fold necessity, comparison
and classification. *First*, spiritual truth is
reached, as is natural truth, only by scientific
systematizing of observed particulars. *Second*,
the terms expressive of spiritual truth, bor-

rowed from the field of material truth, are
to be interpreted as figures, as well as
scanned in their literal meaning. *Third,* the
figures drawn from material truth, to rep-
resent human spiritual conceptions, are to be
made approximate aids to the mind in taking
in the incomprehensible Divine realities to
which, in the inspired New Testament, they
are applied. These three facts make theological science at once the most difficult and
the most exalted of sciences. Our present
effort is to make this application to the
special conception of the Atonement.

The Nature and Method of Theo-logical Science.

All science must begin with a *theory.* As
Newton supposed, from comparing all observations then made by astronomers, the
existence of a principle which harmonized
all the recorded phenomena of the solar
system, so in every age since Christ came,
his statements, and those of his apostles, as
to his mission in his life and death, have
been classified according to principles suggested as theories by leading Christian
scholars, who have sought to harmonize the
doctrine of the atonement with other depart-

ments of spiritual truth. The different theories thus suggested, indicate the necessity of carefully considering, before the attempt at classification, the rules which must guide inquiry and comparison in theological, as well as in other sciences.

First, all known and observed facts must be included in the survey. This is recognized in material or natural science; and hence the long delay and protracted study required in reaching true theories of astronomy, of chemistry and of geology. Any comprehensive theory of the atonement must take into account all the conceptions of men, without revelation; for since a revelation must be given to man in human language, it is manifest that not only the ideas to be established by revelation, but even the words expressive of those ideas, must be already familiar to mankind before they can be used in a revelation. It is an interesting fact, that, while the Natural History of Aristotle, as Agassiz affirmed, cannot be translated into any modern language until discoveries made by him are rediscovered, there has not yet been found a language of mankind, however rude, into which the New Testament could not be translated. The

fact that one of the Twelve Books of the
Laws of Menu the last of the Indian Vedas,
written before Moses' day, is entitled "Expiation,"—the fact that the Budhist system,
which pervades China and all Eastern Asia,
and which was first promulgated about a
century before Christ's day, makes the image
Gaudama, the Divine Being incarnate, to embody the promise of Eden that while the serpent should bruise the Redeemer's heel, the
Redeemer was to bruise his head,—the fact
that in every tribe of mankind, sacrifices,
and ideas of their efficacy, prepare the mind
for the reception of the Gospel statements as
to the sacrifice of Christ,—these facts suf-
ficiently indicate that any consistent and
comprehensive theory of the Atonement
must recognize all these antecedent convictions of the human mind. Our age, taught
by Mission experience, is perhaps prepared
to grasp and group all the terms of Revelation.

Again, since the spiritual truth in the revelations of the Old and New Testament is
embodied in terms necessarily drawn from
human relations, as approximate expressions
of Divine relations, just principles of Scripture interpretation are next called for. In

the first great Christian School, at Alexandria in the second century, this necessity was developed; though Christ had anticipated it when he said, "The words that I speak unto you, they are spirit and they are life." Led by the right conception, that the language of revelation is necessarily figurative, Origen gave currency to a system of "allegorical" interpretation, which has contended with the system of "historical" interpretation down to this day; an interpretation especially mystifying in the study of Christ's redeeming mission. The nice line between the historical and the allegorical, or the literal and the figurative, is seen in the first narratives of Moses as to the creation and promised redemption of man. That God created man's body from the dust, and his spirit by his Divine spiritual energy, are historic facts; but when from the imperfection of human language the Divine Being is pictured as moulding man's body from dust *as with hands,* and as breathing into the moulded form the breath of life as though he had *lungs,* these are, of course, figures of speech. So when it is stated that the Redeemer, with a human body already assumed, walked as the "Lord God," who had made man, in the

garden, with human feet, and spoke to man
in a human voice in reproving his sin and
promising redemption,   these are historic
facts; though the statements as to bruising
the heel and the head are figures. No careful student of the New Testament, and of
theories of the atonement suggested by
Christian scholars, can fail to recognize that
no theory can be comprehensive that does
not carefully follow the established laws of
interpreting human language.

Yet again, that a theory may be comprehensive and consistent, its inception and its
statement must follow the laws of logical
thought. This principle, followed in astronomy but disregarded in modern evolution,
is illustrated and specially confirmed in a
study of the theories of atonement suggested
in different ages. In the earliest discussions
of the structure of the material universe, the
Brahmins of India, and the Greeks afterwards, recognized the necessary laws of observation and of reasoning laid down by
thinking minds; whose guidance met the
false reasonings of their times, and has established the sciences of our day. In the
first place, the four causes for every phenome-
non in nature, are to be combined in the

mind; *first*, a material *cause*, or that which is
acted upon ; *second*, the *formal* cause, or the
manner in which the action takes place;
third, the *efficient* cause, or the Being or energy which produces the act, and the manner
of the movement; and *fourth*, the *final*
cause, or the end had in view and accomplished by the mover in the movement, and
in the manner of the movement. All these
were held in mind by Galileo when he demonstrated the Copernican theory of the
solar system; and when, compelled to recant
before his inquisitor, still in private he declared "E pur se muove"—*and yet it does
move*.

Any theory of the Atonement must hold
in view, first, the sacrifice made; second, the
manner of its offering; third, the being making the offering; and fourth, the end designed
and accomplished by the offering. A careful
scrutiny of the different theories of the
atonement proposed, with these rules of
judging in view, will aid greatly in a right
decision as to the amount of truth each con-
tains.

In the *second place*, the true centre whence
to look out, the original or first cause among
conspiring causes, must be sought and at-

tained; otherwise no consistent or comprehensive theory can be suggested. No mind
ever got a consistent conception of the
material universe, until as by Pythagoras,
Copernicus, Galileo and Newton, the *sun*,
not the earth, was made the centre of observation. So no theory of the Atonement can
ever be consistent unless the observer holds
himself, ever and in all his reasonings, at the
centre and origin of the spiritual universe.

Here it must be noted there are four fields
of study for the theologian: first, God, the
Author of all; second, man made by and redeemed by him; third, Christ the Redeemer,
and his work of redemption; and fourth, the
spiritual world, existing before man's creation
and to be his eternal abode whether redeemed
or not; which four fields modern terminology
styles Theology, Anthropology, Soterology
and Eschatology. Certainly no mind will
ever gain a true, a comprehensive and a consistent theory of the atonement, unless, while
in viewing each of these successive fields, all
of which are to be harmonized, it holds its
eye " single " and fixed on the great author
of all. Even Paul spoke of those, who, " not
holding the head from which all the body "
is consistently joined, beguiled Christ's fol-

lowers. Much more, John, writing some years later, makes Christ's nature his theme; declaring that he alone reveals the Father, he alone knows what is in man's heart, he is the propitiation for our sins and for those of the entire universe, and of Him, in the spirit-world, our future abode, angels as well as men sing forever; his work on earth being the bond which reconciles or sets at one the Creator and all His intelligent creatures.

Yet another principle to be regarded in theological, as in all other sciences, is this: that no knowledge of the essential nature and operation of existences and causes can be attained by any finite mind. Human observation assures us, that the sun's heat, watery vapors and atmospheric currents conspire in producing storms; that heat, moisture and fertilized soil combine to effect germination and the growth of plants; and that muscular contractions, animal instinct and human reason cooperate in the complicated action of walking and of speaking; yet no human mind can comprehend the essential elements of matter or of mind, or can conceive how far these elements act on each other in the mysteries of plant, animal and human life. So Christ and his apostles show

the unreasonable spirit of those who have no
faith, because they cannot know all as to the
union of the Divine and human in Christ
(John 10: 30; 14: 9; 1st John 4: 3); how
regeneration by His spirit, and redemption
by His sacrifice, are effected (John 8: 9; 6:
52); how the Divine and human cooperate
in the sanctification of the redeemed (John
16: 17; Phill. 2: 12, 13); how the future existence differs from this (1 Cor. 15); and how
God's assumed responsibility in creating man
is consistent with man's accountability in
His redeeming some and suffering others to be
lost.   (Rom. 9: 19, 24; compare Isah. 45: 9,
10.)   It is enough that we can no more explain the relation of our own body to our
mind, how our own mental acts are produced,
or the limits of our own responsibility and
of our children's when we assume the relation
of parents.   Science reaches practical truth
by comparing and classifying facts; though
no scientist comprehends any one fact which
he observes.

A final principle to be observed, is this:
that personal experience alone enables any
mind to apprehend the real nature of any
operation observed.   No one but he who has
mastered the mathematical sciences can ap-

preciate the demonstrations of astronomy; and no one that has not experienced the bliss of restoration to health, after sickness, can ever form any adequate conception of it. So no one who has not been born again can "*see* the kingdom of heaven" (John 3: 8); no one that has not the "mind of Christ" can conceive his truth (1 Cor. 2: 6); and no one that has not "*grown* in grace and in the *knowledge* of our Lord and Savior, Jesus Christ," can successfully study the harmony of revelation as to the Atonement. The blind professor may lecture on optics; but his pupils will expect many an inconsistency in his theories of light, whose action he has never seen.

THE LEADING THEORIES OF THE ATONEMENT.

With these rules to guide our survey, in view, we may briefly notice the several theories of the atonement suggested, and their lack, under the scrutiny of all the facts to be harmonized; we may ask if there is not a comprehensive and consistent view hinted in the Old and developed in the New Testament, which includes and gives consistency to all the partial views indicated in figures;

we may then take in the successive statements
of the several inspired writers to see whether
they do not converge to the one centre indicated; and finally we may trace the history
of Christian thought in different ages of the
Church to see how this comprehensive view
has led his disciples out of the mazes in which
partial views have in successive ages involved
heated disputants.

The germ of the theories advanced at different eras may be traced in Paul's allusions to
the partial views of the age styled the "apostolic," which closed with the death of Paul
and Peter about A. D. 67: they are apparent
in John's writings, which appeared about
thirty years later; they are clear in the works
of the Apostolic Fathers and their successors
the Patristic Fathers, in the second century; and they mature in the Gnostic theories
and in the volumes of Origen. They reappear
in the fourth century, in the contest of
Arius and Athanasius as to the nature of
Christ; and again in the fifth century
in the conflict of Pelagius and Augustine as
to the origin and nature of sin and of God's
sovereignty in redemption. They are specially
prominent in the scholastic theology of the
eleventh and twelfth centuries, when Papal

claims to Divine authority in the absolution of sin conflicted with the spirit of independent thought in Anselm, Aquinas, Duns Scotus and Abelard. They have culminated in the discussions since the Reformation among Christian scholars of Switzerland, Germany, Holland, England and America. The special definiteness of the theories enumerated, and the popularly recognized titles and authors assigned to each, are therefore only approximate in statement.

The distinct theories of the Atonement, growing out of views more or less consistent, as to the nature of Christ, the origin and nature of sin and the consequent nature and source of redemption, may be resolved into the following five. In the first three, Christ is not regarded as truly a Divine sacrifice for sin, while in the last two he is recognized as truly God and man in his sacrifice. The five are arranged in the inverse order of their comprehensive and hence consistent embodiment of the entire spiritual and divine truth as to the Atonement.

1st. The *Example Theory*, styled that of Socinus. It regards Christ as only a god-like man, sin as an intellectual error, and Christ's sacrifice as but an example to man

of patience under suffering. Though fully
elaborated by Socinus, the banished Italian
Reformer of the sixteenth century, the theory
was manifestly that of Arius in the fourth
century, and has been that of many successors
since.

Its important, yet partial truth, has its
just foundation in the perfect humanity of
Christ taught everywhere in revelation; in
the element of sin which appeared in Eve,
" who was deceived," and which is embodied
in the Greek word for sin, *amartia*, or error;
and in the fact that Christ in his human
nature is our example, as the command
" follow me," a duty including even a willing-
ness like him to suffer death, (John 13 : 36,
37; 1st John 3 : 16,) indicates.

2d. The *Moral Influence Theory*, now
attributed to the American Bushnell. It
admits the Divinity of Christ, but supposes
his human nature only to have suffered; it
regards sin as *emotional* rather than intellectual, as selfishness or lack of love; and it
makes the efficacy of Christ's suffering to
arise from its moral influence in begetting
love in the sinful heart. Though conspicuous
in the recent treatises of Dr. Bushnell, it was
marked in the theory of Origen as well as of

2

the Gnostics in the second century, and it assumed special brilliance in the writings of the romantic Abelard in the twelfth century.

There is a vital, and yet not comprehensive truth in this theory. Christ's suffering as man was mainly moral, his human soul, both in anticipation and at the hour when his Father left his human soul to be sustained by faith alone, suffering as no merely human being can suffer, (Mat. 26: 32, 39; Heb. 5: 7, 6); sin in its second element is alienated affection, as is seen in Adam who was "not deceived" when he sinned, and is indicated in the Greek word *echthra*, enmity; and the sacrifice of Christ not only is, but is designed to be a moral appeal to both men and angels (Rom. 5: 5, 8; 1st John 4: 9, 11; Eph. 8: 10; Coll. 1: 16, 20.)

3d. The *Governmental Theory*, called that of Grotius. This theory, without committing itself necessarily to the true Divinity of Christ, regards him as the *representative* of the Author and Ruler of all things and beings in his sacrifice. It views sin as the offspring of pride, or ambition, angelic and human; and hence as disloyalty or political criminality. It argues therefore that the Divine Sovereign may remit the penalty of sin by

condoning, mitigating, or reprieving; and
that Christ's submission in living under the
law without sin and yet suffering its penalty,
is the accepted condoning which justifies the
reprieve.

This masterly effort of the Dutch jurist, to
reconcile the conflicts of the Arminian and
Calvinist parties in his little but noble Republican State at a critical era, will always
win admiration from thinking minds. It
embodies transcendent truth; for Christ assumed a subordinate and representative
character in his mission to atone (Phill. 2: 5,
11); and sin in its third element is rebellion,
the ambitious pride of the tempter in Eden
(1 Tim. 8: 6), an element set forth in the
Greek word *anomia*, or lawlessness (1st John
3: 4.)   The failure of the great jurist arose
from two causes: first, the modern science of
International Law, of which he was the founder
and from which he drew his illustrations,
was then in its infancy; second, his view was
theoretical, not experimental, none but a regenerated and adopted child of God ever
realizing to himself and to others the idea of
the relation in which the redeemed soul
stands to its Redeemer.

4th. The *Substitution Theory proper, or that*

of material substitution, styled that of Anselm. This theory maintains that the Divine as well as human nature of Christ shared in the sacrifice for sin ; and that the infinite merit of the infinite sacrifice is a full offset for the innumerable sins of all the human race, and for the eternal suffering those sins merit. Though fully elaborated by Anselm, when Papal absolution for sin was at the height of its claim, it appears in its germ in earlier ages of the Church ; it was so prominent afterwards in the theory of Calvin, as to become that of the school styled hyper-Calvinist; and it is so marked in old Puritan divines such as Emmons, as to have gained the title among modern Unitarians of the " Commercial " or " Mercantile Theory."

There is undoubtedly a truth in the idea that underlies this theory. For though the words "substitution" and "suffering in our stead," often quoted as Scripture, are not Bible statements, and though the phrase "suffered for us " is only found in Peter, who wrote for Israelites accustomed to Old Testament figures (1st Pet. 2: 21; 3: 18; 4: 1), yet the fundamental idea designed to be conveyed by substitution is found in revelation. It is a part of the statements of Isaiah 53: 4,

5, 6, 11, " he was bruised for our iniquities "
" the Lord laid on him the iniquities of us
all "; it is implied in Christ's statements
" God gave his only begotten Son " " my
flesh I give for the life of the world " (John
3: 16; 6: 51); and it is fully recognized in
Paul's expressions " who gave himself for me "
and " who gave himself a ransom for all,"
(Gal. 2: 20; 1 Tim. 2: 6.) As human sin is
committed in the body, as the inherited
source and fruit of sin is partly material, so
the material body of Christ, as well as his
human soul, suffered for sin, and that suffering formed part of the expiatory sacrifice he
offered for us.   When, however, this idea is
made the foundation of a theory, a subordinate teaching of revelation is made fundamental : a tendency to material and human trust
is encouraged; external rites are regarded as
saving; mere men, called saints, are supposed
to have a merit that can be transferred to
wilful and persistent transgressors; the merit
as well as efficacy of Christ's sacrifice is restricted to a class and rendered partial; and,
as De Gasparin [1] intimates, physical penance
and purgatory receive apparent support in
reason.

(1) Des Esprits, Chap. V, Paris, 1855.

5th. The *Ethical or Moral Substitution Theory;* now alluded to as that of Shedd. It takes the view that Christ's sacrifice as both God and man, which sacrifice consisted not only of his death but of his entire life of conformity to the Divine law, met all the demands of law, both in legal justice and in moral equity. It differs from the Governmental theory of Grotius in these respects. It makes the sacrifice of Christ truly Divine, and hence of infinite merit; it meets the demands of equity to the *Divine nature* before law is given, as well as of *justice* after man and angels are created and placed under law ; and hence it realizes the *ethical* demand of God's *holy character* as well as of *his righteous* government. Though conspicuous in its presentation by Prof. Shedd, it is the virtual background of the view of Cocceius, whose theory of the Atonement was but slightly exceptionable; and it is the underlying sentiment of Neander and other modern Germans of the Evangelical School. It is, as Shedd intimates, the view to which Protestant scholarship tends; while that of Anselm marks the drift of Roman theology.

This view is the most comprehensive, in the truth it embodies, of the list thus far con-

sidered; including a wide range of truth, but
leaving omissions which have in every age
caused it to tend to perversion.   It includes
the grand moral view drawn from human
·government elaborated by Grotius; and it
adds the view of Christ as Divine which a
soul renewed by His spirit conceives.   While
viewing Christ, however, as a *substitute*, it
regards him as only standing in a certain
relation to his Father as Creator and Ruler,
thus overlooking the essential fact that Christ
himself is the Creator and the responsible
moral provider as well as sacrificing Redeemer
for man.   It thus omits the main idea on
which Christ's atonement rests; and so weakens
the Divine bond that holds the " whole spirit,
soul and body blameless " in its union to a
personal Savior.   This omission has made the
Arminian theology to lose moral power. It
has become secularized through rationalism
and liberalism, as the Anselmic theology has
become formal through traditionalism and
ritualism.

THE COMPREHENSIVE FACT OF ASSUMED DIVINE RESPONSIBILITY.

Inasmuch as each of the five theories thus
suggested has failed to harmonize all Gospel

truth, the suggestion of another seems natural
and legitimate; namely, *the Theory of Assumed Divine Responsibility.* Its suggestion
is perfectly in accord with human reason; and
yet it lies so completely on the surface of the
Old and New Testament and so accords with
individual Christian experience, that though
made a matter of elaborate demonstration by
the Apostle Paul in his epistle to the Romans,
its very simplicity seems to have left it un-
elaborated in theological science.

This view begins with the central fact that
God in the person of Christ is the responsible
author of all things, and the Creator, Father
and Governor of all beings; that he has
placed angels as pure spirits, and men with
spirits embodied, in their spheres for his own
glory and their happiness; that as a necessity
of their spiritual being they are capable of
error and sin and that for the gift of this
constitution he holds himself responsible;
that the very existence, not to say the exercise of his highest attributes of compassion
and mercy, requires, as Grecian sages recognized to be true of man, the existence of
physical evil to be relieved and of moral
wrong to be met and overcome; that the
Author of our being and of our moral state

holds himself as a father and a governor responsible, as far as and no farther than a human parent and governor is, for fidelity to his relation, including responsibility for the moral conduct of the children whom he has begotten and of the subjects for whom he assumes the administration of government; and that this assumed relation implies the responsibility of sacrifice for the interest of his creatures, especially for their spiritual well-being. Coming then to the mission of Christ, it recognizes that he was truly God and man ; that with this double nature he lived under his own law made for man ; that he kept that law perfectly, yet suffered its penalty, thus submitting himself to all he has imposed on man ; and that in consequence of this sacrifice he secure two results, whose moral glory will make all beings, angelic and human, adore his character as holy, and extol his government as righteous, when at the final day they shall see the complete accomplishment of all his purposes. In the first place, he assumes for all who accept his proffered redemptiom the responsibility of all their past sin : not simply pardoning their sin and remitting its penalty, but positively *justifying them* for having been sinners. In the second place he assumes the responsibility as " surety " for every one accepting his atonement, that in future he shall be made free from sinful character and acts. It recognizes, finally, that the Divine purpose in this sacrifice has been to make known his perfect character to angels as well as man ; to show that he is just in justifying the ungoldly who trust him as their Redeemer; and, yet more, to make all intelligent beings at the final judgment see and confess, that, as in character He is holy, so in goverment He is righteous, when he leaves those who refuse His proffer to the moral result of their own assumed moral responsibility.

The fact, or theory, thus suggested is in itself a complete presentation of the entire truth as to the Atonement. Its final cause is the Divine purpose to win to Himself the supreme love of all his intelligent creatures: thus displaying his own perfection and securing their highest happiness. The efficient cause is the Creator himself, wearing the nature of man whom He was to redeem. The instrumental cause is the sacrifice of that Creator in that assumed nature, reaching its climax in his death on the cross, but including the entire period of that assumed

nature, which covers the entire existence of
the human race on earth. The formal cause
is the moral influence exerted by that sacrifice
on the universe of intelligent beings. The
material cause is the restored spiritual life of
the human race, permitted to sin that they
might be redeemed.

If this view meets all the reasonings of
men without revelation, if it is clearly presented in every portion of the Old and New
Testament, if it is found as an underlying
thought of Christian writers when most imperfect views of moral obligation and of
political authority were dominant in ages
past, if it throws into clear light the partial
truth which must inhere in every specious
theory of the atonement that has held large
classes of minds in successive ages, if above
all it is realized in the experience at regeneration of intelligent Christian converts in every
land and age, then it will have secured the
demands of true science accepted in all other
fields of research; among which Christian
Theology ought to be prominent.

ORDER OF SCRIPTURE SURVEY AS TO THE ATONEMENT.

Holding in mind, then, the fact that the

revelation of the Old and New Testaments must present moral truth in the language of man, and that spiritual relations must be stated in terms borrowed from bodily relations, the order of survey essential in attaining to the truth in the Old and New Testament is suggested. The Books of the Old Testament, from Moses to Malachi, were written by men closely associated with the ancient civilization that clustered at the early seats of Asiatic culture, in Chaldea on the Euphrates where Abraham and Job were reared, in Egypt where Moses was born and educated, and in India whose wise men have maintained ascendency for nearly 4000 years. The Hebrew people, in whose language the Old Testament was written, as the inspired penmen all state, were not only instructors but pupils of the nations around them; and the religious ideas of those people were recognized in the revelation which was for fifteen hundred years the world's only inspired guide.

The Books of the Old Testament, though written successively during eleven hundred years, from B. C. 1500 to B. C. 400, cluster about two great eras in the history of the Hebrew nation and of Asiatic religious progress. There is first the age of the rise and

advancing power of the Hebrew nation, including the period from Moses to Solomon;
during which Egypt, where the Hebrews
were trained, is prominent as the ascendant
nation. There is second the age of the decline and fall of the Hebrew State; the
period of the prophets, from Isaiah to Malachi,
during which period Chaldea, anticipating
the history of Rome and of captured Greece,
was ruled and moulded by her inspired
captives. The first of these periods was the
era of the culmination of Brahminic philosophic religious thought and of Asiatic ritualistic idolatry; the second was the era when
both Asiatic philosophy and idolatry were
declining, and when the age of Asiatic
religious reform began.

The Scriptures of the New Testament,
again, were written during the latter half of
the first century of the Christian era, when
Grecian ideal and Roman practical religious
systems had reached their acme and lost their
power. The ideas and the words of these
people gave the very language in which the
inspired writers both of the Old and New
Testaments were to give God's revelation as
to the Atonement.

IDEAS OF ATONEMENT BEFORE MOSES' DAY.

The advocates of evolution, as distinct from developement, admit that the whole issue between the theory of creation and that of evolution turns on the decision of this question : which is more rational, the belief in a mature created parent, with an intellect fully developed and a religious nature directly instructed, or a germ self-evolved; man advancing through the oyster up to the ape, and beginning his religious experience as the grossest of idolators. These two ideas have struggled from the earliest times in the mind of man; the belief in a personal Creator, and in the golden age as the first and purest of man's history, has triumphed in every age and nation; and Revelation accords with the last deductions of human reason as to this fact.

THE ATONEMENT AT THE ORIGIN OF THE HUMAN RACE.

In the account of the Creation by Moses, God, as a pure Spirit, first appears. In the transition from primitive creation to the stage of the earth's history when man is created the "Lord God" appears, *Jehovah elohim,* or the manifested Deity; God united to

man, with human feet and a human voice,
existing before man, who is made in his image.
Man is matured in body and mind; he dresses
the garden and he names the animals; and
he yearns for a wedded companion, (Gen. 1st
and 2d Chaps.) In his fall, guileless, childlike
woman is the tempter's first victim; and her
sin is error while man's is alienated affection.
When asked the cause of their sin, each throws
the blame on another; and Adam directly
condemns his Maker as the author of his fall.
In the arrest of the penalty of sin, in the
pledge of his own interposition to redeem, in
the figure of the serpent that bites and
poisons before it is crushed, and in the appointment of the rite of sacrificing an innocent lamb, an idea so abhorent if it were not
the Author of all who directs the duty, it is
the Redeemer himself who personally orders
all, (Gen. Chaps. 3d and 4th.)

The positive assuming of His relation as
Father and Redeemer, with all its responsibility, is so palpable in this primitive record
of the origin of man, that no one can mistake
the import of the narrative. Every human
being born from those first parents is equally
conscious that his Creator, not he himself,
has assumed the responsibility of his birth

into the world. Unreasonable or unreasoning creatures, like wayward children, may misinterpret this Divine assumption, as they pervert earthly relations: but human reason has demonstrated and the renewed heart has realized that God could not have been a Father without this assumption; and that no angel ever can be so blessed as can a redeemed man, with the love of such a Creator, Father and Redeemer.

ATONEMENT IN THE RACE BEFORE THE FLOOD.

The most instructive fact is, that the Divine appointment, made by direct revelation to the first human family, is perverted by Cain; an offering of property, in place of the appointed sacrifice of the innocent for the guilty, being presented in expiation. At that earliest era, too, the distinction taught by the apostles after Christ, is made between justification by personal works and justification by faith in the Redeemer's sacrifice; the "Lord God," the Redeemer himself, saying to Cain, "If thou *doest well* shalt thou not be accepted? and if thou doest not well, a sin offering," or the lamb appointed for sacrifice, "lieth at the door,"[1] ready for offering.

It is worthy of note that the facts of this record have entered into the philosophy of ancient Asia and into the ritualism of the religious system that now prevails among two-thirds of the people of Asia. Sanchonia-thon, a Phœnician writer of the age of the Hebrew Judges, whose work, though lost in the original, is preserved in quotations made by a Greek historian of the second century, and whose testimony as to the religious convictions of this age is quoted by Eusebius the Christian historian of the fourth century and by Grotius in the seventeenth century, [2] records this fact illustrative of the perversion of the truth as to the Divine sacrifice originating with Cain. After describing the Creation, much like Moses, he states as to

---

(1) The meaning of this, as of all statements in human language, is determined (1) by the words, (2) by the immediate connection, (3) by the general design of the Scripture records. The word *hattah*, used by Moses more than one hundred and twenty times, is in about four-fifths of the cases translated "sin-offering." The word *rabat*, "lieth," used about thirty times in the Old Testament, is *always* applied to the quiet lying down of domestic animals as herds and flocks; the single exception proving the rule when applied (Gen. 49 : 9) to the lion so gorged that he lies sprawling in his sleep. The latter clause of Gen. 4 : 7, requires the interpretation thus given; the general doctrine thus presented runs through the Old and New Testament; and the early Christian commentators thus understood its teaching.

(2) Philo Biblius; Euseb. Prep. Evang. Lib. I cap. X; Grotius De Verit, Relig. Christ. Lib. I. Sect. 16.

the very first of the human race: "They consecrated the productions of the earth, and judged them gods; and worshipped those things upon which they themselves had lived, and all their posterity. To these they made libations and sacrifices." Here this early Phenician sage mentions just what the philosophic Greeks and Romans observed as to the early Egyptians; who worshipped the lotus on which they fed, the Nile of which they drank, and the cow whose milk fed their children. Again, the revelation in Eden of the Redeemer is preserved in the favorite images of Buddh, the incarnate deity of the Hindoos, of the Chinese and of the Japanese. The Redeemer, Vishnu of the Brahmins, is presented in two images; in one of which a serpent is coiled about the leg of the god biting his heel, while in the other the serpent lies prostrate with its crushed head under the heel of the Deity.

The close of this age, as its history is illustrated in the New Testament, confirms the essential idea of the atonement, by revealing the Divine agency for giving efficacy to its proclamation. The sin of mankind, which had culminated in a sensuality and brutality

like that of the Romans at Christ's day, [1] was
mainly the rejection of the proffer of redemption as positive "righteousness" preached by
Noah and impressed by the direct agency of
the Holy Spirit [2]. Yet more, the righteousness ascribed to men like Noah, combined
two elements: first, justification (more than
remission) for sins committed in the past,
and renovation of the sinful nature (more
than natural morality) leading to a life of
fidelity in all relations; this true righteousness bestowed on man "justifying God"
before his universe in declaring men like
Abel and Enoch and Noah to be "righteous." [3]
Most of all, the Divine Creator, in the result
of this first stage of man's spiritual trial, is
represented not as a stolid and arbitrary despot,
withdrawn from his creatures, but as "grieved
to his very heart," like an earthly parent,
that his fidelity to his assumed responsibility

---

(1) Compare Gen. 6 : 2, 4, 5, 13, and Mat. 24 : 38 with Rom.
1: 24—32.

(2) Compare Gen. 6 : 3, (noticing that "Lord" instead of
"God" in preceding and succeeding verses, is used.) with 1
Pet. 3 : 18—20, as illustrated by 1 Pet. 4 : 6, and 2d Pet. 2 : 5.
These statements of the New Testament show that the idea of
"righteousness" through the assumed interposition of Christ
was known to those "dead" who were living before the flood;
and that the regenerating Spirit strove then with men, and
gave "life" to some.

(3) Compare Gen. 6 : 8, 9 ; 7 : 1, 5, (noticing the words
"Lord," "just" and "righteous,") with Heb. 11 : 4—7, and
Jude 11, 15.

awakens no reciprocation. The tendency of unthinking superstition and of critical philosophy are thus together and alike rebuked; for God, before the flood, had assumed the nature described by the Apostle Paul when he traces the history of Noah. [1]

ATONEMENT IN THE HISTORY OF HEBREW PATRIARCHS.

The record of Moses (Gen. ch. 6th to 50th) gives a simple narrative of religious faith before his day; while the Book of Job, whose age (42: 16) shows that he lived before Abraham, gives us religious reasonings as to the Divine design in man's sinful and suffering condition and as to the ground of his *justifying* human sinfulness, so clear and so deep in thought that it has been the wonder of the ablest statesmen.

The same Lord-God, or " God manifest in flesh," who appeared in Eden, appears to Noah, Abraham and Jacob. He eats, walks and talks with Abraham attesting his perfect humanity; and he claims sovereign sway over men and nations showing his true

(1) Compare Gen 6: 6, with Mat. 24: 30, noting its connection with Mat. 23 : 37, and with 1 Pet. 3 : 20 ; Heb. 1 : 1—3 ; 2 : 9, 18; 11 : 7.

Divine nature, (Gen. 18th.)   Abraham, whose
thought and feeling accord with that of every
thinking and feeling human being, cannot be
reconciled to the Divine rule unless it corres-
ponds to his own conviction when he asks,
"Shall not the Judge of all the earth *do
right?*"

The very end of all revelations made in
the patriarchal age is to show what Paul
elaborated in his epistles; how God is just,
doing right, in his redemption of those who
accept and in the abandonment of those who
reject his offer of salvation.   Abraham's *acts*
showed that he believed in a future world
with its awards, and also believed in the
Redeemer promised in Eden, and to descend
from him ; he saw the Redeemer personally ;
the Gospel was preached to him ; and he knew
that his sin would not be imputed to him if
he believed in that Redeemer.   Moreover,
after this special trial, he saw how his parental
fidelity, in his readiness to sacrifice his son
Isaac, was to be made real when God in his
love should give "His only begotten son " as
a sacrifice for all men. [1]

---

(1) See Gen. 12: 1—3 ; 15: 5, 6 : 22: 7—18 ; and compare John
8: 56 ; Rom. 4 : 1—5 and 9—25 ; Gal. 3 : 6—9 and 14—17 ; Heb.
11 : 8—19.

FAITH AND ITS SIGN IN THE PATRIARCHAL AGE.

Two facts in the record of Abraham's justification are illustrative of the Atonement.
The apostles Paul and James refer for argument and illustration to the fundamental
statement (Gen. 15: 6) that "faith in the
Lord is accounted as righteousness," (Rom. 4:
3, 9, 22; Gal. 3: 6; James 2: 23); and Paul
declares that circumcision in Abraham,
though not in his posterity, was both the sign
and seal (Rom. 4: 11) of righteousness
granted to the faithful.

The English word "faith," as well as the
Hebrew and Greek terms of the inspired
Scriptures, is illustrated by its derivatives
"faithful" and "faithfulness" (Gal. 3: 9). It
is an imperfection of the English language,
that we have no verb corresponding to the
Hebrew *aman* and the Greek *pisteuo;* and
that hence the verb *believe* is used in trans-
lating verbs which combine the ideas of both
exercising and *practicing fidelity.* Faith is
both implicit intellectual belief and a spirit
and conduct conformed to that belief. The
faith of the redeemed under the Old Testament, as Paul declares, (Heb. 11: 1) was at
once the *realization* in act of what they hoped

for, and the *demonstrative proof* of things
transcending the sphere of the bodily senses.
The objects of saving or Christian faith, that
faith which in Paul's strong language is the
" complete making " of the soul's redemption,
(Heb. 10: 38, 39,) are therefore two: *first*,
trust in God's *gift* without us of justification
for past sin ; and *second*, trust in God's work
within us of salvation from future sinfulness.
Of the first of these results of faith Paul treats,
(Rom. 4: 1–5,) while James specially enlarges
on the second (James 2: 20—26.)

The peculiar, and significant rite of circumcision, while in one sense a bodily infliction,
seems for three reasons to have been a special
pledge of fidelity in the parental relation. .
This is indicated, first, in its nature, as
illustrated by the form of oath associated
with it (Gen. 24: 2, 3); second, in the new
parental responsibility which attended its
appointment, (Gen. 17: 9–14,) and the trans-
mission to his son and heir of that responsibility, when a wife was to be sought for him
whose essential qualification was to be
religious fidelity (Gen. 24: 3, 4); and third,
from Paul's connection of the sign with
Abraham as " father of the faithful " (Rom.
4: 11). The important fact to note, is the

place this rite takes in the spiritual teachings of the Old Testament as a sign of the spiritual righteousness received because of the atonement. Moses simply alludes once in his laws to the rite (Lev. 12 : 3); he neglected it in the case of his own children before he received the law, until the superstitious fears of his wife during his sickness led her to perform it (Exod. 4 : 24—26); and under his administration of forty years in the Hebrew State, the rite was not observed (Josh. 5 : 2—9). It is manifest from this record, as well as from the frequent allusions of Moses and of the prophets, that this omission arose because of the danger that the spiritual righteousness, of which the rite was only a sign, would be forgotten from trust in the outward ceremony [1]. The New Testament allusions to this rite, show fully, that, like baptism in the New Testament, circumcision was meant to be, as an expression of human responsibility, the pledge of filial devotion to the Redeemer who pledged his all for us. [2]

---

(1) Lev. 26 : 41 ; Deut. 10 : 16 ; 30 : 6 ; Isah. 52 : 1 ; Jer. 4 : 4 ; 6 : 10 ; Ezek. 44 : 7, 9.

(2) John 7 : 22 ; Acts 15 : 1, 24 ; 21 : 21 ; Rom. 2 : 25, 28, 29 ; Gal. 2 : 3 ; 5 : 2 ; 6 : 12, 13 ; Phill. 3 : 3 ; Coll. 2 : 11 ; 3 : 12.

THE ATONEMENT AMONG GENTILE PATRIARCHS.

The interest of the Old Testament narrative is so centered in Abraham, of the race of Shem, from whom the Hebrew people and the promised Redeemer descended, that the superior patriarchs of the stock of Ham and of Japhet, living in the same age, are too much overlooked in tracing the history of religious truth.

The earliest of the patriarchs is Job, who, from his age, must have lived before Abraham; and who from his residence near Chaldea, and from the cast of thought and expression in his book, seems to be a representative of the Indo-Germanic stock descended from Japhet.

Job is declared to be just and perfect in all human relations (1: 2); and yet he asks "how should man be just with God?" (9: 2.) When his friends argue that his losses and sufferings are proofs of unfaithfulness in his earthly relations, he defends his moral integrity to the last. (31: 5—40.) Yet he repeatedly declares that thereby he is not "justified" before God (9: 20); a fact which is manifest in his murmuring against God, because of his suffering, (3: 3; 6: 9,) and also in his

irritation under the unjust charges of his
visitors. (16 : 2—4.) When thus it is proved
that the very best man will justify himself
rather than God (32 : 2 ; 34 · 5 ; 35 : 3), then
the " Lord," or manifested God, appears and
remonstrates with him; first, because with
limited intellectual comprehension he criticises
the Creator of all things (Chs. 38 and 39) ;
and second, because with *moral* power too
weak to control some of the lowest of animals,
as the crocodile and river-horse (Chs. 40 and
41), he yet " reproved God " and " condemned " his Lord in order that " he himself "
might appear " righteous " (40 : 8). At the
close of the first appeal Job sees and confesses
his special sin, (40 : 3—5,) and at the close of
the second appeal he humbly avows his entire
dependence for justification on the Redeemer
before believed and now seen (19 : 25 ; 42 ;
5). The end of the Book of Job, as seen in
itself, is that God is himself just in all he allows
to befall man, and yet justifies him who
trusts in him ; for, as in Eden, he permits
the temptation that he may recover the
tempted. [1]

A third patriarch, Melchisedek, a Canaan-

---

(1) Job 1 : 12 ; 2 : 5 ; compare James 1 : 13, 14 ; 5 : 10, 11 ;
and note Rom. 3 : 26 ; 1 Cor. 10 : 13.

ite of the race of Ham, is a priest to Abraham.
In ancestral descent he is like Jesus, not of
priestly origin; while Jesus, like him, as the
"seed of the woman," [1] not of a man of the
royal, the Jewish, or of any human line, had
a Canaanite mother of unknown lineage. [2]
The union in both of the kingly and priestly
offices with the designation Lord, the two-
fold name "king of righteousness and king
of peace" so in keeping with that of Jesus or
Savior, and yet again the special Divine appointment of each to his office, seemed to the
great apostle for all nations worthy of note
in presenting to his Hebrew countrymen the
"Lord Jesus Christ;" whose names are an
embodiment of his mission. [3]

ATONEMENT IN ITS RELATION TO REVEALED AND WRITTEN LAW.

In considering the Atonement as embodied
in the laws of the Hebrew nation, three
principles must be observed. First, the laws
of interpretation, applicable to all writings,
but specially studied by jurists and embodied

---

(1) Gen. 3 : 15 ; Mat. 1 : 23, 25 ; Luke 1 : 34, 35 ; Gal. 4 : 4 ;
Rev. 12 : 5.
(2) Josh. 2 : 1, 13 ; 6 : 25 ; Mat. 1 : 5 : Heb. 11 : 31 ; James 2 :
25 ; only her nativity and her faith being recorded.
(3) Gen. 14: 18—20 ; Psal. 110: 1, 5 ; Heb. 5: 6, 10, 11 ; 6 : 20 ;
7 : 1 ; 8 : 13.

in ancient and modern codes, must be reviewed; since their strict application is to be anticipated in God's inspired covenant with man. Second, the doctrines of Expiation which are found in laws whose existence, if not their embodiment, were familiar to Moses when he wrote, must be regarded. Third, the fact must be considered that spiritual truth as to God, as to sin, as to redemption and as to a future world, which was known to Moses and embraced and proclaimed by him aside from his duty as a civil legislator, finds so small a place in his inspired writings.

RULES OF INTERPRETING LAW AND OTHER RECORDS PRESERVED IN HUMAN LANGUAGE.

In all ages the fact is to be observed that as men put different constructions on human language and human acts, so, too, they differently interpret God's words as well as his works. This is seen in the discussions of the Book of Job, in Christ's Sermon on the Mount, and in the allusions of Paul and Peter to men who "handle deceitfully" and who "wrest" the revealed Scriptures. In the second century after Christ, Origen applied to the New Testament rules of interpretation

which have been discussed and elaborated by
Bible students down to our day. In law-
codes, ancient and modern, Roman and
Medieval, German, French and English, the
principles of just interpretation have been
laid down with special exactness. They are
substantially the following : *First*, words
are ordinarily to be taken in their common
or literal signification ; a rule which applies
to the simple narratives of the Old and New
Testament, to moral precepts, and even to
such figurative representations as are found
in the parables of the Old and New Testaments. *Second*, words whose meaning is
doubtful, because drawn from customs or
conceptions not familiar to the ordinary
reader, are to be explained by experts, or by
those most likely to be familiar with the
meaning of such terms. Thus the men of
the later prophetic age, who brought together
the inspired record from the days of Moses
to Ezra's time, " gave the sense " of obselete
words ; and John, in the last Gospel, interpreted Hebrew words and explained Hebrew
customs. So in every succeeding Christian
age, men familiar with Jewish and Christian
antiquities have been the best commentators
on obscure portions of the Sacred Scriptures.

Third, the meaning ascribed to obscure words must always be in harmony with the connection of thought in which the writer uses them, and consistent with his statements elsewhere. This principle is especially to be observed in statements of truths relating to religious experience wrought in the souls of men by the same Divine Spirit which guided the inspired writers; the personal experience of the most illiterate reader being a safer guide than the profoundest philosophy of any age in explaining truth which only Christian experience can comprehend. (1st Cor. 2: 6—16.) *Fourth,* as in law codes the precept of one age and nation aids in the explanation of a statute penned in another age, since natural law, the foundation of all law, is substantially the same in all lands and ages, so in the revealed word of God, all of whose successive writers wrote as they were moved by the Holy Spirit, the earlier writings are made clearer by later, and especially by New Testament writers.

EXPIATION IN LAW CODES BEFORE MOSES' DAY.

Since the idea of redemption involves two elements, expiation for the past and reform in the future, and since expiation has been sought by sacrifices of property and by personal penance instead of by the appointment of sacrifices recognized in Abel's day, it is important to notice what must have been familiar to Moses when he wrote. Moses was "learned in all the wisdom of the Egyptians" (Acts 7: 22). From the earliest times, as the statements of Herodotus and later Grecian and Roman historians attest, the magi, or "wise men," of Egypt, of Chaldea and of India were a common fraternity. Moses alludes to law codes with which his own is compared (Deut. 4: 8); he uses nearly two hundred words of science and art common to the learned world of his day and found in the Sanscrit of the Indian Vedas; and his allusions to the religious convictions of Egyptians and of other nations, as well as the prohibition of religious rites perverted by them, serve to illustrate by contrast his own distinctive teachings.

The last of the Vedas, the Institutes or Laws of Menu, whose statutes if not their embodiment preceded the code of Moses, comprise twelve books. The eleventh of these, filling one-tenth of the volume, is entitled "Penance and Expiation." Of the two hundred and sixty-six precepts no one sets forth anything else than personal penance as expiation. The spirit of the whole book is illustrated in these quotations: "Some of the learned consider expiation as confined to involuntary sin; but others, from the evidence of the Vedas, hold it effectual even in the case of a voluntary offence. A sin involuntarily committed is removed by repeating certain texts of the Vedas; but a sin committed intentionally, through strange infatuation, by harsh penances of different sorts." "Penance, therefore, must be invariably performed for the sake of expiation." [1] The minute details of penances imposed illustrate much in the history of Israel and of medieval Christian times.

While in India, whose philosophy ruled the Colleges of Egypt in Moses' day, penance had usurped the place of sacrifices for expiation, in Egypt the priests continued to offer the sacrifices appointed in Eden and handed down through Noah to all mankind. Herodotus describes minutely the animals sacrificed and the mode of offering them; mentioning that the male rather than the female, the bullock rather than any other

[1] Instit. of Menu. Ch. XI. Sect. 45, 46, 54.

animal, and the red bullock without a black
hair, were the preferred victims; and he
states that over the head of the sacrifices im-
precations are pronounced with the prayer,
"If any evil is about to befall either those
that now sacrifice, or Egypt at large, may it
be averted on this head." In several of their
sacrifices they beat themselves, with wailings;
indicating personal penance associated with
the sacrifices. [1] The doctrine of penance in
the future life, or of expiation for sins committed in the present life by transmigration
into animals or into diseased bodies, prevailed in Egypt, as in India. [2] We are left
to conjecture what special efficacy was supposed by the Egyptians to attend sacrifices;
a clearer light being reserved for the revelation given to Moses at Mt. Sinai. It is important to notice that in this age the idea
that the material world was subject to the
spirit of evil already prevailed, and that
offerings for propitiation were therefore made
to evil spirits.

THE ATONEMENT IN MOSES' WRITINGS, AT
THE ORIGIN OF THE HEBREW NATION.

The actual knowledge of Moses as to the

---

(1) Herodot. II, 39 to 41.
(2) Instit. of Menu. Ch. XII ; Diod. I, 88.

Redeemer and his spiritual work appears only indirectly in his law; it is directly intimated in his life; and its full and true character is presented in the New Testament. Christ says that Moses taught the resurrection, (Luke 20: 37) and that he wrote of the Redeemer (John 5: 46); and he traced Moses' statements as to these truths (Luke 24: 27, 44). Paul quotes Moses as teaching justification by faith (Rom. 10: 5—8), and as believing and preaching the Gospel of Christ and the future life (Heb. 4: 2; 11: 26).

In his life Moses meets the Lord, Jehovah, or the embodied Deity, who had appeared to Adam and to the patriarchs as man's Redeemer (Ex. 3: 2, 4, 7); he explains his peculiar name (Ex. 3: 14; 6: 3); in receiving the law he talked face to face with him (Ex. 33: 10; Num. 12: 8); and hence Paul declares that the Law as truly as the Gospel came through the hands of the Mediator (Gal. 3: 19).[1] Moreover, this Mediator, who was the giver of the law at Sinai, Moses foretells, was to come afterwards and live as a man and really save those not redeemed by

---

(1) Some modern commentators have without due thought referred the word Mediator, in Gal. 3: 19, to Moses. Neither the word nor its idea are ever used except in reference to Christ; and so the old interpreters observed.

the law; a prophecy often referred to by New Testament writers. [1]

As the inspired compiler of God's law for an organized nation, Moses indirectly presents the character of the Divine being as a *ruler*, by teaching that his approved human government was not that of an arbitrary king, but of a sympathizing judge (Ex. 2: 14; 18: 13; Deut. 17: 14, 15); an idea likely to fade from thought after the patriarchal age.

In the *moral* law the Divine authority in permitting sin to affect the third and fourth generation is offset by his purpose of mercy to the thousanth generation (Ex. 20: 5). In the *civil* law, digested in Exodus Chaps. 21st to 23d, amplified in Leviticus and revised in Deuteronomy, these three principles, bearing on discussions as to the atonement, are to be marked. *First*, the idea of condoning for offences by money payment, contrary to the perverted interpretation of Christ's day, is recognized. [2] *Second*, the guardian of the law, as of the people living under it, is the Lord who gave it (Ex. 20: 19; 23: 20; 32: 31). *Third*, the remission of penalties under the civil law partook of the nature of expia-

---

(1) Deut. 18 : 16—18 ; John 1 : 45 ; Acts. 3 : 22 ; 7 : 37.
(2) Ex. 21 : 24 modified by Ex. 21 : 19, 26, 27, and perverted to private revenge, Mat. 5 : 38.

tion made to its Divine author. [1] The *ceremonial* law, again, embodied after the moral and civil law in Exodus Chaps. 25th to 30th, was, as Paul declared, but a material and earthly semblance of spiritual and heavenly influences accompanying the ritual observance (Heb. 8: 5; 10: 1).

It is a fact to be observed, since German scholars have overlooked it, that in his laws Moses recognizes the existence of evil spirits. He twice forbids "sacrifices to devils" (Lev. 17: 7; Deut. 32: 17); the two locations in which these laws were written implying that both in Egypt and in Canaan the practice prevailed. It is yet more important to observe that the Israelites, despite this prohibition, fell into the practice; since David (Psal. 106: 37) records that they even "sacrificed their sons and their daughters to devils."

The distinctive character of the Mosaic *legal* dispensation, so far as the atonement is concerned, is manifestly included in these particulars. The law of man's relations to his fellow beings, *as law*, was more perfectly defined than in any human code, and was de-

---

(1) Compare Lev. 4: 2, 13, 22 with the *double* penalty of crime, Lev. 6: 1—7.

signed in every respect for his well being
(Deut. 6: 24; 10: 3); while the *administration* of that superior law, both in its legislative, judicial and executive departments, was
under the immediate supervision of "The
Lord," or man's Redeemer wearing human
form.

THE ATONEMENT FROM SAMUEL TO SOLOMON, DURING THE SUPREMACY OF THE HEBREW NATION.

During a period of about four hundred
and fifty years, from the majority of Moses
B. C. 1531 till Samuel's retirement about
B. C. 1081, under their judges, [1] the historic
writings of Joshua and of Samuel record the
continuance of the sacrifices, which prefigured the sacrificing Redeemer, and also
declared his occasional appearance and interposition to guard the nation. [2] No
special advance in the revelation of the
atonement, however, is recorded in this age.
During this period the nation was steadily
advancing to the full supremacy promised. [3]

---

(1) See Ex. 2: 11—14 and 1 Sam, 15: 35; compare Acts 7:
23—35 and 13: 20.

(2) Josh. 1: 1, 8; 2: 9, 11; 3: 5; 5: 2 7; 22: 11—31; 23: 6;
24: 24; Judg. 1: 1; 2: 16—18; 3: 4, 8, 9; 13: 6, 7; Ruth 1: 1;
4: 11, 17; 1 Sam 1: 11; 3: 1, 21.

(3) 1 Kings 1: 21; Ps. 72: 8.

A new era dawned when David's line ruled "from the river to the ends of the earth." As the idea of patriarchal government, the type of the Divine Government, was recalled by Moses when its associations were forgotten in the Hebrew State, so an added feature of Divine relationship was brought out when arbitrary kings, realizing in their reign all that Samuel, the last of the judges, predicted (1 Sam. 10: 8—18), became to the popular mind the models of the Divine rule.

Modern speculation has conceived a lack in the presentation of the Divine character under the relation of Father and Son, inasmuch as the maternal element of kindliness is omitted; and out of this idea has grown the seductive perversion of making the mother of Jesus a Divine intercessor. In the inspired writings of the monarchical age the royal penmen are the first to meet this only apparent lack. Both of the inspired kings woo the reader away from thoughts of courts and thrones; and they make the family the type of Divine spiritual relationship. The mother, more than the father, is presented as the source of moral influence, (Prov. 1: 8; 4: 3; 31: 1); and we are told that "The Lord" is more tender and faithful

than either (Ps. 27 : 10). In a picture of his
own only true love, an attachment which
his character as an oriental monarch obliged
him to sacrifice, Solomon sets forth, as did
his father before him, the relation of wedded
union, like to that of Eden, as the type of
the Redeemer's union to those who accept
his love; thus giving the first utterance to a
truth which on the lips of prophets and
apostles, of Jesus and of all who have since
loved him, has proved the power to win alike
the rude and the refined to true love to their
Redeemer. [1]   This added feature of Divine
relationship to his creature man, covering
all the endearments of the love of both
parents, is a new approximation in revelation
towards the reality thus dimly set forth in
human language.

This new revelation of the Divine relationship to man is accompanied by new statements as to the nature of sin and the promise
of the future life; all preparing the way for
a clearer statement as to atonement. The
character of sin, and the grief it gave to "The
Lord" as contrasted with God, had been

---

(1) Compare I Kings 1 : 3 ; 2 : 22 ; Cant. 6 : 13 ; Eccl. 7 : 28 ;
Prov. 5 : 18 for the history ; and for its idea see as specimens
Ps. 45 : 10, 11 ; Isah. 62 : 4, 5 ; John 3 : 29 ; Mat. 9 : 15 ; Eph.
5 : 25, 32 ; Rev. 21 : 2.

stated by Moses in the history of man before
and after the flood (Gen. 6: 5, 6; 8: 21);
but its origin and infant development is de-
duced by David from personal experience
(Psal. 51: 5; 58: 3). The future life and its
awards had been inferred by Job from the
analogy of the sprouting tree and of the re-
descending vapor, as well as from the conscious conviction that the Creator designs the
continued and higher existence of the soul
his special work (Job 14: 7—15); but David
and Solomon not only directly affirm the
spirit's future existence, but also its happy
or unhappy condition dependent on character. [1]

All these more clearly revealed truths, the
parental character and purpose of "The
Lord," the origin as well as the taint of sin,
and the existence and awards of the future
life, are accompanied by new revelations as
to the person and earthly life of Christ, and
of his sacrifice and assumption in atonement.
Prophecy proper, special as distinct from
general statements as to Christ's life, are
found in the eight Psalms called "Messianic"

[1] Psal. 9: 17; 16: 10, 11; 73: 25; 139: 8; Eccles. 3: 21;
12: 7. The question Eccl. 3: 21 is not as to the *fact*, for this
is made clear, Eccl. 12: 7; but the question is whether we can
comprehend the fact, as the word "know" in Eccles. 11: 5 explains.

because they are quoted in the New Testament as referring to the Hebrew Messiah, the Christ or appointed Redeemer. The 40th Psalm describes the assumption of his suffering human nature; the 2d Psalm foretells in detail his trial, the 22d and 69th his death by crucifixion, and the 16th his resurrection; while the 72d Psalm shadows in human analogies his earthly reign, the 110th his heavenly interposition, and the 45th his spiritual union to his people. The natural disposition of man to justify himself and charge sin on his maker is made more clear in this age (Psal. 51 : 4); and the fact that the Divine Maker as Redeemer assumes the imputation of sin for the penitent believer is clearly stated (Psal. 32 : 2). While thus the essential fact of the imputation of sin brings out the *design* and the efficient author of the atonement, the death of Christ as its *instrument*, and the double moral influence of past sin cancelled and of a renewed spirit inwrought in the redeemed [1] is fully revealed.

The special fact that it was moral anguish, rather than physical agony, that became both cause and effect in Christ's sacrifice for atone-

---

[1] Implied Psal. 22 : 22—28 ; Psal. 69 : 30—36 ; stated Psal. 51 : 1—19.

ment, seems to have arrested the attention of David, as it has of many a profound thinker among his adoring disciples. [1] It is specially illustrative of the spiritual design of sacrifices, as a sign of atonement, that their two per-versions are corrected; the sacrifice of the body of Christ for expiation, and the sacrifice of a broken spirit for propitiation, being impressively presented by David (Psal. 40: 6—10; 51: 16, 17).

This latter brings out the special office of the Holy Spirit, only alluded to in former eras of revelation; as first, the renewing and sanctifying agent in redemption (Psal. 51: 10, 11); and second, as the inspirer of Old Testament writers (Mat. 22: 43). The dis-pensation of the unseen Spirit in the latter half of the Old and of the New Testament revelations is as palpable as is that of the seen Son of God in the first half of each; the em-bodied Redeemer being the seen teacher of Adam, Noah, Abraham, Job and Moses, as

---

(1) Sir James Y. Simpson, one of the ablest of Scotch sur-geons, knighted for his eminence, has shown that all the symptoms of Christ's death indicate that his sudden and early death was the result of rupture of the heart caused by mental anguish. This the physical facts of his loud cry, his head erect and not bowed till that cry, and of the blood already clotted and separated from the serum, when his heart was pierced, all confirm ; for each symptom indicates that sudden rupture, not gradual exhaustion, led to his early expiring ; thus making the words, Psal. 69 : 20, to have a literal truth.

He was of the first apostles; while the Spirit of God is the unseen teacher of David, Solomon and of the prophets, as He was of all the New Testament writers.

ATONEMENT IN THE PROPHETS OF THE DIVIDED HEBREW NATION, AND OF ITS DECLINE.

When after Solomon the Hebrew nation became divided, their worship corrupted and the law neglected, for two hundred years no great prophets arose, except Elijah and Elisha who left no record, Jonah whose mission was to Nineveh, and Joel whose prophecy is brief. As to the agency of their inspiration we have the peculiar statement, "the word of the Lord came" to them. [1] In the book of Jonah we find that ancient Phenician sailors had each his tutelary deity; yet all recognized the God of the Hebrews, "The Lord," as the Supreme Ruler; while the people of Nineveh resort to fasting and penitential prayer as an expiation to that Supreme Being. [2] In the Book of Joel the outpouring of the converting Spirit, following the death of the Messiah which David had foretold, is declared with a

(1) 1st Kings 17 : 2 ; 2d Kings 3 : 12, 15 ; Joel 1 : 1 ; Jonah 1 : 1.
(2) Jonah 1 : 5, 9, 14 ; 3 : 5—9.

clearness that impressed the apostles of Jesus
when the prophecy was fulfilled. [1]

In the next century, during which the
kingdom of Israel became completely corrupted and its people were finally carried
away captives into Assyria, five eminent
writers, Isaiah, Hosea, Amos, Micah and
Nahum appeared. Amos foretells the fall of
the northern kingdom, but their future
spiritual union under the expected son of
David not only with Judah but with all the
Gentiles (9 : 11, 12) ; a prophecy recalled by
the apostle James when Greek disciples were
first called Christians (Acts 11 : 27 ; 15 : 16,
17). Hosea at the same time presents the
same facts ; making an allusion to the
infancy of the Hebrew nation (11 : 1) in
which Matthew (2 : 15) afterwards noted a
parallel to that of the infant Redeemer.
Nahum, writing a few years after the captivity which his predecessors foretold, denounces judgments on Nineveh, the chief
city of Assyria, as the captor of Israel. Only
one of the prophets of this age, Isaiah, dwells
at length on the atonement which the promised Redeemer was to provide.

Micah specially presents the Redeemer to

(1) Joel 2 : 28—32, quoted Acts 2 : 17—21.

come and the demand for his interposition.
The heathen around Israel had carried the
idea of the efficacy of penance, or of personal
bodily expiation, to such an extent that kings
sometimes sacrificed their first-born sons,
heirs to the throne, as expiation for sin (2d
Kings 3: 27). The kings of Israel, from
merely admitting into worship forms which
encouraged idolatry (1 Kings 12: 27—30),
came to adopt the grossest idolatry as their
state religion ; under which the priests, while
offering sacrifices, cut themselves with knives
till covered with blood (1 Kings 18: 19, 28).
Some, too, of the kings of Judah caused their
sons to go through the fire, making them
burnt offerings for propitiation (2d Kings
16: 3; 21: 6); a horrid superstition to which
in the next age Ezekiel (23: 37) alludes,
which Jeremiah (7: 31 and 19: 5) condemns,
and which Josiah (2d Kings 23: 10) sup-
pressed. Micah first foretells the moral
blessings of the coming Redeemer's reign (4:
1—4), which Isaiah (2: 2—4) also declares;
he reveals (5: 2), so clearly that afterwards it
guided the eastern magi (Mat. 2: 6), the
place of the Redeemer's birth ; and he adds
a thrilling appeal to the purely moral demands of the justifying Redeemer as con-

trasted with the inhuman barbarity to which
men are driven by superstition when seeking an
expiation made by or for themselves (6: 6—8).

Isaiah, called by preeminence the evan-
gelic prophet, sets forth most fully the design,
the agent, and the instrumentality in the
Atonement. His very opening is a touching
appeal of "The Lord" to His own fidelity
contrasted with man's infidelity in His assumed parental relation (1: 2). He repeats
Micah's statement of the Messiah's coming
to win all nations (2: 2—5); and he records
the sign given Ahaz of Immanuel's birth
from one then a virgin; whose full realization
Matthew afterward recalls (7: 14; Mat. 1:
22). He foretells Christ's spiritual triumph,
beginning with the most benighted and hopeless and extending to every age and nation
(9: 1—7), and he heaps together titles
setting forth the character in him which indicates the moral power by which he rules;
calling him "wonderful" or miraculous [1] in
his twofold nature, "counsellor" or successful advocate [2] in his moral interposition,

[1] Compare Judg. 13 : 18. The word *pala* in the Hebrew,
used about one hundred times, as the word *wonder* in the
English, refers to that which excites wonder not from novelty
but from its miraculous character.
[2] See Isah. 14 : 24, 27 where the word is rendered "purposed"; compare Prov. 19 : 21 and Isah. 46 : 10 with 1st John
3 : 1.

"The mighty God and the everlasting Father"
in his assumed relation, and "The Prince of
Peace " in the bond which binds his creatures
to his sway. His human descent from
David, and his spiritual control over the most
ferocious spirits, is pictured in Oriental
imagery (11 : 1—10) ; and his rightful sovereignty in abandoning those who will not
yield to his sway (29 : 16 ; 30 : 14,) is sustained by the contrasted· blessings of his
reign (32 : 1, 2 and 35 : 1—10). The latter
portion of the Book of Isaiah, from the 40th
to the 66th chapters, is like a Gospel history
written in anticipation ; presenting in order
the ministry of his forerunner (40 : 1—11),
his anointing at his baptism (42 : 1—8), his
own preaching (49 : 1—9), his rejection and
crucifixion (50 : 6 ; 52 : 13 to 53 : 12), and
the success of the Gospel after his sacrifice
(Chaps. 55th and 60th to 65th). In all this
statement the tender relation and the fidelity
of God as a Father and Redeemer (40 : 28 ;
41 : 8, 9 ; 42 : 3 ; 43 : 1, 3), man's special
guilt in not only proving unfaithful but in
charging his Creator with an injustice which
he dares not charge upon an earthly parent
(43 : 22 ; 45 : 9, 10), and the special fact that
through Christ's interposition and sacrifice

even this guilt of man is atoned so as to be
"blotted out" (43: 21, 25) because Christ
took our place in spiritual trial and bodily
suffering (53: 5, 6)—these facts, so palpable to
reason, and so prominent in revelation, are
the thread on which the whole connection
of the book hangs.

ATONEMENT IN THE PROPHETS OF THE HEBREW NATION'S HUMILIATION AND CAPTIVITY.

Of the sixteen prophets, whose books are
preserved, nine belong this age. In the order
of time they succeed each other as follows,
living through about two centuries. Three
of these began to prophecy, Zephaniah about
B. C. 630, Jeremiah 629, and Habakkuk
626, under the last kings of Judah, beginning with Josiah; three others, Daniel, B.
C. 603, Ezekiel 595, Obadiah 587, were prophets of the captivity; two others, Haggai
B. C. 520, and Zechariah 520, were inspired
seers under Zerubbabel the leader in the restoration; and the last, Malachi, B. C. 397,
was the successor to Ezra, Nehemiah and
Mordecai, in completing the records of the
Old Testament revelation. To the records
of these writers must be added about fifty-

three psalms, or songs, written during the same two centuries.

ATONEMENT AT THE OPENING AGE OF CAPTIVITY.

Jeremiah is the most voluminous writer of this era; being probably the compiler of the four books of history entitled Samuel and Kings; as well as the author of the prophecy and the lament bearing his name. The history of the nation from Samuel to the captivity, shows the progress of the unfaithfulness of the people in their assumed and covenanted relation to their Creator, Father and Savior; while it pictures his persistent fidelity to his assumed and covenanted relation. The prophecy sets forth the physical penalty of moral corruption, and the Lamentations bewail the fall of their city as the chief part of that penalty; but both foretell the restoration because of their Redeemer's fidelity. In the lengthy appeal to Israel, drawn from mingled history of the past and prophecy as to the future, the fidelity of " The Lord " and the infidelity of his select people is the refrain in the whole pathetic strain. Israel's depravity, especially in charging God with " iniquity " and excusing their own (2:

5 ; 16 : 10), must, except Divine aid be given, prove like the changeless skin of the Ethiopian (Jer. 13 : 23) ; but the character of the Redeemer (23 : 6), "The Lord our righteousness," offsets this hopeless condition. The very idea of charging upon an earthly parent, or on God, the responsibilities of sin is as irrational as to say that the father's eating a sour grape sets his children's teeth on edge (31 : 29, 30). The admission that "The Lord is righteous" while they have "rebelled," the recognition that "other lovers" have been untrue while "The Lord" remains faithful, is the opening expression in the dirge over fallen Jerusalem (Lam. 1 : 18, 19). The conviction that The Lord will never "turn aside the right of man," and that no "living man" can "complain for the punishment of his sins" (3 : 35—39) is the central truth. The plea "we are orphans and fatherless" when alienated from the Lord, the confession "our fathers have sinned and we have assumed [1] their sins," and the adoring faith "Thou, O Lord, remainest forever" faithful, these are the final expression of the

---

(1) The Hebrew *sabal* indicates a voluntary " taking on one's self " see Isah. 46 : 4 ; the penitent confession being that we h ive " borne " the sins of parents as Christ " bore " our sin. Isah. 53 : 11.

facts of atonement recognized in every age.

The prophet Zephaniah makes the justice of God in the calamities of Judah and His joy in the salvation of those redeemed the points of his vision (3: 5, 17). Habakkuk again makes the hinging truth of his age that which Paul quotes in his special exposition to Asiatics, Romans and Hebrews, of the grounds of the atonement. "The just by faith shall live;" the justified character, not the forgiven condition of the redeemed, constituting that self-satisfaction which makes the bliss of true life.[1]

In the four Psalms written apparently at the fall of Jerusalem, God's attachment to His people, dear as His "turtle-dove," His "covenant" as their assurance of His fidelity, His "own cause" as the end of His interposition, form His plea (74: 19—22). The prayer of His people is "Remember not against us former iniquities" (79: 8); the Redeemer's name "Jehovah" is appealed to as a sufficient pledge (83: 18); and the infinite wisdom and unswerving righteousness of God are the ground for assurance of atonement for sins. In neither the prophecy nor

---

(1) Hab. 2 : 4 quoted Gal. 3 : 11 ; Rom. 1 : 17 ; Heb. 10 : 38.

the psalmody of this age is the personal life
and death of the Redeemer presented; yet
his assumed responsibility and his assured
fidelity to its pledge is the foundation of
religious faith and hope.

THE ATONEMENT IN ASIATIC NATIONS AT THE AGE OF HEBREW CAPTIVITY.

Scholars like DuPerron, the French translator of the Zend-Avesta of Zoroaster, have
significantly noted that the age of the
Hebrew captives in Babylon was the age of
Zoroaster the Brahminic reformer in Persia,
of Confucius the Chinese moralist east of
Persia, and of Phericydes the Grecian teacher
of the ascetic Pythagoras, who studied late in
this age in Babylonia and Egypt. Whether
the Hebrew scriptures, and prophets like
Daniel, were the instructors whose teachings
reached the minds of these reformed religionists, is a question of secondary importance.
The convictions of these men as to spiritual
redemption and their idea of atonement are
of value.

The works of the Persian Zerdusht, called
by the Greeks Zoroaster, and of the Chinese
Confutsee, called by Europeans Confucius,
are translated in part into the languages of

modern Europe; while Zoroaster's more extended writings were known to the Greeks.

Zoroaster found that the Vedas of India
had led on from bodily penance as expiation
to the horrible mutilations of swinging on
the hook and self-immolation; and, going
to the opposite extreme, he conceived of God
as so good that he needs no sacrifice for expiation, because he requires no propitiation.
The *end* of creation is "purity, the best
good" (Khorday Avesta Ch. 1). As "the
Lord's" character in himself is purity " so He
is Ruler on account of purity" (Ch. 2).
Against the Brahminic idea that evil, inherent
in matter, is independent of the Spiritual
God, he contended that Satan, "Ahriman
whose deeds are accursed" (Ch. 3), is an adversary subdued by the Creator; so that man's
redemption is thus provided. The atonement
for sin and for a sinful nature is only pardon
secured through penitence; as is indicated in
the prayer: "All the evil thoughts, words,
deeds, * * which are become my nature,
* * all these sins, bodily and spiritual,
earthly and heavenly. O Lord, pardon; I
repent of them" (Ch. 4). Among the many
names and offices of "Ormasd", the Supreme
Creator, all those in modern Christian

theology are found (Chaps. 7 and 17); while as a necessary consequence of his assumed responsibility his first name [1] is "The not-to-be-questioned," and the second is "The Gatherer." The nature of his redemption is indicated in this ascription of praise (Ch. 14) : " Praise to the Overseer, who rewards good deeds, purifies at last the obedient, and redeems even the wicked out of hell"; this latter of the two parts of man's "restoration " implying the need of expiation. The necessity of meeting the spirit of his time led Zoroaster to tacitly admit a claim to miraculous power; though to his special disciples he explained the natural science on which he seemed to perform supernatural deeds. For the same reason, also, he allowed the worship of the sun ; an adoration which now forms the chief peculiarity of the Parsee religion, and which is commemorated by the word " Sun-day" in all the languages of Europe.

The moral system of Confucius recognizes God's rule as a father's. The fact that the idea of expiation by sacrifices was part of his teaching is worthy of note. He was careful to be present not only at the " great

---

(1) This recalls the address of " the Lord " to Jacob and to Moses.

sacrifice" offered by the emperor, but at
provincial sacrifices. He himself offered sacrifices to deceased men and to higher spirits
"as if they were present." He recognized
that the end of sacrifices was the securing of
a right spirit, and said: "For a man to
sacrifice to a spirit that does not belong to
him is self-adulation." He spoke of the
ancient origin of sacrifices, the record of
which was lost; and when asked to explain
their import he confessed "I do not know."
He declared that contrite feeling was more
important than the sacrificial observance;
and that however grave and serious the emperor and princes might be in the great
sacrifice, if they lacked the virtues they professed to adore, they had no title to preside
at the rites.   When a provincial chief offered
a sacrifice to a mountain, he asked an attend-
ant priest, " Can *you* not save him?" referring
to the unseen fate he feared. When the at-
tendant answered "No"; he again asked,
" Will you say that the mountain has more
discernment than the priest? "   When asked
as to the efficacy of sacrifices for propitiation,
he used this pregnant expression: " The
rites were a subsequent thing;" evidently implying that the purpose to redeem was fixed

by the Divine Creator, before he allowed man
to sin and then taught him by sacrifices to
express his need of expiation (Analects B.
II c. 24; B. III c. 2—12). The dying lament
of Confucius was that his moral system had
failed to redeem those who accepted its truth.

The advanced religious spirit of this age,
its world-wide influence, and its connection
with the advance of true science, is brought out
most fully by Plutarch in his life of Numa.
In astronomy the sun had come to be regarded as the centre of a system in which the
earth was one of the planets; the solar years
were determined to have three hundred and
sixty-five days; the lunar revolutions were
definitely fixed; and the causes of eclipses
were known and their recurrence calculated.
Numa, like Zoroaster, taught that God, as a
universal spirit, should be worshipped without the aid of images, but "through sacrifice"; and that piety consisted in an indus-
trious and virtuous life. Like Pythagoras,
who lived two hundred years later, Numa
taught that sacrifices of vegetables, rather
than bloody animal sacrifices, were preferable;
he required intense attention during these
offerings, and when on one occasion he was
interrupted while presiding, by a herald who

announced, "The enemy is coming," he replied, unmoved, "And I am sacrificing." The religious spirit of the age, especially the reverence for sacrifices shown by this great reformer, is a most impressive testimony to the nature and necessity for atonement.

ATONEMENT AS TAUGHT BY THE PROPHETS OF THE CAPTIVITY.

It would be unnatural if the Hebrew prophets in such an age had not returned to the spirit of Isaiah, and have uttered new visions as to the atonement.

Obadiah condemns the unnatural conduct of Esau's descendants towards Israel in their calamity; and he foretells that the "Savior" is to appear on Mt. Zion, and that "the kingdom shall be the Lord's" (vs. 10, 21.)

Ezekiel's vision is the model of John's Revelation. The Lord appears borne up by four spiritual existences united into one, whose embodiment (1: 5) had four faces, those of a man, of a lion, of an ox and of an eagle (1: 10); these indicating as in the ancient Chaldean and Egyptian sphinx the union of reason, courage, patience and forecaste; which as separate attributes Christian art has conceived to exist in the four evan-

gelists whose four narratives combined present the complete Christ. As in the Apocalyse
the sins of Jerusalem, the ancient Church,
are pictured (Ch. 4th to 24th), under the
name "Sodom" (16: 46—55). The sins,
then of Moab, Edom, Tyre and Egypt, as
those of Rome in the Apocalyse, are rehearsed;
that of the rude Japhetic tribes of Gog and
Magog closing the list (25th to 35th). The
spiritual kingdom of Christ (36th and 37th),
its triumph (38th and 39th) and the restoration of the New Jerusalem (40th to 48th),
as in the Apocalypse, form the third portion of
the vision. The direct presentation of the
atonement is found, first, in the nature of sin,
and second, in the spiritual agent who
restores the soul's life. The unreasonable-
ness of charging God with the responsibility
of sin is presented under Jeremiah's picture
of the sour grapes, and also on the principle
of human equity;[1] and the Lord declares
that He meets its claim, while man does
not reciprocate his fidelity. The essential
idea in the latter portion of the Book is
that of the Divine Spirit's renovation, of

---

(1) Ez.k 18: 1—33; 33: 17—40. The idea of the Hebrew
word rendered "equal," as the old English term borrowed
from the Latin, is in modern English found in the word
"equitable."

which the reviving breezes of Spring are
the emblem; to whose teaching Jesus
directed the Jewish Senator who saw its
fulfillment (Compare Ezek. 37th and John
3d.)

Daniel, himself of the royal line (1: 3),
inserts in the narrative of his book four
visions which Jesus afterwards quotes (Mat.
24: 15). The first is under the Assyrian
Nebuchadnezzar, and foretells how four great
empires shall successively rise and decline;
the last to be followed by a spiritual kingdom
which " the God of heaven " would cause to
hold sway over all nations (Ch. 2d). Under
Belshazzar, in a second vision, the future
spiritual kingdom is more clearly revealed
as that of " the Son of man;" and the four
kingdoms to succeed each other before his
coming are more definitely delineated (Ch.
7th). In a third vision, in the first year of
Darius, the Medo-Persian, the prophecy of
Jeremiah that Jerusalem should, after seventy
years, be rebuilt, overwhelms Daniel with
the conviction that his countrymen were
morally unfitted for a successful restoration
to civil independence; but he is reassured
by the promise of the coming of the Messiah
as a *spiritual* ruler (Ch. 9th). In this vision,

the precise time of the Messiah's appearing, after seven periods equal in length to the seventy years of the captivity, is revealed. Most of all, the fact that contrary to all Hebrew expectation he should be "cut off" in his prime, being rejected as Isaiah had foretold, and crucified as David had pictured, and more than this, that he should be cut off " not for himself," but as Isaiah predicted " for the transgressions of his people;" these form central points of truth as to the atonement. It adds to the intense interest of this revelation, that, when the Assyrian king saw a fourth being walking in the fiery furnace with the three Hebrew youth, he instinctively exclaimed, "The form of the fourth is like the Son of God" (3 : 25). In a fourth vision, in the same year with the third, the names of three of the four empires before announced are given, the Assyrian, Medo-Persian and Grecian; the fourth, unnamed, proving to be the Roman. It is not an unimportant fact that all these four, China only excepted, are the nations already prepared by religious reform to hail the Redeemer.

The Psalms written during the captivity, some fifteen in number, like the songs of all nations, show the ruling thought of the pious

Hebrews. That ruling thought is the "faithfulness" of "the Lord," founded on "justice" and "righteousness" as well as mercy, expected through the Redeemer to come (Ps. 89: 2, 4, 14, 16, 24, 29, 35, 37). The aspiration of their souls is "to show that the Lord is upright and there is no unrighteousness in him" (Ps. 92: 15). Their cry in trouble is, "There is forgiveness" with thee and "plenteous redemption;" · the ground of which is: "He shall redeem Israel from all his iniquities" (Ps. 130: 4, 7, 8). The meaning of these expressions is made clear by the prophets of the same age; and the central truth in all is that God's assumed responsibility constitutes the assurance of atonement.

ATONEMENT IN THE WRITERS OF THE RESTORATION.

Hope realized, restoration not only promised but attained, inspires new views; and to the Hebrew prophets prepared to receive them, new revelations are given. The prophets of the return from captivity are Haggai and Zechariah; the historians of the next generation are Ezra and Nehemiah; a captive narrator of the same age is Mordecai; the

Psalms, as the history of the era, extend over a century; a generation yet later, the last of the prophets closes the Old Testament visions; and all these succeeding writers reveal advanced knowledge of the atonement.

Haggai, writing B. C. 520, sixteen years after the first return of the captives (1: 1; Ezra 1: 1 and 4, 24) when the ardor of the people was checked by opposition, seeks to inspire the people to rebuild their temple (1: 2). His chief appeal is to the fact that the Redeemer, " the Desire of all nations," should appear in it; that its moral "glory" should "exceed that of" Solomon's temple; and that a spiritual power should " shake all the earth" by the "Spirit" of God; prophecies whose fulfillment brightens many a page of the New Testament, and calls forth special mention from Jesus (Mat. 24: 71) and from Paul (Heb. 12: 26). The main point of importance is the historic fact on which these prophecies rest, seen in the history of the age; that "all nations" did desire the Redeemer.

Zechariah, writing at the same era, utters predictions as to the Redeemer to come, minute and vital; whose fulfillment studs the whole of the New Testament. The "branch" to arise from David, a mingled figure drawn from the sprouting of spring vegetation and the upward shooting of the sun's rays at dawn, [1] inspired the namesake of the prophet at the birth of that John, who, as a day-star, heralded the Redeemer's near approach (3: 8, and Luke 1: 78). His figure of the inexhaustible fountain of Divine "grace," drawn not from limited reservoirs but from living olive trees, its two agents being apparently the "everliving Redeemer" and the "living Spirit," [2] forms a hinging point in John's vision of the Gospel's triumphs in ages yet future (4: 2—14; Rev. 11: 4). Zechariah foretells that the "Branch," thus to come, should rear the spiritual temple (6: 12); to which Jesus and his apostles alluded (John 2: 19; 2d Cor. 6: 16; 1st Pet. 2: 5). He pictures, as if it were before his eyes, Christ's riding in triumph into Jerusalem (9: 9; Matt. 21: 5). Under

(1) Gesenius regrads *tsemah*, the "branch," a figure drawn from sprouting plants, as referring to the Messiah, in Jer. 25: 5, and 33: 15, also in Zech. 3: 8, and 6: 12. The Greek translators, who about B. C. 275 rendered it *anatole* or "dawn-ray," quoted by Zacharias at John's birth, evidently understood that there was a double figure in *tsemah*. ·

(2) All explanations of the "two anointed witnesses" (4: 14) that stop short of the anointed Jesus and anointing Spirit fall below the thought of Zechariah and John, as well as of the New Testament generally. See John 1: 41; 7: 39; Acts 4: 27, 31; 10: 36, 44; 2d Cor. 1: 19–22; Heb. 1: 9; 7: 25; 8: 10; 1st John 2: 20, 24.

the figures of the shepherd's two staves,
Beauty and Bands (11: 7,) or gentleness and
firmness, grace and strength, he contrasts, as
Christ did, the true and false shepherd (11:
15, 16, and John 10: 1, 2); he describes
Christ's betrayal, and the traitor's price (10:
12, 13; Mat. 26: 15; 27: 10); under the
figure of a fountain, (13: 1), he anticipates
Christ's emblem of washing his disciples'
feet when most they needed His spiritual
cleansing (John 13: 1, 8); he portrays the
scene of his arrest (13: 7; Mat. 26: 31); he
mentions the very spot from which he ascended (14: 4; Acts 1: 12); thus making
the successive scenes of Christ's last days on
earth pass in prophetic vision before his
readers.

Ezra, one of the many families who preferred a permanent home in Assyria, returning
about B. C. 457, eighty years after the restoration, gives first the history of the early
return and then of his own work of reform.
That reform indicates, that, while in Egypt
formal idolatry was learned, in Assyria the
"lust" (Coll. 3: 5) which is the spirit of
idolatry, remained; and Ezra reveals the
nature of the spiritual redemption provided
for Israel by renewing sacrifices for expiation

and the reading and practice of the law for
renovation (7: 10; 8: 21; 9: 5—15; 10: 5).
Nehemiah, also one of the dispersed, [1] visits
the restored people about B. C. 446, ten years
later than Ezra, and as a civil magistrate
gives an example of enterprise and self-sacri-
.fice; while with executive authority he en-
forces the reform which Ezra could only recom-
mend (2: 12; 4: 23; 5: 10, 14, 15; 13: 21,
28). Meanwhile Ezra continues his moral
work; the sacrifices for atonement, the confession and the new covenant of the people
indicating a returning faith in the Divinely
provided atonement. Meanwhile, as the
most thorough Biblical scholarship shows,
under Xerxes the Great, B. C. 485 to 464, we
have a view of the myriads of Israel in the
" dispersion ": of their continued influence
at the Persian Court; of their distinct and
firm adherence to the faith of their fathers;
and yet more of the propagation of the faith
of the Old Testament " from India to Ethio-
pia," which prepares us for the visit of the
Magi to the new-born Redeemer (Mat. 3: 2),
and for the array of devout men from every
portion of the three continents met as pro-

---

(1) See the distinction indicated by *diaspora*, John 7: 35;
Jas. 1: 1 and 1 Pet. 1: 1.

selytes at Jerusalem when Christ's spiritual reign was inaugurated (Acts 2 : 5, 9, 10, 11), which facts make the Book of Esther the vestibule between the audience chambers of Old and New Testament revelations. The short-sighted eye that is searching for the *name* of "God" in the book, forgets that in the volume of revelation, as of nature, the Father of Spirits writes not his name so much as His character and His will; and that the humble yet believing spirits of Esther and Mordecai, and their aspiration not for worldly honor but for the redemption of their people, prepared the hearts of nations and peoples for that Redeemer for whose coming they lived.

The inspired Psalms of the captivity and of the restoration are historic pictures uniting the age of the prophets to that of the apostles. The fond endearment of the "turtle-dove" (Ps. 84th), the memories of Egypt and Joseph, of Babylon and of many a personal danger (81st, 107th, 114th, 126th), the confident trust in God in the arduous work of restoration (125th, 127th), the assurance of future redemption not only of Israel but of all peoples (102d, 111th), that prayer, sweet to the believer in every age (116th),

and those praises suited to the heavenly host
as well as earthly worshipers (146th to 150th),
will never cease to aid the mind that seeks
to learn God's purpose of human redemption.

The closing of the Hebrew record is doubt-
less the work of Ezra's old age. The Chron-
icles of the kings of Judah trace the line of
Christ's descent from the leader in the restoration to the fifth generation (1 Chron. 3:
19—24). The special appointments made
by David, for national worship, especially
sacrifice, are detailed; the personal temptation of Satan, and the bodily appearance and
interposition of The Lord to David, are recorded (1st Chron. Ch. 21st); Solomon's
special charge of the required sacrifices is
enlarged upon (2d Chr. 8th); the reforms
instituted by Jehosaphat (Ch. 16th and
29th), by Hezekiah (20th to 31st), and by
Josiah (34th, 35), are made prominent; and
the close of the book connecting it with
Ezra's history, shows the special design to
trace the history of faith in redemption.

The Book of Malachi, written evidently
when Ezra was engaged in his last work,
brings out God's full design; his assumed
relation to man, the import of Old Testament
sacrifices, and the nature of spiritual refor-

mation from Adam to Christ. The Lord, as
the "burden" of Malachi's message, declares
his "love," from the beginning, to those
faithful like Jacob; and his remonstrance is,
" If I be a father, where is my honor?" (1: 6.)
Neglect of the "sacrifices" he required is
their sin; because it was a symbol of the
"pure offering" which "all nations" were
yet to bring (1: 8, 11). The Levites appointed to preserve the purity of sacrifice
are declared to have broken their covenant
vows (2: 4—8). All men are "of one father";
and yet Judah and Israel, though brethren,
have been alienated. Yet more, the husband
and the wife of his youth are estranged;
though in Eden God gave man in his sinlessness "one" bosom-companion, to the end
that their seed might be a "godly seed" (2:
14, 15). Nevertheless the promise of Eden
is to be fulfilled; the very Being who gave
the first promise, even "The Lord," Jehovah,
will "come suddenly to this temple," preceded by the forerunner to "prepare his
way" (3: 1). Then his truth and grace will
so shine, and reveal the righteous, that men
can "discern between the righteous and the
wicked" (3: 18). Finally the main ultimate
result, that which as the closing light of the

Old Covenant was caught up at the first dawn of the new,—the parental relation as the very embodiment of God's assumed relation to all whom he has created (4: 6),—will, when Christ *redeems* men, be made real and controlling. It would be difficult to conceive how the *facts* of the atonement, which must all enter into any correct theory, could be made more prominent than in this survey, which closes the Old·Testament revelation.

THE ATONEMENT AMONG THE GREEKS AT THEIR CLIMAX.

The age between Daniel and Malachi was the era of Grecian preeminence in science, art and religious progress. Pythagoras, educated in Egypt, India and Babylonia, taught the true structure of the solar system; Democritus elaborated the modern idea of atomic elements, of their gravitation and their organic union, and Anaxagoras applied this truth to vegetable and animal development; and Aristotle, perfecting logical analysis, so applied it in Natural History that Agassiz often declared he had anticipated and outstripped modern investigations.

Applying this same analysis to religious conviction, both the ideal and material theories of evolution, before taught in India and now revived in Germany and England, were elaborated; while their partial characters had been shown, successively by Anaxagoras, Socrates, Aristotle and Cicero, in the fact that only material and formal causes, to the exclusion of their efficient and final causes, were in these theories brought into view. Socrates urged that it was unphilosophical to trace second causes at all unless the First Cause were admitted. In a demonstrative argument, which, when reconstructed by Clarke, was declared by Newton as convincing as a mathematical calculation, the necessary existence and perfect character of a personal spiritual God was shown by Anagoras, Socrates, Plato, Aristotle and Cicero. As astronomical science, then and now, admits that space is unlimited and time unending though no mind can *comprehend* the fact, so the perfect order of the limitless universe proves the existence and infinite excellence of an incomprehensible personal Creator; since order is to human experience always the result of a designing mind. The same men argued the immortality of the

human spirit; first, from physical science,
which intimates that spirit more subtile than
an atom is indestructible; second, from
moral science, which assures man that his
highest desire, for continued existence, would
not have been created within him unless, like
all his lower desires, provision to meet the
longing were made; the former of which
proofs Butler only repeated, while the latter
is constantly reached in their mature convictions by men like Emerson and Victor
Hugo.

Those special convictions which lead men
to expect an atonement were specially clear
and deep among the Greeks. The "righteousness" of God in permitting evil appeared
from the fact that no high virtue can exist
except by its exercise; compassion being impossible except there be suffering, and mercy
having no place unless there be sin or moral
wrong. Human sin, Socrates taught, must
be in men's nature (*physei*), since, if it were propagated by example, seclusion of children
would secure a sinless succession (Plat.
Meno.); Aristotle regarded it as inherited,
(*suggenes*, Nic. Eth. iii. 15); Cicero declared
it a "depravity in religious convictions"
beginning in infancy (Tusc. Quest. iii. 1);

Ovid pronounces it incurable (Metam. vii. 18—22); and Seneca states that it is universal, corrupting all men and prevailing from childhood to old age (De Clem. I, 6).

Redemption from sin, these sages taught, has two elements; expiation and renovation. In early times the Greeks offered even human sacrifices; the fate of Iphigenia moving not only the poets Homer and Euripides, but also the statesmen Plato and Cicero. Xenophon indicates how fundamental the idea of expiation was in Grecian religious thought by stating this as the palpable proof, that Socrates in teaching that there was but one Spiritual God did not encourage irreligion: "he was always conspicuous in offering sacrifices, oft-times at home and oft-times upon the common altars of the city" (Mem. I, i. 2).

The purity of character essential to righteousness was elaborated to the last degree in the teachings of Socrates and in the writings of Aristotle, Cicero and Seneca. Socrates pictured the ideal of a man loving and practicing right for its own sake, meeting public odium on himself by resisting injustice, and bringing on himself martyrdom and even "crucifixion" (Plat. Rep. ii. 3); a portraiture

which seemed to some early Christian scholars
to be a prophecy of Christ, and which in its
contrast as an ideal with the future real "Just
One" (Acts 3 : 14, 15), led even Rousseau to
write in his Emile: "the life and death of
Socrates were those of a sage; the life and
death of Jesus were those of a god!" In his
final "defense," when on trial, Socrates expressed the conviction that an effectual Redeemer, so much needed, would yet be sent
by the Deity to save men from moral ruin;
as also Cicero in his "Divination," dwelling
on the inadequate impression made by sacrifices and their spiritual intimations, uttered
the conviction that a more reliable revelation
would some day be made.

ATONEMENT IN WESTERN EUROPE BEFORE CHRIST'S DAY.

As the New Testament revelation was to
be in the Greek language, and as that language was an embodiment of the ideas of the
people who used it, it is necessary, in studying the Gospel statements as to the atonement, to gain all the knowledge possible of
the common ideas incorporated into that
language just before the New Testament was
written. This is the more necessary because

the distinctive ideas as to religious truth held by the Greeks and Western nations before they became Christians, are the clue to their future distinct history as Churches.

While many philosophic and cultured Romans, like Cicero, were Grecian in their religious convictions, the Romans were Asiatic. Their order of priests was a caste, with a monarchical "pontifex maximus" as their head. They recognized the whole range of deities, Greek included, over which their world-wide empire extended; but specially recognized the seven celestial powers, the sun, moon and five greater planets, after which the names of the days of their week, still preserved in the Italian, Spanish and French languages, corresponding to the quartering of the moon, were framed (Dio. Cas. 37 : 81). They offered sacrifices to evil or infernal deities as well as to good, or celestial deities; making a notable distinction in these two classes of sacrifices. The animal offered to the celestial deities was white, the priest dressed in white, the neck of the victim was bent upwards, the knife was plunged into the jugular vein from above, and the blood caught in cups was sprinkled from above on the altars. The victim for the in-

fernal deities was black, the priest dressed in
black, the neck was pressed down, the stab
was beneath, and the blood was poured into
an excavation in the earth. Prayers and
other rites, minutely described by historians
and poets, accompanied the sacrifice. The
"aruspices" inspected the inwards when laid
open, especially the liver; and from their
appearance professed to divine good or ill
fortune. In the early days of the kings,
human sacrifices were offered; a law of
Romulus making traitors sacrifices to the infernal deities; but one of the humanizing
influences of the republic, as Pliny records
(Nat. Hist. 30: 1, 3), was a decree of the
Senate "Ne homo immolaretur." There is
reason to suppose that civil rather than
religious reasons prompted the law of Romulus; and that, as in the "burnt offering" of
Jephthah (Judg. 11; 31, 39), in the "atonement" of David, from which his nature
shrank before Rizpah's resistance (2d Sam.
21: 1—13), and in Josiah's sacrifice of Baal's
priests on their altars (2 Kings 23: 20), the
idea of expiation was secondary; as it was in
the slaughters at the tomb of Julius Cæsar,
ordered by Augustus (Dio. 48: 14). The an-
nual human sacrifices, however, practiced from

the days of the kings to the emperors, even under the Republic (Macrob. Sat. 1: 7, and Dio. 43: 24), were for atonement.

Among the early people of Central and Western Europe, the religious order of Druids had supreme civil as well as military authority throughout Germany, Gaul or France, and the British Isles. They retained the ancient name of inferior celestial powers, designating the days of the week, still retained, in Saxon corresponding to their Latin designations; yet they forbade the forming of any image, and worshipped only a spiritual deity. Sacrifices of animals and human beings were their chief rites. Strabo describes how the priest would gash a man on the back and divine from his convulsive throes; sometimes impaling or crucifying the victim; and sometimes framing a colossal image, filling it within with hay, wood, animals and men, and setting it on fire. Cæsar states that excommunication, or exclusion of any one from the sacrifices, was the most fearful penalty; since he was driven from his home and family, and no one was allowed to furnish him food or shelter. [1]

---

[1] Cæsar de Bel. Gal. vi. 13, 14 ; Strabo B. IV. c. iv, Sect. 4, 5 ; Tacit. Germ. c. vii to xi, Agric. c. xi. The use of "Greek letters" by the Druids, mentioned by Cæsar, indicates their Pelasgic and Brahminic origin.

The perpetuation in the Roman Church of this civil power after the Gothic conquest, its incorporation into the Gothic and old German codes, and the sanguinary penances imposed by priestly power, will be seen to have an influence on views of the atonement which the German Reformation could not fully meet; since it was not reform but eradication which the Gospel proposed.

·

A REDEEMER FROM THE EAST EXPECTED AT CHRIST'S DAY.

The opening of Matthew's Gospel, picturing "wise men" of the East following a star westward in search of the "king of the Jews," is but an allusion to a wide-spread idea, on which the writer at his day had no occasion to comment. The statements of this expectation among the Jews made by Tacitus (Hist. 5: 13), may perhaps be traced, as Gieseler (Eccl. Hist. P. 1, D. 1, Sect. 16) intimates, to Josephus, from whose Jewish history Tacitus quotes; but Suetonius (Vespas. c. 4) refers to it as "an ancient and constant opinion in the entire East," and Virgil pictures it in his Pollio a century before Josephus wrote.

·

This expected ruler, though not to be an expiatory sacrifice, was in the record of Roman writers as truly a restorer of moral and religious "righteousness" as the Messiah pictured by David. Among Greeks and Romans this idea was so controlling that the successors of Alexander and the first Roman emperors, availing themselves of it, took such names as "Soter" Savior, and "Euergetes" benefactor (Cicero in Ver., Philo Legat. and adv. Flac.); to which Christ himself alludes (Luke 22: 25).

The rise of Budhism, whose doctrines began their spread eastward from Northern India after the moral systems of Confucius in China, and of Zoroaster in Persia, had failed to redeem, indicates the nature of the Redeemer who was "the desire of all nations." It arose some three or more centuries before Christ; and, as Mohammedanism arose five centuries after Christ, in the disappointed expectation of moral redemption from former religious systems. Its author was the heir to the throne of a vast empire, whose aspiration was to "*know*" eternal truth, the idea in the name "Budha"; knowing which, as he declared, "I can give lasting peace to mankind," and "become their deliverer."

His effort was to become perfect in every moral and religious virtue; his followers regarded him as divine as well human; his perpetuated life as an embodied divinity is symbolized in the images of Budha in India and China, and is realized in the grand Llama of Thibet. The prevalence of Budhism over the moral system of Confucius indicates man's felt need of a personal Redeemer; while its inefficiency to redeem is now recognized by the practical Japanese in the suggestion of their statesmen that Budhism be renounced for Christianity.

THE GREEK LANGUAGE AS FITTED TO EXPRESS ATONEMENT.

In several respects the Greek language had, when the New Testament writers employed it, become fitted to express the new truths to be revealed. Under the Macedonian Empire, beginning with Alexander, it had come to be the learned language of Asia and Africa as well as of Eastern Europe; under the Roman Empire, as Cicero states, (Orat. pro. Arch. c. 23) it prevailed over the Latin "in all nations"; and as Cæsar mentions (Bel. Gal. vi. 14), it was used even by the Druids of Central and Western Europe. In the progress of two or three centuries before Christ, its completeness for the expression of all the common spiritual ideas of mankind had been tested; some new compound terms indeed being formed in itself, and some names of new objects being incorporated; while, however, it became afterwards so little changed that the Greek of the present day is being brought back to the classic purity. Its copiousness furnished words for spiritual ideas adapted to express the limited and general terms of the rudest tribes; while its elaborateness met the demand for nice discrimination in expressing special distinctions in spiritual conception. Its firmly fixed forms at this era, made it like the Hebrew of the Old Testament, an unchanging repository for a permanent record of truth whose full meaning was to be developed in the progress of ages of future spiritual experience.

THE ATONEMENT IN THE GREEK TRANSLATION OF THE OLD TESTAMENT.

In the early period of the Macedonian sway, the Old Testament was translated into Greek as a literary treasure under Ptolemy II, B. C. 277. In this translation three distinct aids to the conception of the atonement as held by the Hebrews are offered; since that translation is directly quoted often by New Testament writers.

The chief of these aids is the comparative correspondence of Hebrew and Greek conceptions indicated by the use of one term for another. This is specially to be noted in the significant name Jehovah; which is rendered *kyrios*, or Lord; which designation in modern Greek has come to 'mean no more than kindred words in other modern European tongues equivalent to "Mister." The kindred ideas in *nesphesh* and *ruach*, rendered *psyche* and *pneuma*, "soul and spirit," and the use of the words for salvation, justification, redemption, &c., are noteworthy. The special word for "make atonement," *exilaskomai*, stronger in form than that of the New Testament, in its full signification meaning to "secure expiation from," is used from Moses to Daniel; and it even supplies the word "forgive" (Ps. 78: 38).

Subordinate to this chief aid is the occasional filling out in the Greek translation of the Old Testament of what was the writer's unexpressed conception. Thus in Ps. 40: 6, instead of a part for the whole "mine ears hast thou moulded," we have the full idea "a body hast thou remodelled for me"; which rendering, with its wider import, Paul adopts (Heb. 10: 5). The knowledge of "God" learned from nature is extended to that of the "Lord", indicated in Ps. 19: 1, 4, 7, and confirmed Rom. 10: 18. Again in Deut. 32: 43, in addition to the subordinate idea "Praise him ye nations his people" the Greek translators inserted "Praise him ye heavens, and let all the angels of God worship him"; and, though a similar yet unlike sentiment is found in the Hebrew as well as. Greek in Ps. 97: 7, Paul quotes the enlarged statement of the translators given to Moses' words, whose bearing on the doctrine of the atonement has been noted by Christian scholars in many an age.

THE ATONEMENT IN THE HEBRAIC-GREEK OF THE APOCRYPHA.

A minor addition to the Old Testament view of the atonement is found in the books entitled Apocrypha; volumes not found in Hebrew; written after the age of the Old Testament; having historical and scientific errors, which, as scholars of the Roman Church allow, disprove their inspired character; but which like Greek and Roman

writings give important illustrations of
human convictions as to the atonement. The
Books of the Maccabees record the fact of
the prohibition of the Mosaic sacrifices and
other rites by one of Alexander's successors,
and that some Israelites offered Grecian sacrifice instead (1 Mac. 1: 45—52). In contrast with this, Josephus records the Roman
reverence for the Jewish sacrifices; the emperors from the first favoring Jewish sacrifices, and the priests offering them on their
behalf; while the war which destroyed the
Jewish State originated in the neglect of
these sacrifices (Wars B. II, 17: 2, B. VI, 2:
1; Apion B. II, 6, 24). In the act of prohibition, promulgated by the Greek ruler,
occurs the significant expression that the
Israelites should "change all the justifying
offerings," *dikaiomata*. Hints of truths
brought out in the New Testament are found
in the picture of the "just one," declaring
himself the "Son of God," yet rejected
through "the envy of the devil" by which
"death came into the world" (Wisd. 2: 12—
24); again in the perfect "righteousness"
attributed to God (Wisd. 12: 12—16); and
again in the injustice, as well as sin of mankind, who, *from* Adam and *like* Adam, have

charged God as the Author of their error and its penalty (Wisd. of Sir. 15: 11—22). The absurdity of this charge is illustrated in the suggestion "He hath set fire and water before thee; stretch forth thine hand to whichever thou wilt." The error and corruption of sacrifices, which subsequently appeared in the medieval Roman Church, is indicated in this age by the ritualistic error of "sacrifices for the dead" (2 Mac. 12: 43), and by the opposite rationalistic error "to depart from unrighteousness (*adikia*) is expiation (*ilasmos*)." (Wisd. of Sir. 35: 5).

Special Greek Terms used in the New Testament bearing on the Atonement.

The New Testament idea of atonement is revealed by statements of Christ's nature as its author, of men's character as its object, of Christ's sacrifice as its means, and of its influence on men and angels as its end. The teachings of Jesus and the preaching and writings of his apostles, extending over a period of sixty years, indicate an increasing definiteness in the use of terms and a growing completeness of view corresponding to the preparation of men to appreciate the revelation.

The relation of God to man is pictured as that of a "*father*" in all the precepts and parables of Christ; the idea of a *kingly* rule being denied by Christ before the people and the Roman governor (John 6: 15: 18; 18: 37). Christ as Divine is the "I am" who appeared to Moses, the "Lord" described by David, and the "Word" or spiritual God of Grecian Sages; all of which terms involve the idea of a revealed Supreme Being (Mat. 22: 32, 43; John 8: 58). In his assumed human nature the Divine Being has a "sympathy" with man impossible unless directly experienced (Mat. 8: 7; John 1: 14; Rom. 8: 3; Heb. 2: 14). His human soul, left alone to resist sin in his extreme agony, was saved, as any man's, by submissive faith (Mat. 27: 46; John 12: 27; Heb. 5: 7). With this double nature Christ was the direct Creator of the universe and of man; and as such assumed the authority and responsibility of their government (Mat. 28: 18; John 1: 2; Coll. 1: 16; Heb. 1: 2).

The personal existence of evil spirits, and of Christ's power over evil, is made distinct; Christ meeting the tempter by stronger tests than did Adam, and permitting during his own incarnation bodily possessions by evil spirits that he might prove his Divine control over them (Mat. 3:1—11; 12:22—29); this power of evil spirits over the body having entirely ceased when John wrote, and only their spiritual power being alluded to in the epistles of the apostles. The chief tempter of Christ is declared to be the "old serpent" of Eden, the "Satan" of the Old Testament, the "Apollyon" of universal history; his spiritual power in all opposition to Christ is recognized; and this opposition is always avowed to be put forth against Christ as the "Son of God" and the Redeemer of the Universe. [1]

The end of Christ's mission, as wide as his creations, has a direct relation to angels as well as men. They hailed His incarnation before man's creation (Heb. 1:6), and they heralded his birth; declaring the two ends of his mission to be the "glory of God in His highest sway" [2] revealed in the "peace" He gives and in the "good will" He shows to man. Hence they discriminate human character, they rejoice over penitents, they

---

(1) Mat. 4:3, 10; 16:23; Mk. 1:24; 5:7; Luke 10:18; 22:3, 31; John 13:27; Acts 5:3; 19:15; 26:18; Rom. 16:18; 2d Cor. 11:14; 2d Thess. 2:9; Rev. 2:9, 13; 3:9; 12:9.

(2) The word *hypsistos* elsewhere has this meaning, and hence seems to have it in the "hosanna" of the angels and of children, Luke 2:14; 19:38.

are moral guardians of childhood piety, and
are ministering spirits to heirs of salvation
(Mat. 13: 41; 18: 10; 25. 31; Luke 15: 7,
10; Heb. 1: 14; 12: 22). More than this,
Christ's mission to man had a direct reference
to angels; that they might have new and
complete knowledge of the Divine character
(Eph. 3: 10); and that as *man* is "reconciled," *katallasso*, by the "atonement,"
katallage, (Rom. 5: 10, 11) so the *angels* are
"re-reconciled," *apokatallasso*, (Coll. 1: 20),
this being the *higher* "intent" of the long
unrevealed and when "revealed" the un-
searchable riches of Christ (Eph. 3: 3—10; 1
Pet. 1: 12).   This view, intimated at Christ's
birth, confirmed by his words, fully developed
in Paul's later epistles, led to the employ,
especially by John the latest New Testament
writer, of the Greek word *kosmos*, familiar
to the readers of Plato and Aristotle, and
noted by Christian scholars of many an age.
Its original meaning of "order," extended to
the Universe as a perfect whole, is manifest
in the expression "foundation of the world"; [1]
it is intimated in the allusion of John and of
Paul to Christ's creative work. to God's love,

---

[1] Mat. 13 : 35 ; 25 : 34 ; Luke 11 : 50 : John 17 : 5, 24 ; Acts
17 : 24 ; Rom. 1 : 20 ; Eph. 1 : 4 ; Heb. 4 : 3 ; 9 : 26 ; 1 Pet. 1 :
20 ; Rev. 13 : 8 ; 17 : 8.

to the "crisis" at Christ's crucifixion, to the field of Satan's influence, to the extent of faith exercised in Christ, to the glory thus brought to God, and to the scenes of the judgment; [1] and many have inferred that a share, at least indirect, in the expiatory sacrifice offered by Christ is participated by the entire Universe of spiritual beings. [2]

In its teachings as to the character of man, specially redeemed by Christ, discrimination in the use of terms is to be observed. His threefold nature, with bodily appetites, *sarx*, animal passions, *psyche*, and an immortal spirit, *pneuma*, is recognized; first in the law for their control (Mk. 12: 30), second in the impulses to which they are subject (Heb. 4: 12), and third in the Divine power controlling the redeemed (1 Thess. 5: 23). The special discrimination between these terms is not found in the popular language of Jesus (Mk. 8: 35, 36); though he does note it in quoting the Old Testament law; but it is oftener observed by Paul, as when he declared that the *psychical* nature, or animal soul, is to perish with the body (1st Cor. 15: 44—46).

---

(1) John 1 : 10 ; 3 : 16 ; 10: 36 ; 12: 31 ; 14 : 30 ; 16: 11 ; 1 Cor. 4: 9 ; 6 : 2 ; Coll. 1 : 6 ; Heb. 10 : 5.

(2) John 1 : 29 ; 6 : 33, 57 ; 2d Cor. 5 : 9 ; 1 Tim. 3 : 16 ; 1st John 2 : 2.

The sin of man is two-fold; first, even those not giving sway to the "lusts" or undue desires (1st John 2: 16) of either of these three natures, "come short" of the "perfect" obedience which constitutes "righteousness" (Mat. 19: 21; Mk. 10: 21; Luke 18: 22; Rom. 3: 23; 10; Gal. 6: 10; James 2: 10; 3: 2); and second, all men delay to accept and faithfully improve the proffer of redemption provided by Christ (John 3: 19; 16: 9; Heb. 2: 3). The depravity of man's nature making his sin irrecoverable without Divine interposition, is error, *amartia*, in the finite intellect, selfishness, *echthra*, from alienated affection, and self-will, *anomia*, from pride and unsubmission to law; of the first of which Eve is an example, of the second Adam and of the third Satan. [1]

The universal prevalence of sin, aside from other proofs, is a necessary inference from the fact that Christ "died for all men" (2 Cor. 5: 14). The origin of sin is in man's "nature" (Eph. 2: 3); the foundation of its universality is a spiritual "deadness" to religious truth and duty (Eph. 2: 1, 5), a

---

[1] Error Luke 11: 4; John 9: 41; Rom. 3: 20; Jas. 1: 15; 1st John 1: 8; 5: 7; compare 2d Cor. 11: 3. Alienation Rom. 8: 7; Eph. 2: 15; Jas. 4: 4; compare 1st Tim. 2: 14; 1st John 2: 15. Self-will Mat. 7: 23; Rom 6: 19; Tit. 2: 14; Heb. 8: 12; 1st John 3: 4; compare 1st Tim. 3: 6.

"death" inherited from Adam (1 Cor. 15:22);
for which bias, leading to "one" or each
man's *first* transgression, we are responsible
because we endorse it as ours by yielding, as
did Adam when sinless, to the first temptation; so that all men, even those who from
Adam to Moses had no express revelation,
and who in this one particular do not sin
"after the similitude of his transgression,"
are nevertheless responsible for their own
sin, sinning actually against more knowledge
than he (Rom. 1:32; 5:12—16). The "inexcusableness" of man's sin is twofold; first,
that, knowing "the law" in its application to
others and himself, he does not obey it (Mat.
7:3; Rom. 1:20, 32; 2:1, 8); and second,
that the knowledge which all nations have
had of "redemption" has not been improved
(John 9:41; 15:22, 24; Acts 14:17; 17:
27, 30; Rom. 10:18).

The redemption provided by Christ, is presented in the provisions themselves, in the
means by which they are provided, and in
the conditions in man essential to their
appropriation. In itself redemption provides
the cancelling of past sin and restoration to
future holiness; in each of which provisions
distinct elements are to be observed. The

means Christ employs are his death and his
life; his human trial on earth from birth
till he expired, constituting the sacrificial
offering or gift that cancels the past; while
his spiritual power, put forth from his first
assumption of human nature before the
creation of Adam till his resignation of it
after the last of the redeemed shall have
been taken from earth (1st Cor. 15 : 28), constitutes the work of redemption which restores man for the future. The grace of
" faith " secures for its possessor Christ's interposition in both parts of his redemption
(Rom. 5 : 1; 1st John 5 : 4, 5); the grace of
" hope " prompts the redeemed soul to a life
of faith (Rom. 8 : 24; 1st John 3 : 3); while
these two secure the reign of the ultimate
grace of " love," which is the law of Heaven
(Rom. 5 : 5; 1 Cor. 13 : 13; 1st John 2 : 5—8;
4 : 7, 8).

The general provision of redemption is
righteousness, *dikaiosune*, embracing three
ideas; first, righteousness in the character
and government of God in all His redeeming
work for man (Rom. 1 : 17); second, righteousness in man so far as his past sin makes
him guilty (Rom. 3 : 25), and third, righteousness in the life of him thus redeemed

(Rom. 6: 13). In the language of Jesus, as in the Sermon on the Mount, these two latter ideas are included (Mat. 3: 15; 5: 6, 20; 6: 1, 33; 21: 32; John 16: 8, 10). The verb *dikaioo*, rendered justified, is restricted by both Jesus and Paul to "justification" for the past (Luke 18 · 14; Acts 13: 39; Rom. 3: 20). In the discriminating argument of Paul, *dikaioma* represents the righteous act in itself of God; who, through His fidelity to His assumed relation to man and the sacrifice of Christ in his human nature, proves to His intelligent Universe his justice in justifying the redeemed (Rom. I: 32; 2: 26; 5: 16, 18; 8: 4). In that same special use of terms *dikaiosis* represents the Spirit which possesses the redeemed (Rom. 4: 25; 5: 18). With equal discrimination the new feeling thus awakened towards God in the redeemed is called *katallage*, "reconciliation" (Rom. 5: 10, 11; 11: 15; 2 Cor. 5: 18—20); the English translators in their one only employ of the word "atonement" (Rom. 5: 11) manifestly recognizing the universal meaning elsewhere given to the Greek term. This provision in redemption is called *dorea*, a "gift," as that which is bestowed from without, (John 4: 10; Acts 2: 38; Rom. 3: 24;

5: 15, 17; Eph. 3: 7); its meaning being rendered distinctive by the use of *dorema*, for the gift in itself (Rom. 5: 16), and of *doron*, for the general provision of entire redemption (Eph. 2: 8). Careful attention to like nice discriminations in terms used by Paul is essential in studying the doctrinal portions of his epistles; as it is also in all his practical statements regarded morality in life and order in Church organization.

The second provision of redemption, a future holy life, begins in repentance, *metanoia*; a change of mind which involves "reconciled" feeling and a "faithful" life (Mat. 3: 2, 8; 4: 17; Luke 15: 7; Acts 2: 38; 17: 30; Rom. 2: 4; 2 Cor. 7: 9, 10). The inward change wrought by Divine power that accompanies repentance, is sometimes called regeneration or "new birth," but oftener "resurrection" or "new life." [1] The term sanctification, though sometimes only apparently used in a general sense, indicates the "setting apart" of the regenerated to a

---

(1) The word *gennao* used by John 3 : 3, 5, 6, 7, 8, and 1st John 2 : 29 ; 3 : 9 ; 4 : 7 ; 5 : 1, 4, 18, and also *anagennao*, used by Peter 1 Pet. 1 : 3, 23, indicate "new birth." The word *anothen*, rendered "again," John 3 : 3, usually refers in the Gospel to the *character* rather than the *source* of the act mentioned ; as Mat. 27 : 51 ; Mk. 15 : 38 ; Luke 1 : 3 ; John 19 : 23. The more common representation of "new life" is seen Luke 2 : 24 ; John 5 : 21, 25 ; 6 : 63 ; Phil. 3 : 10 : Coll. 2 : 12 ; 3 : 1 ; Eph. 2 : 6 ; 5 : 14 ; 1st Pet. 3 : 18.

new life. The progress of the Christian life is specifically called "salvation"; and as distinct from the "gift" of justification it is called a "work," having its beginning, and advancing progress toward completion. To indicate the *completion* of this "work" the special term "glorify" is used. The subduing of the will to preferred obedience in this new course of life is called "freedom"; the redeemed keeping the law from choice and therefore without the feeling of "bondage."

The Greek word *hagiazo*, "sanctify," is derived from a root signifying a thing "set apart;" as an image of a deity, or an offering, sometimes expiatory, presented to a deity. The adjective *agios*, used more than two hundred times, is applied first to the "Hòly Spirit"; second, to Christians, rendered "saints," or personally consecrated; third, to things or persons dedicated by others, as the heavenly city (Rev. 21: 9), the earthly sanctuary (Heb. 9: 1), the Scriptures (Rom. 1: 2), the kiss (1 Cor. 16: 16), and children of Christian parents (1 Cor. 7: 14). The verb is used about thirty times; and is applied twice to the name of God as "hallowed" (Mat. 6: 9; Luke 1: 2); thrice to Christ

(John 10 : 36; 17: 19; Heb. 10: 29); once
to God in his people (1 Pet. 3 : 13), and once
to influence of parents on each other, as on
their children (1 Cor. 7: 14); and thrice to
things set apart (Mat. 23 : 17, 19; 1 Tim. 4:
5). It is applied to Christians by Christ
twice (John 17: 17, 19), by Paul in his
addresses and epistles thirteen times, and by
Jude and John each once; in all which cases
it must have a signification as limited as the
adjective rendered saints so far as the *attainment* of the "holiness" to which the one
set apart is concerned; since, though the
"Spirit of God" is *perfectly* conformed to
the character of God, the Christian is only
gradually conformed to it, as Paul and John
in their extreme old age declare (Phill. 3 : 12,
13; 1st John 1: 8; 3: 3.) The noun
agiasmos, rendered "sanctification" or "holiness," used ten times by Paul and Peter, has
the same limitation as the verb; a limitation
specially indicated in Paul's addresses to
critical Greeks and Romans (Rom. 6 : 19, 22;
1 Cor. 1: 30). The word *agiotetes* (Heb. 12:
10), indicating a progressive *active* attainment,
and the word *agiosune,* a character *perfect*
in Christ (Rom. 1 : 4) and gradually "perfecting" in Christians (2 Cor. 7 : 1; 1 Thess.

3 : 13), confirm the special meaning of this important term, and indicate the error of those who attribute to it the meaning of other terms yet to be considered. This is further confirmed by the use of the word *osios* and its derivatives [1] when inherent character as distinct from active energy is indicated; a word whose derivation, like that of the word "holy" in English and other languages of Europe, denotes that *wholeness* of character belonging only in reality to God, and which in finite beings is an ultimate aspiration rather than a realized attainment.

The word "salvation" is the general word employed to indicate the second part of redemption effected by the atonement. The verb *sozo* is used about three hundred times; and its specific meaning, as the gradual work of spiritual restoration following after justification, is seen in such expressions as "save *from* sins" (Mat. 1 : 21), they that "*endure* shall be saved" (24 : 13), in the connection of statements (John 3 : 17; Acts 2 : 40), in contrasts (Rom; 5. 8; 8: 24; Heb. 7 : 25), and in the efficacy of acts and ordinances which influence conduct though they are

_____

(1) Employed Luke 1 : 75; Acts 2 : 27 ; 13 : 24, 35 ; Eph. 4 : 24 ; 1 Thes. 2 : 10 ; 1 Tim. 2 : 8 ; Titus 1 : 8 ; Heb. 7 : 26 ; Rev. 15 : 4 ; 16: 5.

not in themselves tests of character (James
2: 14; 1st Pet. 3: 21). The title *soter*,
"Savior," used about twenty-five times, has
its specific meaning often indicated (Eph. 5:
23; 1 Tim. 4: 10; 1st John 4: 14). The
noun *soteria*, "salvation," is illustrated in
Isaiah's prophetic contrasts (33: 5, 6; 62:
1); in Christ's teachings (Luke 19: 9; John
4: 22); in the special records of the Apostolic
history (Acts 4: 12; 16: 17; 27: 34); in
Paul's contrasts where the use of "justification" for "salvation" reveals the distinction
(Rom. 10: 10; 13: 11; 2d Cor. 7: 10; Phill.
1: 19; 2: 12; 2d Tim. 3: 15; Heb. 2: 10; 6:
9); and in the allusions of Peter (2d Pet. 3:
15) and of Jude (v. 3.) The special noun
soterion, "salvation bestowed" (Luke 2: 30;
3: 6; Acts 28: 28; Eph. 6: 7), and *soterios*,
"salvation operating" (Titus 2: 11), show
the nicety of expression which guided the
pens of Luke and Paul.

Among the minor yet important terms
filling up the Gospel view of atonement are
the words "conversion, glorify, free and redemption." The word "convert" in the Old
and New Testament is that rendered "turn"
and "return." It indicates the act of the
redeemed when regenerated; and of the

advanced disciple who, after wandering, is restored to fidelity; and the introduction of the word "regenerate" for "convert" will test their difference (Mat. 13: 15; 18: 3; Luke 22: 32; Acts 3: 19; 15: 3; James 5: 19, 20). The word "glorify" indicates the point in Christian advancement when the *triumph* of salvation is attained; its employ by Paul instead of any other in his full analysis for the Romans of all that Christ's atonement implies, showing its import. Having stated the nature of sin as "coming short of the glory" (Rom. 3: 23), and that the gift of justification and work of salvation cause the "sanctified," or those *consecrated* to Christ, to "rejoice in hope of the glory of God" (5: 2), he completes his climax by the declaration "whom he justified them he also glorified" (8: 30). The term "free" indicates, *not* freedom "*from* the law," but a will so conformed to the requirements of the law that its commands are the preferred guide and spontaneous aspiration of the redeemed; a transcendent blessing of the Gospel on which Jesus loved to dwell (Mat. 5: 7, 48; 11: 30; John 8: 31—36); a truth whose perversion Paul was called often to meet (Rom. 3: 31; 6: 7—22; 7: 22; 8: 2;

Gal. 2: 4; 4: 7, 31; 5: 1, 16—18); an essential feature of redemption forming in James'
epistle a key to his peculiar statement that
we are "made righteous by works" (James
1: 25; 2: 12—24). Finally the term "redemption" indicates the perfect deliverance
from the power as well as the penalty of sin,
following the entire work of Christ for and
in man; the complete result of the "ransom"
(Mat. 20: 28; Mk. 10: 45) which Christ declared his "life" would secure, which his
disciples hoped for, and which He promised
(Luke 21: 28; 24: 21); whose completeness
even in recovering the body from the power
and penalty of former lust Paul pictured to
the Romans (3: 24; 8: 23); whose fore-
shadowing was the "substance" of Old Testament rites (Heb. 9: 15), while in Christ's
sacrifice on earth it was consummated (Eph.
1: 7; Coll. 1: 14; Tit. 2: 14); and whose
"glory will be realized" at "that day" in the
hour of perfect "revelation" (Eph. 1: 14; 4:
30).

The *means* by which Christ effects redemption are, first, his sufferings, cross, death,
blood, each term indicating a special part in
his comprehensive sacrifice; and, second, his
words, life, spirit; the one securing the gift

of justification, the other the work of salvation. In his sacrifice Christ's human body, soul, or life, and spirit have a share; while the association of the Divine with the human makes the Divine assumption of man's sin and its penalty to be the chief element in atonement. Since man, unlike angels, (Heb. 2: 14, 16), has a body and a soul, or life, animating it, Christ took that nature; that body and "soul" were a prey to death till his resurrection; while his "spirit" was kept from sin (Heb. 4: 15; 5: 7—9), and was saved by faith.[1] So, too, redeemed man has spirit, soul and body redeemed from the power of sin in this life (1 Thess. 5: 23; Rom. 8: 25) and rescued from the grave like Christ's hereafter (2d Thess. 4: 14; 1 Cor. 15: 20). This bodily suffering during a human life-time, and this agonizing death, are the *material* cause in redemption; but the teachings of Christ and of his apostles always

(1) The word *psyche* is used more than one hundred times in the New Testament; like the Hebrew *nephesh* it is rendered "life" nearly fifty times, as Mark 3 : 4 ; Acts 27 : 10 ; it is the source of worldly enjoyment in man, Mat. 6 : 35 ; Luke 12 : 19, and its loss by vicious indulgence is the loss of all the world, Mat. 16 : 25, 26 ; it was part of Christ's sacrifice, Mat. 2 : 20; 20 : 28 ; John 10 : 11 ; 12 : 27 ; and with the body it went to the grave (Ps. 16 : 10 ; Acts 2 : 27, 31). Christ's "spirit," *pneuma,* yielded up to God, was with the redeemed thief at once in Paradise, Luke 23 : 43, 46 ; John 6 : 5, 23 ; 17 : 11, as also the spirits of all Christians are, Phill. 1 : 23 ; Heb. 12 : 33, and 1 Pet. 3 : 19.

make it subordinate to his offering of himself
before the foundation and until the consummation of the universe. [1]

The "day of the Son of Man" is the day
when *as such* he will judge the "world" or
universe (Mat. 25 : 31; John 5: 22, 25; Acts
17 : 31; Rom. 3 : 6). It will be the day of
the "revelation" of judgment (Rom. 2: 5),
because the judgment which decides each
spirit's destiny will have already been made;
while the full revelation of that judgment
can occur only when the whole work of
human redemption is complete. The angels
will then judge men (Mat. 13 : 41), and the
saints will judge the "world" including
"angels" (1 Cor. 6: 2, 3), because every
being in the universe, seeing the entire
result of Christ's atonement, will *ratify* for
himself the decision as "righteous" (Rom. 2:
5; 14: 11; Phil. 2: 10). It will appear to
all beings righteous because the sentence of
the unredeemed will be "banishment" from
that very presence and power from which
they have always shrunk (2 Thess. 1: 5—10);
and it will appear righteous as to the redeemed, because they accepted Christ's re-

_____

(1) John 6: 51—63 ; 10: 17—29; 12 : 32 ; 2d Cor. 5: 15—21 ;
Heb. 7 : 22 27 ; 9 : 26—28 ; 1 Pet. 1 : 20, 21 ; Rev. 5: 9, 10 ; 13:
8 ; 14 : 4—13.

demption. He only who suffered for man's sin can "condemn," and He is the very one who "justifies" them, assuming as His own their sin (Rom. 8: 1, 3, 34; 2d Cor. 5: 21). Hence in Heaven the redeemed will be a peculiar throng, having a "right" to its glories, having a personal relation to God and Christ unknown to angels, and singing a "new" song, a part of which only can angels make theirs (Rev. 5: 8—13; 22: 4).

ATONEMENT IN THE GOSPEL HISTORIES.

Christ's life, unwritten by himself, is presented by four disciples, whose narratives together make one whole. As history and the records themselves attest, Matthew wrote for Jews at Jerusalem probably about A. D. 55, while traditions of Christ were common; at the era when the mission of the twelve apostles as distinct from Paul's was fixed at Jerusalem and proclaimed to the churches, and when Paul's first inspired epistles were written (Acts 15: 22; 16: 4; and 17: 1—13; 1 Thess. 2: 16; see Mat. 28: 15, 20). Mark wrote for the Romans, using many Latin terms (2: 4;) and citing points impressive to Romans, guided by Peter (1 Pet. 5: 13; 2d Pet. 1: 15), and giving full accounts of facts

specially known to Peter when only James
and John beside were present. Luke wrote
for the Greeks, in classic style, with care in
historic statements and with logical reasonings (1 : 1—4; 10 : 1; 24 : 13—48), finishing
his treatise nigh the close of Paul's ministry
(Acts 1: 1; 28: 30). John wrote thirty
years after the death of Peter and Paul, when
philosophic perversions of the Gospel called
for added records of Christ's deeds and words
(John 20: 30, 31; 21: 25).

Matthew traces Christ's human descent
from Abraham through David to Joseph,
whose *adopted* son Christ was; adoption
both among Asiatics and in Roman law being
the essential title to heirship. He cites the
Asiatic expectation of a "king of the Jews"
who should rule all nations in righteousness;
and quotes parallels between the infant life
of Jesus and the history of the Hebrew
nation. He records how John and afterwards
Jesus met the Pharisees and Sadducees (3 :
7; 5: 20; 16: 1, 12; 19: 3; 22: 15, 23, 34,
23: 1—12), the ritualists and rationalists
who controlled the Jewish Church and State;
and how the people at large hailed the
doctrine of radical reform through faith in
Christ, and flocked to the new rite which

embodied the new doctrine. He relates how
Christ, filled from his baptism with the
Divine Spirit, met the personal tempter, who
from Adam's day had triumphed; and, over-
coming him, made the first conquest in re-
gaining for man the Paradise lost through
Adam. He intimates Christ's mission to all
nations by the mention that Christ's ministry
was first and mainly to the darkest and the
Gentile regions of Israel's possession (4: 15,
16); while the very first to exercise perfect
faith in him was a Roman soldier (8: 10).
He reports at length Christ's discourse on
"righteousness" as man's need; this including remission from past sin and deliverance
from future evil, both given in answer to
prayer, but one the gift of God as a Father,
and the other His work in man (5: 6, 48; 6:
1, 13, 14; 7: 11). His miracles and preaching attest his authority to remit (*aphiemi*)
sin (9: 9; 11: 5, 6); penance and external
rites are a yoke he removes (9: 14; 11: 29;
15: 2, 3); and his assumed nature as the
"Son of Man" before man's creation made
him Lord of the Sabbath, the first external
religious institution (12: 8). A series of
parables illustrates the progress of his spiritual reign; first, in its varied fields; second, as

to the opposing evil it meets; third, as to its
outward spread; fourth, as to its inward
working; fifth, as to man's desire for it; sixth,
as to man's sacrifice to attain it; and seventh,
as to the final separation of the redeemed and
unredeemed which must result (Ch. 13th).
Christ only indirectly alluded to his death
(12: 40) until nigh its occurrence; and then
Peter spurned the suggestion (16: 21, 22).
Peter's avowal of faith in him as " the Christ
the Son of the living God," Christ declares
the foundation truth [1] on which his Church
was to be built; while he denounces as Satan's
delusion the idea that his death and resurrection were not a chief element in that same
truth (16: 16—23).   He then reveals to
Peter, James and John the heavenly view
taken of his death and of its glory by Moses
and Elijah (17: 1—9; Luke 9: 31).   He
soon repeats the announcement of his death

(1) Christ's expression "*epi taute te petra*," upon this the
rock, feminine not masculine, refers to the *sentiment* not the
name of Peter ; as Jerome, the Latin translator of the Roman
Catholic Vulgate, recognizes in his version and declares in his
comments ; in which he is followed by the leading Roman
Catholic translators at the dawn of the Reformation, as
Diodati in the Italian, DeSacy in the French, and S. Miguel in
the Spanish.   Peter's leadership in spurning Christ's death
(16 : 22), in worldly conformity (17 : 25), in denying Christ (26 :
31), and in misinterpretation of the Gospel for the Gentiles
(Gal. 2 :14), confirm this interpretation.   The added power of
"binding and loosing" is explained by Christ himself in the
connection as belonging to his Church as a body (18: 17, 18) ;
as also by Paul (1 Cor. 5: 4, 5) and by John (2d John 10, and 3d
John 10).

(17: 22, 23), shows Peter and all his disciples that political conformity to the world and its ambition, utterly opposed to the childlike spirit of his true followers, to the sympathy of angels and to his own self-sacrifice in giving his life an *atonement, katallage*, to redeem men, suggested their shrinking from the ignominy of the death he was to meet (17: 24 to 18: 10; 20: 20—28). Christ shows that the Old Testament law, both in the ten commandments and two precepts, was not kept by the best of men (19: 16—23; 22: 35—40), In fulfillment of prophecy he rides as king into Jerusalem; he is believed in by children and by the abandoned (21: 16, 31); he teaches the limit of civil duty (23: 21); he proves from Moses and David his Divine nature and man's immortality as assured through Him (23: 32, 44); and he foretells the earthly calamities (Ch. 24th) and the condemnation at the judgment (Ch. 25th) which their rejection of his offered redemption would bring. The tender relation in which he will then appear to all the universe is pictured as that of a bridegroom coming to take his bride; while the ground of this wedded union is a character like His, prepared indeed for them before the

world's foundation, but possessed and ex-
hibited in their life among men.

In describing the events of his betrayal,
death and resurrection, the relation of Christ's
sacrifice to the atonement is specially brought
out. Of the cup he says, "This is my blood
of the new Covenant, shed for many for the
remission (*aphiesis*) of sins." The high
priest understands that he claims to be "The
Christ the Son of God"; and under the oath
laid on him Christ affirms it and foretells
His future coming in glory (26: 63, 64).
The denial of Peter (26: 69) and the remorse
of Judas (27: 4) add bitterness to his trial.
The dream of Pilate's wife, bespeaking the
continuance of a former conviction, awes the
Roman governor with the conviction that
Jesus is a "just man" (27: 19); while his
name, "the Christ," and His Divine claim
makes Pilate the convict before the Judge of
all (27: 22, 23). The incidents of his last
hours, the darkness three hours from noon-
day, his expiring cry, the earthquake, the
dead raised, make his Roman executioner
exclaim, "Truly this was the Son of God"
(27: 54). His miraculous resurrection and
the effort of the Jewish rulers to conceal it,
preserved in tradition at Jerusalem when

Matthew wrote, indicate the time when and the people for whom Matthew wrote (28: 15). Christ's last commission proves, first, the universal mission of His Gospel; second, the order of its three duties; third, the essential unity of Father, Son and Spirit, incomprehensible in conception but instinctively recognized in the Christian's personal dedication in baptism; fourth, the supreme and univeral authority of Christ in his assumption of man's redemption (28: 18—20).

Mark, Roman-like in brevity, opens his full yet condensed record, with the essential point: "The beginning of the Gospel of Jesus Christ the Son of God." His mention of Peter as Simon (1: 16, 30), his allusion to his wife's mother hinting that he was not a celibate (1: 30), his late allusion to his " surname" (3: 16), his details of incidents specially known to Peter (5: 23—43; 9: 15—29; 13: 3; 14: 51, 52; 16: 5—22), all indicate his relation as amanuensis. His special address to Romans is seen in Latin words such as *grabbatum* (2: 4) and *kenturion* (15: 39); in his explanation of Greek in Roman coin (12: 42); in his special mention of the Sabbath as " made " for all men (2: 27), and of political as distinct from religious parties

(3: 6; 8: 5; see Mat. 16: 6; 12: 12; 15: 10);
in his allusions to Christ's reception among
heathen (3: 8—11), to his reported insanity
(3: 21), and to the use of natural remedies
in miraculous healing (6: 13; see James 5:
14); in parables, and in added incidents in
miracles, illustrating Christ's Divine saving
power (4: 26; 5: 4—43); in the impression
made on Herod as Roman governor by John
(6: 14—19); in Christ's withdrawing from
political partizans (6: 31); in the mention
of the mixed races of Shem, Ham and Japhet
in individuals blessed by Christ (7: 26); and
in explanations of Jewish traditions (7: 2—13)
and of Hebrew words (7: 11, 34). Added
views of Christ's redemption are brought out
in the questions of his disciples when he first
announced his death and resurrection (9: 10);
by incidents in the scene following the transfiguration (9: 15, 21—29); in disputes as to
superior rank (9: 35); in the peculiar moral
significance attributed by the Romans to
both fire and salt in sacrifices (9: 49, 50)[1]; by
the conformity of Christ's law of divorce to

(1) In Hebrew sacrifices the idea in the use of salt was sub-
sidary (see Lev. 2: 13; Josephus Antiq. 3: 9, 1 and 12: 3). In
the Roman sacrifices the preparation of meat by "fire and
salt" had an added significance, indicating the *moral influence*
produced by sacrifices (See Plin. Nat. Hist. 31: 44; Virg. Æn.
2: 133; Ovid. Fast. 1: 337; and especially Plutarch Symp. 7,
Plut. Quest. 9).

the Roman law which allowed *no* cause of
divorce (10: 11, 12, compare Mat. 19: 9); by
Christ's expressions of tenderness to children,
of love to moral youth, and of the moral
danger of riches (10: 16, 21, 24); by mention
of the unbroken colt taken for Jesus' trium-
phal procession (11: 5—7); in the envious
plot of the "priests" against him (11: 18);
in his repeating the law of human forgiveness
like that of his "Father" (11: 25, 26); by
the case of the lawyer "not far from the
kingdom of God" (12: 32—34); in the poor
widow's superior sacrifice (12: 41—44);
in his deportment when arrested, afterwards
cited by Peter (13: 9—11, compare 1 Pet. 3:
18—16); in the political crime of Barabbas
(15: 5); in the Roman relationship of Simon
(15: 21); and in incidents of the resurrection familiar to Peter (16: 5, 8—22); all of
which facts and principles throw new light
on the atonement and its appeal to the practical mind of every age.

Luke, in his memoirs of Jesus and of his
apostles, like Paul his companion, writes
after that careful investigation which studious
minds require (1: 1—4); citing dates and
historic associations (1: 5, 26, 57; 2: 1, 2);
tracing connections of events (2: 21, 22, 41,

and 4: 5, 9, compared with Mat. 4: 5, 8);
naming eminent followers of Jesus (8: 3);
mentioning the three languages in the in-
scription on his cross (23: 58); minutely indicating the place of his ascension (24: 50;
Acts 1: 12)[1]; and alluding to the succession
of emperors and governors which invited
historic investigation (Acts 11: 28; 12: 20
—23; 13: 7; 18: 2, 12; 24: 27; 25: 13; 28:
7). He uses technical terms for diseases and
bodily affections, indicating professional accuracy (4: 38; 8: 44; 22: 44; Acts 16: 16;
28: 8; see Coll. 4: 14). He records minutely the childhood history of Jesus; citing
clear prophecies of the "remission of sins"
and "salvation from sin" united in redemption (1: 17, 55, 69, 72—79) and making the
nice Greek distinction between holiness and
righteousness (1: 75); he gives new testimonies of Christ's Divine paternity (1: 32, 35)
and of his natural maternal descent through
Nathan the son of David and through Heli
Mary's father (3: 23, 31); he pictures the
joy of angels, as well as of good men, at his
birth as the "promised Savior"; who brought

(1) The traditional locality, as Jerome in the fifth century
showed, is reliable ; being on the line separating the territory
of Bethany in Judah and Jerusalem in Benjamin (Josh. 15 : 7;
8) on the summit of Olivet, as Zechariah (14 : 4) prophesied.

glory to God among the heavenly host and
salvation to all nations of mankind (2: 11,
14, 31, 32, 38); and he records his devotion
and promise as his human body, mind and
moral nature were developing (2: 40, 52.)
He shows the moral influence of Christ's redemption on men of other nations; quoting
John's addresses to the people, to publicans
and to soldiers (3; 10—14); citing Christ's
use of the miracles of Elijah and Elisha in
Phenicia and Syria (4: 16, 30); giving his
own abstract of the Sermon on the Mount
(6: 20—49); and mentioning the religious
worth attributed by Jews to the Roman
whose faith Christ commended (7: 3—6;
compare Mat. 8: 5—8). Most of all he
devotes a large portion of his narrative to incidents in the last three months of Christ's
life (9: 51); when "seventy" chosen disciples
(10: 1) added to the twelve (6: 13) in accordance with the Jewish idea of the seventy
distinct families of mankind (Gen. 10th Ch.),
go before him into Samaria (9: 52), to the
vicinity of Jerusalem (10: 38), to the east of
Jordan (11: 1; 13: 22, compare John 10: 44),
back through Galilee and Samaria (17: 11),
by Jericho (18: 35) to Jerusalem (19: 28).
In this Gentile tour the imperfect view of

"righteousness" seen in those who sought to
"justify" themselves by works (10: 27), the
repetition of the Lord's prayer for past forgiveness and future deliverance from evil (11:
4), the answer to that prayer in securing the
"Holy Spirit's" regeneration (11: 13), the
condemnation of the "lawyers" who rejected
Christ as did their fathers the prophets (11:
46—53), the principles of the Sermon of the
Mount repeated amid incidents enforcing
their truth (ch. 12th), the need of repentance, and Christ's authority over the Sabbath
(13th), the welcome of the humble to His
kingdom (14th), the sympathy of the angels
and of true men in this welcome (15th), the
necessarily wretched doom of those not in
sympathy with it (16th), the spirit of forgiveness, faith, devotion, and gratitude constituting the "kingdom of God *within*" (16: 4,
6, 10, 15, 21), the doom of those not his (16:
22—37), the cry for expiation (*ilaskomai*, 18:
13, 14) which justifies the plea for mercy
(*eleeo*), the faith which secures "salvation"
(18: 38—42), the "fruits" of righteousness,
when the Son of Man seeks and saves a
"sinner" (19: 7—10), final acceptance or
rejection dependent on fidelity to spiritual
trust (19: 11—27)—all these accumulated

testimonies addressed by Luke to studious Greeks, give new clearness to the union of expiation and salvation entering into the atonement. In this new presentation, the constant recognition of the *necessity* as well as nature of atonement shines out in the Magdalen's love following forgiveness (7: 43, 48), in the far-reaching "end" of Christ's sacrifice (22: 37), in the moral anguish which produced the physical agony in that sacrifice (22: 44), in the dying malefactor's plea and his acceptance (23: 40—43). To add demonstration to confirmation, Luke cites Christ's argument from the moral necessity, back of his own purpose and of the revealed promise and meeting all the demands of human "reason," that by his death only could he secure atonement (24: 15, 26, 46) ; a final argument, which as Paul's companion he had seen to meet all the skepticism of minds like that of the Greek Cleopas "reasoning" upon the facts of Christ's life to learn their meaning.

A new age of thought and a new world of investigation and confirmation opens, when John, writing under Nerva, about A. D. 98, more than thirty years after the martyrdom of Peter and Paul, meets the subtleties of

Asiatic-Grecian philosophies by an introduction which for centuries has riveted the attention of idealists and rationalists from Justin and Origen in the second, to Neander and DeWette in the nineteenth century. Jesus embodied in "flesh" was the "word," or manifestation of God the Spirit; a nature in which He created all things, in which he appeared repeatedly, though unrecognized, in the world, or universe, being the only revealer of the Father, but fully manifest when he appeared. As such, John, his forerunner, testified, that he was the "Lamb of God" whose sacrifice was to redeem the world; and John's disciples became believers in him as the God of Jacob's vision and of Abraham's personal meeting (ch. 1: 1—51; see 4: 12, 24; 8: 56). At his first appearance in the temple, Jesus in figure announced his death and resurrection (2: 22); in his first private reasoning he spoke of his expiatory sacrifice as the theme of "heavenly" interest, while man's reformation excited "earthly" interest (3: 12); declaring that condemnation rested only on those who rejected his redemption (3: 18, 19). When baptism was misinterpreted as in itself purifying, John taught that faith in Christ alone saves (3: 25—36).

From the first the Samaritans and Roman
noblemen recognized his Divine mission (ch.
4th). When he healed the body he assumed
authority to remit sin; and, when the Jews
saw this was a claim to equality with God,
he declared that He, the Son of Man, had
"authority" to raise the spirit now and the
body hereafter to life; and that John and
Moses taught this truth (5th). He showed
the people that their bodily desires made
them neglect the spiritual provision he brings
(6th). His language to Jews leads them to
anticipate that he will go to the Gentiles (7:
35). Assuming supreme authority even over
civil law, he clears a guilty and condemned
woman, her accusers recognizing his righteous judgment (8: 9, 11); and then he
declares his mission to make men under the
written law as free as Abraham was before
that law was written, his indwelling power
making them of their own free choice keep
all the law's requirements, even as Abraham
bowed to his will when as the "I am" he
was present with him (8: 12—58; Gen. 12:
1; 18: 1; Ex. 3: 14, 15).

He shows that sin blinded the Pharisees
(9: 41) who rejected the "Shepherd" as well
as the "Lamb" who gave himself for sin

(10: 11); declaring that his voluntary assuming, as equal with the Father, the responsibility of redeeming man, called forth God's
love as well as Heaven's admiration (10: 17,
29). His raising Lazarus proved him the
author of spiritual as well as bodily resurrection (11: 15, 25, 26, 45); and led Caiaphas
to announce that principle of human government which shows expiation to be an essential idea of human nature (11: 48—53).
When told that Greeks wished to see him,
he illustrated in planted wheat the influence
of his death in winning all men and breaking
the power of evil (12: 20—30). At the
supper, by washing his disciples' feet he
taught the complete spiritual renovation
which his death for sinners would secure (13:
1—17, 34); and in a lengthy discourse showed
how his death would secure the Divine
Spirit's redeeming and inspiring efficacy (14:
12, 16, 26; 16: 7, 8, 13; 17: 11, 17, 21, 24,
26). His words to Pilate announcing his
Divine authority as spiritual ruler (18: 36,
37), the authority to which Pilate himself
was responsible (19: 11), so awed the Roman
governor that he put forth earnest efforts to
change the purpose of those who sought his
death. The careful statement of facts attest-

ing his death and resurrection (19: 25 to
20: 29), which Greek objectors had opposed
by declaring that God in the person of Christ
had only apparently not really assumed a
human body (1st John 4: 2, 3), John declares
must in all ages and to all men make sure
and clear the fact and the nature of Christ's
atonement (20: 31). An added chapter gives
yet farther confirmation of Christ's united
Divine and human nature; and brings out
the extreme old age of the inspired penman
(21: 23) when he wrote this final revelation.

ATONEMENT IN THE ACTS OF THE APOSTLES.

Luke's second treatise, like his first, covers
about a generation; from A. D. 33 to 64.
Alluding to the still cherished error of the
apostles that Christ's mission was only
"restoration" of civil "kingdom" to Israel
(1: 6), he traces the acts of the apostles;
among whom Peter for ten, and then Paul
for twenty years was leader. The promise of
Jesus on the night of his death (John 14th
to 16th) is repeated (1: 18) and is soon fulfilled (2: 17, 33). Prayer is offered to Jesus
(1: 24); the fulfillment of prophecies begins
(1: 16—20; 2: 18, 30); in Peter's first dis-

course Christ's death and resurrection are
recognized as preordained; and repentance
and faith are followed by remission of sins,
a confession of Christ, and a devoted life
(2 : 23—46).   In his second discourse The
God of Abraham is declared to have glorified
his Son Jesus; in whom "holiness and right-
ness" are met, and who has brought the true
"refreshing" looked for by Moses and all the
prophets (3 : 19—26).   In his.third address,
the wider fact is declared that no other
Savior or salvation meets the need of all men
(4: 12).   False profession prompted by
worldly motives, is marked as sin against
the Holy Ghost (5: 1—11).   Rationalistic
opposition from the Sadducees is met by
Peter's attestation of Jesus' resurrection
which they denied (5: 17, 32).   Ritualistic
opposition from the Pharisees is condemned
in Stephen's argument; that as Abraham,
Joseph and Moses were rejected through
"envy" of their "righteousness," so was
Jesus; and that as their fathers were idolaters
under Moses' "law" so they were desecrators,
as Jesus said, of His "temple" (6th and 7th
chaps).   At Samaria true believers multiply;
but the false apostate is unmasked (8: 21).
The first era closes with three select conver-

sions; that of the docile Ethiopian, who in the heart of Africa had read Isaiah (ch. 8th): that of the bigoted Asiatic, resisting the truth of the Old Testament (ch. 9th), and that of the European soldier devoutly and earnestly seeking atonement by nature's teaching only (ch. 10th); all alike trusting in Christ when fully revealed to them (8: 35; 9:17; 10: 35, 38). The report of this last case brought out a new revelation (11: 18) and introduced a new era in the acts of the apostles (11: 19—26); even the name given to the disciples assuming a new Greek form.

The interposition of the Roman civil power (12: 1—3), not attempted for nine years after Christ's death, removed Peter from the leadership (12: 17). [1] The fact discovered to Peter that the Gentiles without revelation were looking for redemption (10: 35) and had heard of Christ (10: 37), and its confirmation at Antioch (11: 19—21) opened the meaning of Christ in his last commission,

---

(1) No fact in early Christian history is more fully attested than the statement of Eusebius, Jerome and others that Peter went to Rome under Claudius, who reigned A. D. 41 to 54 (Acts 11: 28 to 18: 2); where he "was eminent" (praefuit) for twenty-five years, from A. D. 42 when Cornelius was converted, to A. D. 67 when Peter was crucified (John 21: 18; 1st Pet. 5: 13; 2d Pet. 1: 14) at Rome, the Babylon of Christian prophecy.

first stated on the evening after his resurrection (Mk. 16: 15), then in Galilee (Mat. 28: 19), and then at his ascension Acts 1: 8). Paul, now assuming a Roman name, becomes prominent in the new work (13: 2, 9) ; and he realizes the promise given nine years before (9: 15) in his influence over Roman rulers, and false teachers who had controlled their counsels (13: 8, 12). In his first address his countrymen in Asia Minor are met by him as a son of Abraham ; the history of their nation in Egypt, under judges [1] and two kings, from the second of whom Christ descended, is traced ; and the gospel narrative of his life, death and resurrection is stated ; its end, justification through faith instead of the law, is urged ; and the prophecy that the Savior of Israel would be rejected by his own nation is made a thrilling appeal (13: 16—41). This first discourse won the Gentiles (13: 42, 48); while the Jewish leaders through " envy " rejected Paul, as they had Jesus (13: 45; Mk. 15: 10) ; from which event Paul's

(1) The four hundred and thirty years of civil rule under judges as distinct from military rule under kings, must, and naturally in Paul's as in Stephen's argument does, extend from the first Divine appointment of Moses as "judge and deliverer" of Israel B. C. 1531, to the time when Samuel retired from office about B. C. 1081. See Ex. 2 : 14; Acts 7: 25, 27, 35 ; also 1 Sam. 7 : 15 ; 15 : 35 ; and compare Deut. 17 : 14—20 ; 1 Sam. 8 : 4—18.

mission becomes fixed. The influence of
Jewish opposers drove Paul and Barnabas
from city to city (13: 50; 14: 2, 5), yet
many Jews and Gentiles believed (14: 1).
The imperfect views of the people and of their
heathen priests, prompted by trust in Grecian
sacrifices for atonement, led them to imagine
the apostle a deity to be worshipped (14: 11—
13): but Paul by an appeal to their own
knowledge, through nature, of God and of
his providence leads them to Jesus as the
redeemer (14: 14—18). Jewish opposers
again prevail; but Christians are confirmed
and churches are organized (14: 19—23).
The report made by Paul and Barnabas at
Antioch of their first mission tour settled
the question of Gentile preparation to accept
Christ's atonement.

A new stage of progress was reached when
after five years of experience a question as to
the saving efficacy of rites, especially of Old
Testament circumcision, arose (15 : 1). Two
questions were involved ; first, the *religious,*
and second, the *civil* obligation, at issue ;
questions which have for eighteen centuries
influenced theories of the atonement. The
Christians who had been ritualist Pharisees
before their conversion, contended that Old

Testament rites were essential (v. 5); the apostles and elders listened to facts and conclusions of Peter, Barnabas and Paul (vs. 6—12) ; when James gave opinion that Divine foreknowledge, which provided redemption before Abraham and Moses, and prior to both circumcision and the law, had anticipated and decided the question (vs. 15—19), that while the Old Testament, read in all nations, had prepared the world to receive Christ, *natural* law existing prior to and as the ground of Mosaic statutes was to rule Gentile Christians (vs. 19—21); a decision which met the approbation alike of the Jewish and the Gentile Church (vs. 19—31). This discussion manifestly led Paul farther than his brethren; a separation, personal in part but yet on principle, made him a special leader ; and he entered on another stage of progress in views of the atonement (vs. 36—41). The Gospel of Matthew, as history attests, was written soon after this juncture. Its full recognition, in its opening (4 : 13—16), of Christ's mission to the Gentiles, could not have been written before the decision of this council A. D. 50 ; and the circumstances already cited show that it could not have been many years later. The era called for the first written revelation; and the Jews in their blindness had the greater need, as well as the first claim under Christ's promise.

The opening of his new work reveals in Paul the nice application of the principle just settled. Meeting Timothy, universally esteemed as a Christian, the child of a Jewish mother and trained as a Jew, though as his father was a Greek circumcision had been neglected, Paul, who before the council had not circumcised Titus for principle's sake (Gal. 2 : 3), now for principle's sake circumcises Timothy (16 : 3). All his future acts and teachings show that he regarded it a civil duty to observe religious rites as binding when not in conflict with the Gospel; that, hence, a Jew was bound to observe Jewish rites, ordained of God through Moses, as long as the Jewish State lasted; [1] while, however, the rites of Grecian and heathen State-

(1) Paul personally paid Nazarite vows (Acts 18 : 18), observed Mosaic purification and made legal offerings (21 : 18–26). He takes for granted that Hebrew Christians did the same (Heb. 5 : 1 ; 8 : 3) ; but neither he nor his Hebrew fellow-Christians took part in the sacrifices, now superseded by Christ's sacrifice (Heb. 9 : 10; 10 : 1). As he himself paid respect to the high-priest as a Jewish citizen, only appealing as a Roman to the higher Court when compelled by sense of duty (Acts 23 : 5, 35 ; 25 : 10, 11), so he taught Gentiles to be faithful to their rulers (Rom. 13 : 1—7). As he observed the Jewish rites and Jewish festivals, yet taught Jewish Christians not to abuse them (Acts 18 : 21 ; Coll. 2 : 16 ; Gal. 4 : 10), so he enjoined on Greeks and Romans a similar care as to their national feasts (Rom. 13 : 13 ; 14 : 1—23 ; 1 Cor. 5 : 7 ; 8 : 1—13 ; 10: 20, 21).

religious were to be abandoned if connected
with idol worship (1 Cor. 8: 1—13.)   A new
field, that of Europe, opens for Paul's new
mission.   A Roman colony among Macedon-
ians, or Northern Greeks, is first entered;
and three marked conversions, first, of an
Asiatic-Greek merchant-woman, second, of a
Grecian female devotee, and third, of a
brutalized Roman jailor, all illustrate the
common faith in Jesus (16: 15, 18, 31), and
show that all minds were prepared to accept
Christ's atonement.   Proceeding to the chief
Jewish centre in Macedonia, Paul, following
his custom, first preaches Christ to Jews;
availing himself of their Sabbath to reach
them, and arguing, as did Jesus, the *necessity*
in itself of the Scripture teaching that the
promised Redeemer must first suffer and then
rise again (17: 2, 3).   At Thessalonica and
Berea many searched the Scriptures and
tested the doctrine (17: 4, 11, 12).   Driven
by Jewish opposers from Northern Greece
he goes to the centre of Grecian culture,
Athens; and he meets leaders of the two
dominant schools and then the Athenian
Senate.   He appeals to their knowledge of
the one spiritual God, known to them as a
providing Father, requiring penitence for

sin, and holding every man to account at
the judgment; and he proclaims the fact
that the man Jesus is both Redeemer and
final Judge; who will "in righteousness"
judge all the "habitable earth" (*oikoumenen*)
since God has given ground for "faith" in
him by "raising" him from the dead (17:
18—34).

Silas and Timothy, left at Thessalonica,
here join him; they proceed to Corinth; he
goes first, again, to the Jews there; when
the persistent rejection of Christ by European
as well as Asiatic Jews calls forth his first
inspired epistles (18: 1—6; 1st Thess. 1: 1,
2, 14, 15; 2d Thess. 1: 1); as the contrasted
reception of Christ by the Greeks had called
out Matthew's Gospel for the Jews.

An added trial now brings out more fully
the truth of the Gospel. Aquila and Priscilla,
coming from Rome, spend a year and a half
with Paul at Corinth, accompany him to
Ephesus, and there await his return while he
takes the Greek bounty to Jerusalem (18:
1—21). Just before his return by way of
Antioch, Galatia and Phrygia, Apollos, a
Jew trained at Alexandria, the seat of former
Grecian and later Christian ritualism, having
embraced crude views of the new religious

reformation reported as preached by John,
comes to Ephesus and by his finished rhetoric
attracts and misleads Christian hearers (18:
23—25). Taught more perfectly by Paul's
fellow-visitors at Corinth, Apollos becomes
an intelligent and efficient Gospel herald;
and as such goes on to Corinth commended
by the brethren (18 : 26—28). His teaching,
however, which had been mere self-reform
without knowledge of the atoning Savior
and renovating Spirit, left a leaven of rationalistic error at Ephesus which followed him
to Corinth (19: 1—10; 1 Cor. 3: 4—6; 4:
6). Meanwhile, and prior to this event, an
opposite ritualistic error had been propagated
by the former leading apostle Peter; whose
fickle natural impulses led him back to old
Jewish prejudices; and who, after the council
at Jerusalem, had followed Paul to Antioch
(Gal. 2: 11), thence through Asia Minor (1
Pet. 1: 1; 2d Pet. 1: 16; 3: 2), and thence
to Corinth (1 Cor. 9: 5). This special trial,
the necessity of meeting in Christian leaders
the two perversions of the redemption of
Christ which priestly superstition on the one
hand and human philosophy on the other
had already opposed, led Paul not only to
put forth his second succession of inspired

epistles addressed to the Asiatic Galatians and the Greek Corinthians, but also to take a more systematic and logical method in meeting errors as to the atonement.

With new "boldness" towards his Jewish opposers, and with new care in "separating" true from unstable disciples, he assumed the form of *dialectic*, or argumentative discourse; following it for three months among the Jews (19: 8) till it seemed of no avail, and then resorting to a Grecian school (v. 9) where for two years he engaged in daily discussions (v. 10). Moreover, special miraculous testimonials were given him (v. 12); his Divine spiritual power meeting and subduing the pretenders who before had ruled religious belief (vs. 13—20). At length the self interest of image-makers created a popular outbreak; before which the great apostle, after three years of persistent antagonism, yielded, purposing to make Rome the next great centre of his effort (19: 22; 20: 31). Proceeding through Macedonia to Corinth, in Greece (20: 1, 2), prevented by some cause from his bold purpose of going at. once to Rome, whence Aquila had been driven (18: 2; 19: 21), Paul penned that master-piece of dialectic statement of Christian truth, the

epistle to the Romans, which will always
stand as the Divine Spirit's *complete revelation* of "the truth as it is in Jesus" (John
14: 26; 16: 14; Rom. 2: 8; 15: 8; Eph. 4:
21).

Returning again from Corinth by Troas to
Ephesus, he reminded the elders of the
Church that his whole mission had been to
testify both "to Jews and Greeks repentance
towards God and faith toward our Lord Jesus
Christ"; and declared that in this he had
"not shunned to declare the whole counsel
of God." As if to show the completeness
and consistency of the Gospel for both Jews
and Greeks as revealed in his preaching and
epistles, on reaching Jerusalem, at his own
and James' suggestion, he goes into the
temple to perform his special religious obligation as a Jew; taking with him, though
not into the temple, the Greek Trophimus,
that their different duties might be made
more conspicuous (19: 18—29). The tumult
which followed, in God's Providence, brought
Paul to the final fulfillment of Christ's early
declaration, "he is a chosen vessel unto me
to bear my name before the Gentiles and
kings, and the children of Israel" (9: 15).
Always making his countrymen first in

thought (Rom. 9: 1), yet specially successful in reaching the Greeks, he was now, after one more effort, to proclaim the Gospel to governors, kings and the emperor himself.

Rescued from the mob by the chief captain, respected by him for his culture in speaking Greek, and permitted to address his Hebrew countrymen, he chooses their own cherished vernacular, recounts his youthful life at Jerusalem known to them, and relates his conversion and baptism. Passing over the three years of his ministry elsewhere, he declares that, in a vision in the temple itself, he was directed to leave the holy city; that he had argued against the vision that his share in the martyrdom of Christians made it specially his mission to be the witness of the "Just One" to his "fathers and brethren" in Jerusalem; but the mandate was repeated that he should go thence to the Gentiles (22: 1—21). The simple word "Gentiles" raised such a storm of passion that only his Roman citizenship and the chief Captain's firmness saved him from following his Master and Stephen to instant death (20: 22—29). Brought now the next day before the Sanhedrim, made up still, as at Christ's trial twenty-six years before, of

ritualists and rationalists, Paul's consciousness of right, both as a Roman and a Jew,
led him to a course less forbearing and more
worldly in its policy than his Master's;
showing indeed that the indwelling of
Divine inspiration did not always attend him,
but yet leading on to the mission for which
his nature had been given him (23 : 1—10).
A third hearing before his countrymen followed at Caesarea, the Roman capital of
Judea; where, before Felix the Roman governor, the high-priest, with a Roman bar-
rister as his counsel, appeared against him.
Here, as in Christ's case, the high-priest's
charge was a political one; but as in Christ's
case the very reverse of the charge was shown
by Paul to have marked his mission, since he
brought "philanthropic alms" and religious
"offerings" to his people and their temple;
and then, appealing to the Hebrew law and
prophets, he maintains his faith in the resurrection through the Christ, who, it was prophesied, should rise from the dead.

To make the parallel between the trials of
Christ and Paul yet more complete, as Pilate
had been forewarned by his wife's faith (Mat.
27: 19), so Felix had, evidently through his
wife, received "more perfect knowledge"

(24: 22) than the high-priest had supposed of Christ and his history. Adjourning the court till the chief-captain could be sent for, Felix showed that it was Roman faith, as well as his Jewish wife, that influenced his counsel; for he sent for Paul in order to hear from him " the faith concerning Christ"; and when Paul, like John before Herod, appealed to Gentile convictions, the result was kindred (Mar. 6: 20). As he "*reasoned* of righteousness, temperance and judgment," of justification for past, and of self-restraint from future sin, and of the " righteous judgment of God " believed in by Romans (Rom. 1: 18, 32; 2: 5), the religious conviction of the man, as in Pilate, was stifled only by the ensnaring policy of the ruler (24: 25—27). When after two years a new governor succeeded, less susceptible to Christian influence, when the Jews came again from Jerusalem to renew their charges and Paul cleared himself under both Jewish and Roman law, when the vacillating policy of Festus, as of Felix, compelled Paul to appeal to the Emperor at Rome, and the necessity of sending a specific charge in accord with Roman law gave Paul the opportunity to present the Gospel to a new audience, when with all the pomp of

oriental princes King Agrippa and his queen,
Festus and a retinue of military and civil
dignitaries, were assembled to listen, Paul, at
the zenith of his power as a Christian advocate, held his hearers spell-bound. Appealing to king Agrippa's thorough acquaintance
as a writer of Jewish history with customs
and questions peculiar to the Jews, he cites his
own early life and the common hope of
Israel in the resurrection; 'and then he
reviews his own Christian conversion, declaring that Christ announced personally to
him, as to his apostles, what Moses and the
prophets had taught both as the fact of and
the necessity for his death and resurrection
in order to secure " remission of sins " and
" sanctification by faith " in him. The effect
of Paul's address not only satisfied this
august assembly of his innocence but of the
truth of his doctrine.

After a long and eventful voyage, Paul
reaches Rome. He calls together, first, his
countrymen ; and from morning to evening,
out of Moses and the Law, urges the truth
of the Gospel he proclaimed. Failing again
to secure their assent, he turns finally to the
Gentiles. This instructive history of the
progress of revelation as to the atonement

and of its reception by different peoples, closes with the significant fact, that while the new doctrine of atonement through Christ met with opposition from Old Testament adherents, it was welcomed by the Gentile mind, and its preaching was upheld under Roman law [1] (28 : 31).

THE ATONEMENT IN PAUL'S FIRST TWO EPISTLES, MEETING JEWISH OPPOSERS.

The first inspired epistle of Paul was written on the return of Silas and Timothy, left in Macedonia when the first mission of Paul aroused Jewish opposition (Acts 18 : 5 ; 1st Thess. 3 : 2, 6); and was designed to confirm Gentile converts in "faith, hope and love" under trial (1 : 3 ; 2 : 14 ; 5 : 8). The second, soon following, corrected a misinterpretation of his first epistle in its allusion to the second coming of Christ; the fruitful theme of imaginative errorists in Christian history (2d Thess. 2 : 2 ; Acts 1 : 6, 7 ; 2d Pet. 3 : 8). In both epistles he writes by an amanuensis; adding his signature to assure

(1) The Roman law as to new religions was, "Let no new or foreign gods, unless publicly acknowledged, be privately worshipped" (Cic. Leg. II, 8). Christ's defence, under Roman law "I always spake openly" (John 18 : 20), was satisfactory (Luke 23 : 14) ; and Paul, before Roman magistrates, was charged with inciting insubordination, not with preaching a new religion.

their authenticity and inspiration (1st Thess. 1: 1, 5; 2: 13; 4: 2, 18; 5: 27; 2d Thess. 1: 1; 2: 2, 15; 3: 14, 15).

Their former character as Gentiles, indicated by idolatry, lust, avarice, debauch and revenge (1: 9; 4: 5, 12; 5: 7, 15), is declared to be transformed by "imitation" of Christ (1: 6, 7; 2: 5, 10). The change thus wrought is designated as "sanctification" or life-long consecration (4: 3; 5: 23) showing itself in "increasing" love, purity and the work of "salvation" (3: 12; 5: 8, 22, 23). The agent in this work is the Lord Jesus (3: 11; 5: 9); the means is his resurrection as well as his death (1: 10, 3: 12; 4: 14; 5: 10); and the end is his glory in the redeemed at his coming (1: 10; 3: 13; 5: 23). The final glorified state of his followers is attested by Christ's bodily resurrection and by the spiritual resurrection already effected in his redeemed (2: 12; 4: 14).

In this first epistle Paul had declared, as did Christ, that the "time" of the final judgment was unknown (Acts 1: 7; 1st Thss. 5: 1); yet they, like Christians of many an age, mistook imagination for fact. Writing his second epistle, Paul thanks God that their "faith" in essential Gospel truth

"abounds" despite their errors. He declares
that the present spirit of those who accept
and of those who reject redemption is a sufficient "token" both of the nature and the
necessary "righteousness" of their final
award; since the latter "shall *honor justice*
(*diken tisousi*) in their endless destruction
from the presence of the Lord and from the
glory of his power" (1 : 9), while the former
will equally honor that justice, because Christ
will be "glorified in his consecrated" ones,
and will be "admired in all them that
believe." In order that Christ may thus be
"glorified" in them, Paul cautions them
against vain dreams as to the nature and the
time of Christ's "coming" and of their
"gathering to him" (2 : 1). He intimates
that the opposition of his countrymen, begun
in Christ's condemnation and death (1 Th.
2 : 15), was the working of Satan, who
prompted the Jewish rulers sitting in judgment on Christ and claiming Divine authority as God in his temple; that this
spirit was an iniquity already at work; an
assumption which would culminate in the
adversary's final struggle before Christ's
final triumph, when he should come to be
"admired" in his saints and "glorified" by

all beings. [1] The presentation of Gospel redemption is the same in this second as in the first epistle; the surpassing love of God as a Father, and of Christ as a Redeemer, being set forth in the work of salvation rather than in the gift of justification (1: 11, 12; 2: 13—17; 3: 5).

ATONEMENT IN PAUL'S SECOND THREE EPISTLES, MEETING CHRISTIAN ERRORISTS.

When, about two years after writing his first two epistles, Paul wrote three others, two of them from Ephesus, it was not opposition without, but error within the Church, which he was inspired to meet. The epistle to the Galatians corrects the ritualistic error which Peter introduced from Jerusalem; and the two to the Corinthians the rationalistic error brought in by Apollos from Alexandria.

_____

(1) As Irenæus (Haer. c. 24—30) taught less than a century after John wrote, it was to a *present fact*, illustrated in Christ's ministry (John 10 : 35 ; Mat. 23 : 2 ; 27 : 18), experienced by himself (Acts 13 : 8 ; 13 : 19 : 17 : 18 ; 18 : 13 ; 19 : 13), confirmed in Peter's history (Acts 8 : 10, 19 ; 1st Pet. 4 : 12 ; 2d Pet. 2 : 1—3), brought out by John in the Apocalypse (Rev. 1: 3, 7 ; 22 : 10, 12, 18),—it was to a fact then witnessed Paul directed the Thessalonians (Acts 17 : 5). By tracing the connections afterwards recorded (Luke 10 : 18 ; 22 : 31, 53 ; John 13 : 37, 31 ; 14 : 30 and 1st Thess. 4: 13—18 ; 2d Thess. 2: 3—17), Paul's allusions, so clear to the view of early Christian writers, may appear.

Five years after the Council at Jerusalem (Acts 15th Ch.), about A. D. 55, led by the fact that Peter's actions, not his words, on a visit to Antioch had given a wrong impression as to the efficacy of Jewish rites (Gal. 2: 11), which error had extended to the Celtic Galatian Christians, Paul wrote that brief but pregnant epistle which since the day of the long and heated discussion between Augustine and Jerome in the fifth century has been the central ground of debate between Roman ritualists and their opposers. Paul first maintains that he, in distinction from the twelve apostles to Israel, had received a special revelation as to Gospel truth for the Gentiles not of Israel (1: 1, 8, 16, 17); which fact was recognized by those apostles in the Council at Jerusalem (2: 9). The aim of Christ, who " gave himself for our sins," was to " deliver us from this present evil world " (1: 4); which aim no rite, such as circumcision (2: 3, 16), could effect. It is " faith," or fidelity, like that of Christ, which gives efficacy to his " life " within us, and to his " death " for us (2: 17—21). Hence the Spirit's work (3: 3, 5); and hence the Gospel promise, or covenant, given to Abraham four hundred and thirty years before the law by

Moses; "faith" only availing when man
fails to "continue in all things written in
the law to do them" (3: 8—10.) Hence
again the central Old Testament truth, "The
just shall live by faith" (3: 11); which
removes the curse for the past (3: 13) and
adds the Spirit's promise for the future (3:
14). Hence, still again, the peculiar wording
of the Covenant, "in thy seed"; not seeds,
as if it was a boon from the Jewish nation
by which "all nations shall be blessed" (3:
16). The law, indeed, so far from annulling
the former promise, was but "added to it
until the seed should come"; the law being
given to Moses through the very mediator
who was to fulfill the promise; he, as the
mediator of both, making them harmonious[1]
(3: 17—21), since the design of the law was
so to reveal man's spirit of transgression as
to drive him to Christ (3: 19, 21—24). The
source of Gospel righteousness, thus, is not
man's natural power to keep the law; but it
is that faith in the death and resurrection of
Christ indicated by baptism (3: 27 as Rom.

[1] The early Christian interpreters note that Moses is not
named in all this connection, nor ever styled a "mediator";
but that Christ is elsewhere declared by Paul to be the only
mediator (1 Tim. 2 : 5); while the mediation here referred to
is not the general "reconciliation" between God and man
but the mere harmonizing, as mediator, of the Law and the
Gospel.

6 : 4). Its result is not the slavish obedience
of a servant like Hagar's son (4: 1, 3, 22, 24),
but the filial obedience of an adopted child
longing like Christ and Isaac to show his
love (4: 6, 26). The "liberty" of the Gospel
leads the Christian to serve his brethren, as
well as his Lord, from love; the fruits of the
Spirit are "love" and all like graces (5: 1,
13, 22); in whose exhibition Paul admits
that he himself failed when not under the
Spirit's control (6: 1 compare 2: 11, 14).

At Corinth, "the eye of Greece" in Paul's
day, pride of intellect, fostered by the style
if not by the thought of the eloquent Apollos
(1st Cor. 3: 5, 6; 4: 6), led to a rationalizing
tendency; while also, since extremes meet,
Peter's mode of presenting truth (1: 12; 3:
2; 9: 5) aggravated by its counter influence
this drift of Christian sentiment. It showed
itself in the spirit of sensuality, litigation
and luxury, which an erroneous view of
"liberty under law" begets in one who trusts
to his own intellectual strength, as well as in
one who trusts to rites for spiritual redemption (ch. 5th to 8th). To meet this error
and its corrupting influence Paul declares
that to the "sanctified in Christ, elected
saints," it is not superior intellect which

proves the "power" and the "wisdom" of
God; but it is Christ Jesus, who "is made
unto us by God, wisdom, righteousness, sanctification and redemption" (1: 2, 20, 24, 30).
This end, again, is effected not by any
natural intellectual energy either in the
believer or the preacher; but it is wrought
by the "Spirit of God," which gives us "the
mind of Christ" (2: 4—16; 3: 5—11). The
only motive that can control a Christian is
the longing to honor Christ (5: 7; 6: 15, 20;
7: 24; 8: 6); and the energy giving effect-
iveness to this motive is the fact that we "are
washed, sanctified and justified in the name
of the Lord Jesus and by the Spirit of our
God" (6: 11). He cites his own special revelation for Gentiles (9: 1, 2, 21), the error of
Israel under Moses (9: 9), their own inconsistency in mingling with their idolatrous
countrymen (10: 9, 21), the indecorum of
their religious assemblies, the perversion of
the Lord's Supper, as proof that nothing
but the rule, "do all to the glory of God,"
and the aim to "show forth the Lord's death
till he come," could secure Gospel redemption
(10: 31; 11: 16, 20, 26). Yet more the
intellectual "gifts" of which they were
proud, whose diversity, administration and

operation Father, Son and Spirit united
to bestow, direct and energize (12: 4—6),
these gifts, proved fruitless without the
"graces" of "faith, hope and love" (13: 1,
13); a fact practically illustrated in the
effect on unbelievers produced by the "gift"
of tongues and the "grace" of prophecy, or
speaking of religious experience [1] (14: 1, 2,
23—25). Finally the spiritual fitness for the
future life, the spiritual and bodily resurrection, the perfect redemption secured by
Christ's death for sin and by his resurrection
so fully attested, the failure to realize which
after all Christ's sacrifice to secure it would
make the professed Christian more wretched
than the heathen, the attainment of what
Christ purposed for man when he made
Adam and for which during man's whole
earthly history Christ humbles himself by
wearing an assumed human nature, that new
life of which baptism is made the symbol and
for whose heralding Paul had suffered such
hardships—all this leads Paul to exclaim
"Awake to righteousness and sin not" (15:

---

(1) In all classic Greek usage from Homer down, and in all
Old and New Testament history from Abraham, prophesying
is the revealing, not of secular events, but of the *religious duty*
which these events impose. In the apostles' age the power
thus to reveal religious duty comes from spiritual regeneration; which both teaches and realizes that duty in the
Christian.

1—30).[1]   Yet more, the recognized power-lessness of boasted reason to conceive, before experiencing it, the nature of that future life of promised glory, and the fact that only its present realization in the "victory" Christ's grace may now give can ever realize that promise, this should prompt the Christian not only to be "steadfast and unmovable" in his present attainment, but to be "always increasing" in the work his Lord has made essential to redemption (15: 35—58.) The apostle closes with the earnest appeal that any being who does not "love" such a being as "the Lord Jesus Christ," God wearing man's nature from the creation to the judgment in order that he might be his Savior and as such anointed from the foundation of the world,—such a man *must* be accursed when that day shall come.

Paul's second epistle to the Corinthians is

---

(1) The word "saved," v. 2, held in mind till the conclusion is reached, v. 34, is the key to this chapter and to the epistle. The placing of v. 19 in connection with v. 32 is inconsistent with Paul's utterance at Ephesus shortly after this epistle was written (Acts 20 : 24) ; it is the supposing of a connection he does not indicate ; and it overlooks the elevated sentiment of the entire epistle. The reasoning in vs. 20—23 is illustrated in his epistle written shortly afterwards (Rom. 5 : 12—19) ; while the statement, vs. 24—27, gives emphasis to that first assuming of a responsibility which has, at length, an end. The moral significance of baptism, v. 29, as contrasted with circumcision in the two epistles closely associated with this (Gal. 2 : 3 ; 3 : 27 ; Rom. 4 : 11 ; 5 : 4), finds its natural interpretation in those epistles.

written from Macedonia (2: 12—13; 9: 4; Acts 20: 1, 2) on his way to Corinth two years after his first. He pictures his anguish, like to that of Christ, which as his inspired apostle to the Gentiles he had experienced (1: 5, 9) when his first epistle and the delay of his promised visit had been misconstrued (1: 13—17; 2: 1—4). He urges that as Moses wrote things not comprehended, so he, writing by revelation, found that even Christ's disciples misunderstood the truth he revealed (ch. 3d and 4th). This trial, however, was relieved by faith in future glory and by the present love of Christ (5: 1—14); a suggestion which leads to one of Paul's graphic statements as to the atonement (5: 14—21). To him it was a logical conviction, as well as a revelation, that "if Christ died for all," then first, " *all*," he and his Corinthian brethren, "were dead " to Christ's love; and, second, that Christ offered such a sacrifice that those made spiritually alive "should not henceforth live unto themselves but unto him who died for them and rose again." Hence he inferred that no "personal knowledge " of Jesus during his fleshly life, such as Peter and the first apostles enjoyed, (11: 22, 23) gave new spiritual life; but that a new spiritual "creation" is its source. Hence "all things" constituting redemption "are of God." The "atonement" (*katallage*), received by the Christian and to be preached by Christ's ministers, is this chain of connected truth; each link in which is necessarily implied in the one fact of Christ's death for us. The author of atonement is God manifest in Christ; its design was the reconciling of the world to himself; its formal procuring cause was his own assumption of the responsibility of the transgression of those who accept his redemption, he not imputing their trespasses to them; and its material cause was Christ's sacrifice, he "who knew no sin being made sin for us, that we might be made the righteousness of God in him." To this comprehensive statement farther allusions conspire; the motive to Christian sacrifice being Christ's example (8: 9); no bounty given by a Christian comparing with God's "unspeakable gift" (9: 15); Paul's zeal in preaching where other apostles had not gone falling below Christ's (10: 7, 14, 16); all perversion of Christ's gospel being from the same adversary whom Christ met in Eden (11: 8, 14); all inspired men, despite their revelations, showing personal imperfections, he as well as Moses and Peter (3: 15; 11: 22; 12: 7), while, nevertheless, the Spirit's power shown through the truth was the testing seal of apostleship (12: 12). He closes his epistle, for the first time, with the apostolic benediction; recognizing the union of Father, Son and Spirit in the work implied in the atonement (13: 14.)

PAUL'S LOGICAL STATEMENT AS TO THE ATONEMENT IN THE EPISTLE TO THE ROMANS.

Paul's delay in Macedonia, his circuit in Illyricum and his duty at Jerusalem having postponed his intended visit to Rome, he writes from Cenchrea, the port of Corinth, about A. D. 59, that comprehensive and convincing argument as to Christ's atonement matured in his discussions at Ephesus (Acts 19: 8, 9, 21; 20: 3; Rom. 1: 13; 15: 19—25; 16: 1; 2d Cor. 2: 11, 12).

Beginning with the fact of Christ's Divine and human nature as admitted, he asserts his special inspiration as the expounder of his mission to the Gentiles (1: 1—5, 14). The design of the Gospel is to effect the work of "salvation" by the gift "of righteousness," "from a faith" inwrought by Divine power "to a faith" exercised by the man saved (1: 16, 17). The necessity and the justice of its application to all men is the fact that the nations without revelation "hold the truth," first, as to God (1: 19—21), second, as to their duty (1: 28), third, as to the penalty of sin (1: 32), and fourth, as to the efficacy of repentance and expiatory sacrifice for redemption from sin [1] (2: 4, 8, 14, 15). All men then, are "inexcusable" for sin because they "hold the truth in unrighteousness"; perverting their knowledge of God (1: 21—25), judging others than themselves justly (1: 32; 2: 1—4), resisting conscience (*suneidesis*) when self-convictions (*logismos*) contend within them (2: 14, 15). Calling attention, then, to the essential fact of "his gospel" for Gentiles, that the final judgment will be a simple "revelation" of the "secret" convictions of men as to themselves, and that its decisions will turn on their own conviction that they had rejected redemption as provided by "Jesus Christ," the *principle* of

---

[1] The word *agnoeo*, rendered "not knowing," in Greek classic usage, like its Latin and English derivates, indicates an ignorance arising both from inexcusable oversight and from willful rejection of knowledge ; the first of which is seen in the maxim "ignorance of law excuses no one," and the second in the charge "he ignores the law." That this is Paul's use of the word is manifest in his speeches Acts 13 : 27 ; 17 : 23, 30, and in this epistle Rom. 6 : 3 ; 7 : 1 ; 10 : 3 ; 11 : 25, and from his own experience 1 Tim. 1 : 13.

whose "salvation," though not the manner of its provision, had been known to "all men" (2: 5—16), Paul sets forth the yet more manifest inexcusableness of the Jews; who, having a revelation of God's plan of redemption, so perverted its truth that the Gentiles "blasphemed" the "Redeemer" of the Old Testament on their account (2: 17—24).

Inferring thence that no outward rite, as circumcision, is saving (2: 25—29), Paul declares that the Jew has special advantage over the Gentile in having the "lively oracles" (*logia* or logically stated truth) of God; and he meets three syllogistic objections of the Jews to this limitation of their "advantage" (3: 1, 2). First, God must be faithful as a father, though the Jew, his acknowledged child, is unfaithful; to which, in the words of David their great king, Paul replies, that God allows his children to "judge" him, while David declares He is "clear" after that judgment (3: 3, 4; Ps. 51: 4). Second, if the "unrighteousness" of the unfaithful "commends God's righteousness" God would be "unrighteous" if he inflicts "wrath" (*orge* as 1: 18); to which the reply is that God is the final authority in ruling the entire Universe, and there can be on the

principles of human government no possible
or reasonable appeal from his decision (3 : 5,
6). Third, putting the objection on moral
rather than legal ground, if God's truth is
made by my lie more to promote his glory
how can I be judged as a sinner?; to which
the reply is that a counter decision would
lead to that principle condemned by the
common conscience and reason of mankind,
" Let us do evil that good may come " (3 : 7,
8)! Every form of objection thus being met,
the conclusion is that all have sinned and
hence cannot be accepted on their own merit;
the essential nature of universal sinfulness
being that " all come short " of the glory of
God," their character and life lacking complete perfection in duty to God and man (3 :
9—20, 23.)

Thus shut up to a provision outside of
personal merit Paul states God's gratuitous
provision for the perfect righteousness of
sinful man. Its material provision, stated in
the Old Testament, is a positive " righteousness " for those not righteous (3 : 21); its
condition is man's faithful appropriation of
that righteousness, which is offered " to all,"
and is efficacious " for all that are faithful "
(3 : 22). Its formal or procuring cause is

God's grace working in and for man through
the redemption (*apolutrosis*) provided by
Christ Jesus (3 : 24). Its ultimate author is
" God," and its instrumental provision is the
propitiatory offering (*ilasterion*) of his blood,
received by faith (3: 25). Its result, or final
cause, is entire remission of all past sin; and
that consistently, not with the mercy merely,
but with the perfect " righteousness " of God
(3: 25, 26). This provision is in harmony
with the law, since " faith " or fidelity meets
the provision of the law (3: 31). It is illustrated in Abraham, whose faith was counted
to him as righteousness (4: 3); and yet more
in David, who in his own case saw that only
by " not imputing his sin " to him could God
" impute righteousness " to him (4: 1—8).
The efficacy of ceremonial law, as that of
"circumcision," is apparent in Abraham's
case; the " sign " being a " seal" of the
righteousness granted because of his faith
before his circumcision. In his case (4: 9—
12), therefore, there is an illustration, how
by faith and hope righteousness is imputed,
irrespective of ceremonial.as well as moral
law, to all believing in Jesus (4: 13—23);
and that because that faith rests, first, on the
Being who was the author of Christ's atone-

ment raising him from the dead (4 : 24), and
second, on Christ's sacrifice, his death being
an expiation for our offences, and his resurrection securing our justification (4 : 25).

Justification for the past being thus
secured, the " work of salvation " follows ; it
consisting first in peace with God, then in
an inwrought " grace " which not only makes
us " stand " but also advance in attaining a
character and life conformèd to " God's
glory "; trial " working " patience; patience
developing a gradual experience ; that experience awakening hope for the future;
and that hope not disappointing the believer
because its nature is " love to God " and its
author is the " Holy Spirit " (5 : 1—6).. This
work of salvation, as truly as the gift of
justification, was provided by Christ's sacrifice, since " when we were without strength,"
for the future, as well as guilty in-the past,
Christ died for us; so that as our justification, including our reconciliation (*katallage*
or atonement 5: 10, 11), is secured by his
death, so our salvation is secured by his
" life " resumed at his resurrection (5: 6—11).

To show that the atonement cancels sin
in all ages and in all men alike, Paul goes
back to Adam the " father of all men "; as

before he had cited Abraham the "father of
the faithful." While sin entered the world
by one man, and so death, its bodily and
spiritual penalty (see ch. 7th and 8th) passed
on all because all are alike sinners, a fact
manifest since all "from Adam to Moses," with
the exception before made (3 : 2), have
"sinned after the similitude of Adam's transgression," Adam was in his relation to
universal human sinfulness a counter-part [1]
of the Redeemer to come (5 : 12—15). This
general truth two facts and the conclusion
from them establish. First, as sin began
with one man's voluntary wrong, it must be
that this loss to man would be more than
counter-balanced by the grace inwrought and
the gift of justification, both of which are
surpassing in Christ's atonement (5 : 15).
Second, while after his first sin Adam sinned
as all other men with a sinful nature, and as
only our first sin is affected by his first offence,
Christ's atonement avails for any number of
our offences. Hence the truth is established
that while only through one sin of our human
father, death, the penalty of sin, for a time

(1) The word *typos* rendered "print" John 20 : 25, "fashion"
Acts 7 : 44, "example" 1 Cor. 10 : 6, "pattern" Heb 8 : 5, has
in all cases the force of its ordinary classic signification, drawn
from its literal meaning, of "counter-part; as the wax impression of a seal, or a coin struck from a die.

reigns over us, a grace triumphing over our
sinful bias, and a gift of righteousness cancelling countless sins, secure life, the bliss of
heaven, throughout eternity as the provision
of Christ's atonement. Returning then to
his first comparison, Paul repeats that while
as its material cause the sin of one man introduced temporary condemnation, on the
other hand the righteous-offering (*dikaioma*)
of one proffered to all men a permanent personal righteousness (*dikaiosis*) securing endless life (5: 18); and, again, while as its
instrumental cause the disobedience of one
made the many sinners (*amartoloi*), or erring,
on the other hand the obedience of one made
the many righteous (*dikaioi*) or perfectly
free from sin (5: 19).

Returning to note the fact that God gave
a law which man, as was before known,
would never keep, Paul declares that the law
was indeed given that sin might abound,
but because thus only could grace abound
(5: 20, 21); and when, then, it is objected
that we may "continue to sin that grace may
abound," he replies; that this objection is
self-contradictory, since "grace" implies
deadness to sinful inclinations and a new life
opposed to sin, of which baptism is an ex-

pression (6: 1—5); that this new life prompts
to free, because preferred, service to God as
the fountain of holiness and the bestower of
righteousness (6: 6—23), since the redeemed
spirit is united as in wedlock to Christ and
inspired by love to fidelity (7: 1—4). To
show, then, how the law makes grace abound,
he cites the fact that impulses of appetite
and passion by their fretting against the
restraints of law reveal their own depravity,
the flesh warring against and triumphing
over the mind, till the wretched victim longs
for the redemption of Christ (7: 5—25).

The perfect triumph of Christ's redemption is two-fold in its action; and that action
is complete in its moral results. It, first,
removes all sense of condemnation for the
past, thus giving hope for the future (8: 1);
which in itself frees us from the law of sin
and its penalty (8: 2). For, Christ's personal
sinless life showed the possibility of a sinless
life in those led by his Spirit, and condemned
sin even in bodily impulses, since the
Divine Spirit of God and of Christ rules over
them. This reign of grace, second, is gradual;
beginning with the aspiration of our new
adoption; but awakening an earnest expectation in man with his present bodily organ-

ism [1] to secure even bodily redemption.

The focal truth, the hinge of the balance on which human judgment turns in deciding that God is righteous in having made man to be a sinner that as such he might be redeemed, is now presented. Man with his earthly organism (*ktisis*) was not of *his choice* made subject to his frail condition (*mataiotes*); but "by reason of," to accomplish the design of "him who subjected him," not to hopeless exposure to be lost, but in hope of that "glorious freedom of the sons of God" for which every suffering being at times longs (8: 20—22). Even after spiritual adoption the redeemed have only the "first fruits" of a redemption yet to be fully realized; since, if saved completely at once, the grace of "hope," the promise of God's Spirit in us, would have no place in us (8: 23—26). That hope is assured because we know that God foreknew and predestinated the redeemed to

(1) The noun *ktisis*, as well as its verb *ktizo* and its abstract *ktisma*, are in classic and New Testament usage either general or special in signification; referring sometimes to the organized Universe, but oftener to one particular organism, especially that of man. This is seen in Mk. 16: 15; 2 Cor. 5: 17; Gal. 6: 15; Coll. 1: 15. 23; Heb. 4: 13. The word rendered "whole," v. 22, as Stuart agrees, must be rendered "every." Paul's logical method, his special argument, his connection of statement, and his use of words throughout the chapter, forbid the idea that he speaks of material creation, of plant or animal organisms, as "groaning" and as "hoping for redemption." It is the "sanctified spirit, soul and body" (1 Thess. 5: 23) to which he is calling attention.

be perfectly conformed to his image; to the
end that he (v. 3) might be the first-born of
many having his family likeness; following
up his predestination by calling, then justifying and finally glorifying them; thus making
"all things" in their history conspire "for
good to them" (8: 28—30). "What then,"
exclaims the apostle, "is the necessary inference as to the final result of atonement" (v.
31)! The fact of Christ's death once admitted, then all the chain of truth implied is
assured (v. 32)! For "who can lay anything
to the charge," sinners though they have
been, of "God's elect"? For, who has any
claim to "condemn" except the Redeemer who
alone has suffered on their account? And
he is the one who not only died for them,
but having risen, ever puts forth interposing
power to finish the work he has begun (8: 33,
34). Add then to this, the gift of Christ's
righteousness, the work of salvation to which
it must prompt; and "who" or "what," exclaims the enthusiastic apostle, can "separate
us from the love of God which is in Christ
Jesus our Lord!"

The admitted fact of God's "election" of
the redeemed is the last point as to the atonement to be harmonized with God's righteous-

ness. Here Paul's deep sensibility, gradually
kindled by his enraptured view of the
atonement, breaks out in an appeal to his
countrymen as the last among men to object,
as God's former elect, to its necessary truth;
since in Abraham's favored line they were
the heirs, first of elect Isaac, and then of elect
Jacob. On the other hand Pharaoh's curse
came only after persistent disregard of God's
proffer, against the protest of his wise men,
and in defiance of his people's appeal; God
designing in his case to show the inexcusableness of all who will neither keep his law
nor accept of his redemption when warned
by its penalty. The utter folly of resisting
God's natural law, set forth in the ancient
figure of the clay thinking to resist the
potter, men universally recognize. Much
more, the aggravated guilt of resisting God's
moral law, the child's refusing to be reconciled
to a father ready to sacrifice everything for
him and waiting long for the unnatural
spirit to relent, needs only the statement to
make its truth manifest. Certainly God is
righteous, then, when he receives the Gentiles
who having no other hope, accept this righteousness; and he is equally righteous in
leaving to their choice the Jews who trust to
their own merits (9: 1—33).

Appealing again to his countrymen he states the special ground of their error in rejecting Christ and his atonement. Ignorant, as was the apostle (1 Tim. 1: 13), of God's righteousness because they would not submit to it, not recognizing that Christ, as Moses taught, accomplishes "the end" sought in the giving of "the Law," overlooking Moses' statement that Christ's redemption, promised in Eden, was "nigh to," though neglected by the (Deut. 30: 11—14) Israelites of his day (Heb. 4: 2; 11: 26), Paul declares that the *principle* of the gospel from the first was plain to Jews and Gentiles (10: 1—8). Only by outward profession and inward fidelity to the profession that the Redeemer promised in the Old Testament is the crucified and risen Jesus, can justification for past sin and salvation from sin be expected (10: 9, 10), as Joel (2: 32) and Isaiah (52: 1) taught; while in clear prophecy of Christ's atoning sacrifice (10: 11—21) Isaiah foretold that the Israelites would reject him (53: 1—12), and that the Gentiles would accept him (65: 1, 2). That the Gentiles had, without the Old Testament revelation, the means of knowing God's provided redemption, David taught, when he intimated that he himself had been led to the Lord Christ by the teachings of nature as well as of revelation (10: 18; Psal. 16: 7, 8; 19: 1—13).

The question arising whether Israel were finally to fail of accepting Christ's atonement, Paul cites his own case and that of the seven thousand in Ahab's reign, also David's statement (11: 1—10), as proving that many accept while many reject promised redemption. He argues from the success of his own appeal to the "emulation" of his countrymen, that, when the Gentiles at large are enjoying the earthly blessings of redemption, all Israel will long to share the inheritance (11: 11—16). In a figure, specially true to natural and revealed law, [1] he intimates that as the engrafted scion retains its inherent form and fruitage when grafted upon a stock bearing fruit of another type, so Gentiles grafted on the stem of Jesse (Is. 11: 1) do not exclude from their native stock Israel for a time unfruitful (11: 17—24). Citing again Old Testament confirmations of this principle, that God, as a Father, never recalls his gifts

---

[1] As a pear graft upon a quince gives the fruit of the scion with the spicy flavor of the stock. and as a rose graft upon a barberry is in form a rose but tinged with the delicate yellow of the stock, so a Gentile graft on the stock of Israel was a Gentile still in his worldly associations, yet one with Christ in spirit, taking on but a new savor and hue.

however obdurate his children prove, the
apostle breaks out, in closing his argument
(11 : 25—36), "O, the depth of the riches
both of the wisdom and knowledge of God!"
and concludes with this ascription to the
Lord Jesus Christ, "For of him, and through
him, and to him are all things: to whom be
glory forever, Amen!"

The argument is supplemented with some
paragraphs of practical conclusions; as to
self-culture (12 : 1—3); as to Church co-
operation (12 : 4—8); as to social interchange (12 : 9—21); as to civil obligations
(13 : 1—14); and as to Christian influence
(14 : 1—23). Citing his own extended and
self-sacrificing labors as examples (15 : 1—
33), Paul adds (16 : 1—24) a list of individual
personal messages which embodies for all
time a picture of the simple organization of
the primitive Church; so indirect that it has
been unsuspected by those who in dark times
might have erased the record; so needful in
later ages that its clear teaching seems a
new revelation when re-studied. Thus the
closing paragraph is as deep in the Divine
wisdom which inspired it as is the master-
piece of logic preceding.

THE ATONEMENT IN THE EPISTLES OF PAUL'S IMPRISONMENT.

After writing his epistle to the Romans, about five years, from A. D. 59 to 64, were spent by Paul, including four years of parole imprisonment at Cæsarea and at Rome, in preaching rather than writing; when he successively wrote, under close confinement (Eph. 3: 1; 4: 1; Phill. 1: 7, 14; Coll. 1: 24; Heb. 13: 19, 23), the Epistles to the Ephesians, Phillipians and Colossians, to Philemon and to the Hebrews. These epistles, except the last, are practical rather than argumentative; and yet are studded with suggestions of new truth as to the atonement.

To the Ephesians, specially tempted to Asiatic pride and luxury (2: 2, 3), Paul specially dwells on the eternal purpose of God in redemption (1: 5, 11; 2: 10), the end of moral perfection sought (1: 4, 5, 12), the means in Christ's death and resurrection (1: 7, 20), the agency of the Spirit (1: 13, 18), and, especially, its moral influence on angels (1: 10, 14; 3: 9, 10). The infinite power exercised in regeneration (1: 19; 2: 1, 5), the oneness of the redeemed from all nations (2: 14—19), the special purpose to call forth angelic adoration (3: 10) demonstrates the

Divine efficacy of the atonement; and the ground of fidelity in all human relations, in the Church (4: 1—16), in society (4: 17 to 5: 21), and in the family (5: 22 to 6: 9) is the attained result of the spiritual power thus bestowed.

To the Philippians, whom Roman virtue animated (1: 5; 3: 15; 4: 1, 15), Paul opens the limitless height of possible Christian attainment (1: 9, 27; 2: 2, 12; 3: 15, 17; 4: 8) ; and he urges as motives to its attainment Christ's honor at the final day (1: 6), the perfect righteousness he provides by his Spirit's work (1: 11, 19), Christ's condescension in his sacrifice to provide it (2: 5—8), Christ's exaltation dependent on that sacrifice and its result (2: 9—11), the Christian's co-operation in the Divine work of salvation (2: 12, 13), the self-sacrifice thus inspired in Christian workers (2: 16—30), the new spiritual resurrection witnessed in each stage of ever upward (*ano*) Christian attainment (3· 10—14), the bond of Christian sympathy thus created (4: 1), and the assurance as to the future thus given (4: 19, 20).

To the Colossians, among whom, at the centre of Asiatic superstition and false philosophy, the power of redemption made slow

progress (1: 6, 21, 23; 2 : 1, 4, 8), as John
afterward noted (Rev. 3: 15—17), Paul
exults in the Gospel's promised triumph (1:
3—12) and gives minute lessons for Christian
guidance. The "grace" of Christ effects a
"translation" (1: 2, 13), as actual as Enoch's
(Heb. 11: 5); remission of sins by Christ's
death is its provision (1 : 14); its Author is
He " by whom and for whom all things were
created" (1: 15—19); and the "reconciliation" of angels as well as men is its result
(1: 20—22). As it had conquered Paul's
pride of ancestry and trust in rites so it would
theirs (1: 23 to 2: 8); for Christ is the
Divine "completeness" (*pleroma*) which
their sages dreamed of; imparting the Divine
life of which Jewish "circumcision" and
Christian "baptism" were symbols (2: 9—
13); and furnishing an expiatory sacrifice
that forbids any longer dread of infernal
deities and propitiatory offerings to them (2:
14—28). The test in them of the spiritual
power of Christ's atonement is their elevation
above earthly allurements (3: 1—7) their
Christian oneness (3: 11—17), their family
fidelity (3: 18 to 4: 1) and their access to
God in prayer (4: 2—6). The brief note to
Philemon, sent with this espistle (4: 9) by

his converted servant Onesimus, shows that
the Gospel duty of giving to servants what
was "just and equitable" (Coll. 4: 1) was
realized in the daily life of Christians even in
Asiatic communities (Philem. 10—21).

In the Epistle to the Hebrews, to whose
authorship Paul's own allusions are a sufficient testimony (13: 19—23), Paul presents,
first, the two-fold nature, and then the two-
fold office of Christ, in an argument drawn
from Old Testament revelations. Christ's
Divine nature was manifest in his declared
character (1: 2, 3), in its recognition by
angels (1: 4) and in God's announcement to
the universe before man was created (1: 5—
14). His human nature appeared in his un-
likeness to angels (2: 1—5), in David's inspired statement (2: 5—8), and in the necessity of his redemption (2: 9—18); while the
"purging away" of sin accomplished by his
sacrificial death and his living power demanded the union of these two natures (1:
3, 13; 2: 3, 10, 14, 17). His double character of "apostle" and "high-priest," indicating his double office as effective advocate and
sufficient propitiator, are seen in the contrast
between Moses as "the servant" and Christ
the "Son in his own house" (ch. 3d); in the

spiritual "rest," symbolized at creation by
the "Sabbath," and sought by Joshua and
David as a lack when their earthly "rest"
was most perfect (ch. 4th and Josh. 23 : 1—
16); in its prefigurement by the names given
to the priest and his city, the "king of righteousness and of peace," to whom Abraham
paid tithes; and in the perfect sacrifice of
Jesus, whose human spirit was saved in his
own assumed sacrifice for man (ch. 5th).
The demonstration that this sacrifice was the
atonement is seen in the impossibility that
man's imperfect spirit be either justified or
saved but by an immutable "counsel," back
of and conspiring with the fulfilled immutable
"promise," which gave "full assurance" to
both the faith and hope of redeemed men (ch.
6th).   The ground, again, of this assurance,
is in the character of the being who carries
through that "immutable counsel and promise"; whose earthly descent was aside from
all laws of human conception, as that of
Melchisedek was from Hebrew ideas of legitimate succession; and whose Divine authority
gives "the power of an endless life," making
him the "surety" of his own "covenant"
with His redeemed (ch. 7th).   The "sum" of
all this chain of truth as to Christ's atone-

ment is this; the "covenant," for whose fulfillment Christ is "surety," has two provisions; first, an expiatory "offering" meeting the Divine and the universal moral necessity; and, second, an imprinting of the whole Divine law on the heart so that without any direct requisition every man will in himself know and keep it (ch. 8th). As to the first provision, an adequate expiatory sacrifice, reason and revelation agree that the infliction of death on an innocent animal rather deadens than gives life to the human conscience; while such an offering as that of Christ, of which the sacrifices offered in all nations from Abel's day have been but symbols, satisfies reason and "purges" to its central core the most "corrupted" conscience (ch. 9th). In fine, the sacrifices from time immemorial observed everywhere among men, whose design was unknown till the Old Testament revelation from Daniel to Christ showed that they were symbols to cease when the true Jehovah the Anointed Redeemer, implied in the title "Lord Jesus Christ," should come to offer his sacrifice, [1] those

(1) See statements before quoted from Menu and Confucius as to the universality of "sacrifices"; especially Menu's statement (Instit. V. 22, 23) before Moses wrote, that "in the primeval sacrifices of holy men" the bodies of "beasts and birds of excellent sorts" were presented to the deities "; and,

sacrifices which no rational mind could believe would take away sin, were only a "shadow" keeping in memory the fact that in the volume of God's eternal counsel, preceding his promise, it was declared, "sacrifices, and offering and burnt offerings and offerings for sin thou wouldst not, neither hadst pleasure therein;" though the law prescribed them as the remembrancers of Christ's own declaration before He made man in Eden, "Lo, I come to do thy will, O God" (10: 1—9). All this, the last days of Jesus' mission on earth, his one offering, his ascension to His seat of spiritual power, the Holy Spirit's outpouring fulfilling all Christ promised, the perfect cancelling of sin by His sacrifice and the annihilation of its power by His spirit's work, the utter end put to Jewish rites when at Christ's cry, "It is finished," the temple vail was rent from top to bottom and the waiting worshippers first gained access through Christ's death into that holy place where only the high-priest before could go—all this stupendous fulfillment of the promise demonstrated the nature

associated with this Asiatic practice, the declaration of Daniel that the Messiah by his death after a ministry of "half seven" years, should "cause the sacrifice and oblation to cease" (Dan. 9: 27); a prophecy familiar to Eastern wise men, Greeks and Romans, as we have seen, when Christ came.

of the eternal counsel, preceding the promise, and held in memory through the sacrifices of all nations till Christ's day (10: 10–
22). The experience of Hebrew Christians
then living (10: 28—39) the faith of the
patriarchs from Abel to David and the prophets (11 : 1—40), the example of Jesus himself, and of the cloud of witnesses including
"an innumerable company of angels" and
"the spirits of just men made perfect," this
tested result on men for four thousand years,
and its influence on higher beings, attest the
truth as to Christ's atonement (ch. 12th) and
assure its controlling power over Christians
(ch. 13th).

THE ATONEMENT IN PAUL'S PASTORAL EPISTLES.

Early Christian history confirms the fact
that Paul realized his aspiration once more
in old age to herald with his voice the redemption of Christ. Released from prison,
going thence westward to Spain, thence to
Crete, Greece, Macedonia and Asia Minor,[1]

_____

(1) The concurrent and repeated statements of men relied
upon for authentic Christian history during the first five centuries, such as Clement, Eusebius, Jerome, Chrysostom, cannot be rejected without destroying the very sources of historic
truth. The expectation of Paul as to visiting Spain as well
as Rome may be reasonably supposed to have been only de-
ferred, but not frustrated (Acts 19 : 21 ; Rom. 15 : 24—29). His

Paul's ripened experience and latest inspiration is embodied in three letters addressed not to Churches but to their pastors; letters studded with new gems of truth as to the atonement of Christ.

To Titus he writes, that as men are to be won by Gospel truth embodied in the preacher's life (1: 3—16), to which all Christians should be conformed (2: 1—10), the essential points of that truth should be maintained. The central truth in Christ's salvation, is, present purity of life in hope of perfect glory at Christ's appearance; since he "gave himself for us" to attain two ends; first, to redeem us from all iniquity, and second, to purify for himself a people truly his own, eager for good works (2: 11—14). This end he accomplishes not through our full performance of the works which constitute

_____

confident assurance of release for the same reason must be supposed to have been realized (Phill. 1: 25; 2: 24; Philem. 22; Heb. 13: 19, 23). The line of visits indicated (Titus 1: 5; 3: 12; 1 Tim. 1: 3; 2d Tim. 4: 13, 20) accords with no previous tour. Most of all, his sending to Troas, which prior to his first imprisonment he had not visited for more than five years (Acts 20: 6; 24: 27; 28: 30), for "books and manuscripts" evidently needed in his second "defence" (*apologia*, 2d Tim. 4: 13, 16), and especially for a thick Roman overcoat (*paenula*) never used in southern latitudes but needed and before used by Paul amid a Roman winter (2d Tim. 4: 21), are testimonies compelling the conviction that Paul was arrested on an old grudge at Miletum the port of Ephesus and was hurried thence to Rome to undergo a six months' imprisonment and a beheading under Nero in the spring of A. D. 67 (Acts 19: 24—27; 1 Tim. 1: 20; 2d Tim. 4: 14, 15, 20).

righteousness; but first by the regeneration symbolized in baptism, the renewing of the Holy Spirit, and second by justification through His grace; both of which conspire to realize the " hope of eternal life " (3: 4—8).

To Timothy he declares that the end (*telos*) of the gospel requirement (*paraggelia*) is "love," the product of "a pure heart, a good conscience and a sincere faith" (1: 5); he cites his own conversion as proof of its universal power (1: 8—16) ; and he avers that fidelity to Christ's redeeming mission, " who gave himself a ransom for all men," will accomplish the salvation even of kings, as his experience had proved (2: 1—7). He urges therefore that Christians, male and female, and especially their appointed leaders (3: 1—14) remember that they are " the house (*oikos*) of God," the very columns and foundations which adorn and maintain the temple of His truth (3: 15) ; an impressive fact which calls forth a climactic utterance as to the comprehensiveness of that truth.

As all must confess, " great was the hidden provision of the atonement now revealed: God was manifest in flesh, justified in Spirit, beheld by angels, preached to the nations of men, believed on in the universe, taken up into

glóry" (3: 16). Rehearsing then the duties
of various classes of Christians (4: 1 to 6: 14),
and citing as a model Christ's own "good
confession," he utters this ascription to "the
Lord Jesus Christ," as "the blessed and only
Potentate, the King of kings, the Lord of
lords, who only hath immortality, dwelling
in light which no man   can   approach
unto; whom no man hath seen nor can see;
to whom be honor and power everlasting,
Amen."

In his last inspired letter, written just
before his martyrdom, the memories and
the prospects natural to such a man at such
an hour add their final radiance to his view
of Christ's atonement.   His childhood convictions like those of Timothy (1: 3, 5), the
logical consistency of Gospel truth (1: 7),
the clear light thrown on the character and
purpose of God and the present and future
welfare of man by his provision before creation in Christ (1: 9, 10), Paul's perfect
knowledge of his personal Redeemer and
trust in him, all of which Timothy had seen
in his life (1: 12, 13) should · prompt his
" son in the faith " to a like life (1: 13 to 2: 6).
The essential truth of his "gospel" is that
" Christ, of the seed of David, was raised from

the dead" for an end to which he could not
but prove "faithful" (2: 7—13); which end,
desired during his first and second imprisonment at Rome (Phill. 3: 11, 18), consists in
a spiritual resurrection not yet complete, but
sure of final accomplishment, since it rests
on these firm foundation-principles of Christ's
redemption, first, Christ's perfect knowledge
of "his own," from personal sympathy with
them, and second, the complete separation
from all iniquity which the taking of the
name "Christian" implies (2: 14—19).
This truth alone can save the preacher
(2: 20—26), meet designing opposers like
those of Moses' day (3: 1—13), keep alive
the power of childhood-trust in God's inspired word (3: 14 to 4: 5) and realize a
happy review of life and confident assurance
of a reward as "righteous" at Christ's appearing (4: 6—8).

THE ATONEMENT IN THE EPISTLES OF JAMES, JUDE AND PETER.

While Paul was writing his last practical
epistles for Gentiles predisposed to rationalism, and for Jews predisposed to ritualism,
three of the twelve apostles were addressing
their Hebrew countrymen; James of Jeru-

salem writing for foreign Israelites in the "dispersion" in the valley of the Euphrates (John 7: 35; Jas. 1: 1); Jude, James' brother, whose home was in the East, to the same "dispersion;" and Peter to the "dispersion" in the West or Asia Minor. All are inspired to correct errors among Israelite Christians, as to the person and office of Christ (Jas. 2: 1; Jude 4; 1st Pet. 2: 4; 2d Pet. 2: 1), as to the spiritual transformation which constitutes his redemption (James 1: 18, 26; Jude 8; 1st Pet. 1: 16; 2: 11; 2d Pet. 2: 20; 3: 11), as to the nature of Christ's "coming" as a spiritual reign in the heart rather than a fleshly appearance addressing the eye (James 5: 7—11; Jude 14—21; 1st Pet. 3: 19, 22; 4: 7, 13, 17; 2d Pet. 1: 11; 3: 4, 8, 13); and, yet more, as to "faith," conceived by the Israelites to be a substitute for, instead of a stimulus to the "works" which God's law requires (James 2: 14—26; Jude 3, 20; 1st Pet. 1: 5, 9; 5: 9; 2d Pet. 1: 5). All allude to teachings and writings of apostles and prophets confirming the truth they affirm (James 1: 22; 5: 10; Jude 17; 2d Pet. 1: 10—21; 3: 2); Peter quoting Paul's epistles as generally known (2d Pet. 3: 15, 16).

James urges that spiritual "wisdom" and

"grace" are the direct gift of God (1 : 5, 17) ; that they are given in answer to the prayer of faith (1 : 6), and that they imply a spirit eager to keep the "perfect law" both of self-restraint and of active charity (1 : 21—27). The "faith" of Christ "the Lord of glory," forbids arrogance (2 : 1— 7), and makes "love" the "law of liberty" by which we "shall be judged" (2 : 8—13); that "faith" being not a sentimental feeling but "fidelity" in duty to others (2 : 14—26). It especially subdues the spirit of domineering (3 : 1), ruling the tongue (3 : 2—12), and eradicating envy which prompts intolerance (2 : 13 to 4 : 6) ; and it cultivates humility before God as the judge of all (4 : 7—12), dependence on his fatherly care (4 : 13—17), self-distrust (4 : 16, 17), a life that will be a solace in adversity (5 : 1—6), patience in well-doing (5 : 7—11), reverence, faith and prevalence in prayer (5 : 12—18), and efficiency in saving the erring (5 : 19, 20).

Peter in an opening sentence sums up the provisions of redemption as "election" by the Father and "sanctification" by the Spirit, resulting in obedience and spiritual cleansing through the blood of Christ (1 : 2); and he puts himself on a level with his breth-

ren as a sharer of its blessings and privileges
(1: 8; 2: 9; 5: 1).   The fruits of redemption
are "hope" of the spiritual resurrection
Christ gives, a "faith" that leads on to "salvation," and a "love" to the unseen Savior
which makes faith as effective as sight (1:
3—9); which salvation, and the sufferings of
Christ that procured it, inspired prophets
and angels have longed to comprehend (1:
10 — 12).   Since redemption, then, is by
"the precious blood of Christ, the lamb
without spot," and its purifying is wrought
by the Spirit of God, spiritual sacrifices like
to that of Christ (2: 5), perfections like those
of the Father (2: 9) and a conduct controlled
by the Divine Spirit in all human relations
(2: 11 to 3: 7) ought to possess those whose
sins Christ bore that they might be dead
to sin and live to righteousness (2: 24).
Especially, in the tests to which persecution
was subjecting them, the spirit of Jesus who
suffered the just for the unjust to bring us to
God, the renewing power of the Spirit which
raised Jesus from the grave and had worked
even from Noah's day on the hearts of sinful
men, the vow of baptism as a recognition of
the raised Redeemer sitting in Heaven at the
head of all power (3: 8—22), ought to arm

them to resist every temptation and to meet every Christian duty (4: 1 to 5: 9); faithful always to "the God of all grace who has called us unto eternal glory by Christ Jesus" (5: 10).

In his second epistle, Peter, again, avows the "like faith" in himself and his brethren (1: 1); he repeats that Christ's redemption makes every disciple a "partaker of the divine nature" and an heir to every "virtue" (1: 2—4); but he declares that faith is only the first among many graces which make the Christian's "calling and election sure" (C: 5—11); and he reminds them of the perpetual duty imposed by the truth which he, as an apostle, and the prophets of old time were inspired to reveal (1: 12—21). He warns them that selfish deceivers, like the "angels that sinned," scorners like those of Noah's, Lot's and Moses' day, still misled men by "denying the Lord that bought them," and betrayed even believers into the "pollutions" from which through "the knowledge of the Lord and Savior Jesus Christ they had escaped" (2: 1—22). He exhorts them, therefore, to take as true the teachings of "prophets" and "apostles," especially of "our beloved brother Paul," who foretold the

"day of the Lord;" on which day Christ's
atonement would not prove to be a cloak to
cover cherished sensuality and selfishness,
but the power which had wrought in them a
life of "holy conduct and godliness" (3:
1—16). His last apostolic appeal, the sum-
mary of his own trying experience as to the
efficacy of Christ's redemption, is embodied in
the words, "Grow in grace and in the knowledge of our Lord and Savior Jesus Christ.
To him be glory both now and forever."

THE ATONEMENT IN THE APOCALYPSE AND THE EPISTLES OF JOHN.

About fourteen years after the inspired
epistles last mentioned were published, under
Domitian, about A. D. 84, the Apocalypse
was written; which was followed about fourteen years still later, A. D. 98, by the Gospel
and the epistles of John. The experience of
added years required the added light they
throw on the atonement.

During the political troubles of the sus-
picious Domitian, John, the last surviving
apostle, has a vision of his Master. On the
"Lord's day," fitly recalling that Master,
viewing from the heights of Patmos seven

representative Churches in whose circuit his last days were spent, John points to Christ as "the faithful witness, the first begotten of the dead, who hath loved us and washed us in his own blood and made us kings and priests unto God" (1: 4—10). He sees his Master, more glorious than at the transfiguration, holding the seven Churches in his right hand as on a candlestick with seven branches, and walking amidst the burden as if it were slight (1: 11—20). The errors of doctrine and faults of practice peculiar to each as representatives of all Churches, errors and faults increasing in guilt from simple lack of "first love" (2: 4) to loss of all religious interest (3: 16), sins dishonoring God the Father (2: 27; 3: 5, 21) and grieving the Spirit who revealed their character (2: 7, 11, 17, 29; 3: 1, 6, 13, 22), are met by the ever varied perfections of Christ, developing more and more from the first promise in Eden (2: 7) to the final glory of His triumph at the last day (3: 14, 21).

Turning now from his vision on earth towards heaven, God the Father is seen supported by four living powers, indicating in Him the union of fortitude, patience, intel-

ligence and foresight,[1] and is surrounded by
twice twelve witnesses representing the redeemed of the tribes of Israel (4: 1—11). In
His right hand is seen the book of His eternal counsels and his revealed promises;
which book "the Lion of Judah," in whose
nature is blended also "the Lamb," receives
and prepares to unseal the book. Before
"the Lamb" the same witnesses from Israel
bow, hailing him as "slain" to redeem them;
while the angels, also, adore his sacrifice as
revealing the exhaustless "power and wisdom," as manifesting the "authority," as
vindicating the "honor," as exalting the
"glory," as promising the "blessing" of the
Divine Redeemer (5: 1—14).

Turning again to earth, the opening seals
successively display the judgments of military
conquest (6: 2), of war (6: 4), of famine
(6: 6), of pestilence (6: 8), of ecclesiastical
persecution (6: 9), and of political dissension
(6: 12, 13) sent on the ancient people of God.
The seventh seal remains unbroken while

(1) The effort to symbolize the union of Divine attributes,
seen in the sphyuxes of Assyria and Egypt, which unite portions of the bodies of the lion, the ox, the eagle and of man,
is an absurdity in elaborated sculpture, as Horace (Ars Poet.
1—5) declares ; yet to the Oriental mind this representation
seems necessary. The permanently recognized idea is equally
a necessity in European conception ; as the British lion and
the American as well as Roman eagle are proof.

thousands redeemed from Israel (7: 4—8),
and countless numbers of Gentile converts
among whom Israel had been dispersed (7: 9)
are gathered as the fruits of Christ's atonement in ages past (7: 13—17). The fearful
calamities foretold by Christ at the final fall
of the Jewish state, pass in review (Chs.
8th to 10th); whose significance is indicated
by reference to Ezekiel's measurement (11:
1, 2); by Zechariah's two witnesses (11: 3,
4); by Christ's crucifixion, and his appearance to John and his brethren after three
and a half days, giving them new life, on the
evening after his resurrection (11: 8—11);
by the fall of Jerusalem amid darkness and
terror (11: 12—15); and by the spiritual
triumph of Christ's redemption amid these
catastrophes (11: 15—19). In closing this
vision, the mission of God's first chosen
people, foreshadowed in Joseph's dream
and its fulfillment (Gen. 37: 9, 10; 49:
24), and realized in Christ's transient life
on earth (12: 1—5), is declared to be
a continued trial, yet as brief as Christ's
own three and a half years' ministry foretold by Daniel (9: 27); the angels in
heaven and even earth itself aiding the
triumph of the truly redeemed over eccle-

siastical opposition and Satan its instigator
(12 : 6—17). [1]

In a second series of visions (chs. 13th to
18th) the judgments that fall on political
powers opposing Christ's mission are por-
trayed. A power presented first under the
symbol of Daniel's visions (ch. 13th), fully
interpreted afterwards (ch. 17th), whose empire in John's day had its type in the Babylon of Daniel's age (17: 5, 18), a power imperial in sway and ruling over many kingdoms
(17: 10—18), yet ruled, as are all tyrannies,
by false religious teachers claiming religious
homage for the despot (13: 11—15), a power
whose name, unlike that of fallen Jerusalem,
could not safely be revealed in John's day
(13: 18), but which was privately held in
memory till revealed after the Roman Empire
became nominally Christian,–this power, often
wounded as if unto death (13: 3), was to suffer
like calamities with fallen Jerusalem (ch.
16th) and finally to fall as low (ch. 18th). The
grand spiritual triumph of Christ, like that
under Moses amid the plagues of Egypt (13:
13, 14) and of true Israelites on the Euphrates
(16: 12), runs like a linking chain through

---

(1) See confirmations of this view in preceding statements
on the visions of Ezekiel, Zechariah and Daniel, on Mat. 24th
ch., on Christ's last hours, and on Acts 2d ch.

all these historic visions; the brief period
of Christ's suffering being the limit of his
followers' trial (13 : 5); the names of each
being guarded "in the book of life of the
Lamb slain before the foundation of the
world" (13: 8); they that "follow the Lamb
whithersoever he goeth," His "redeemed,"
who keep "the faith of Jesus," being "without fault before the throne of God" because
of Christ's atonement (14: 1—13); He, as
the Lord of lords and the King of kings,
triumphing ever (17: 14); and his people
being separated from the calamities that befall
the corrupt nations (18: 41).

A third series of visions presents the future
triumphs of Christ's spiritual reign ; following up the two previous series and ever
repeated in past and in coming ages (chs. 19th
to 22d). In this vision a prophet of the Old
Testament day utters the significant statement that the testimony of Jesus has been
"the spirit of prophecy" in all ages, and that
all "holding his testimony," however imperfect their knowledge from revelation, are
brethren ; their common head being the
"Faithful and True," whose "vesture is
dipped in blood" and his name "The Word
of God" (19: 10—13). In his continued

future conflicts, so protracted that a thousand
years will witness the struggle, rude Japhetic
tribes, as in Ezekiel's day, will be deceived,
but finally enlightened, becoming partakers
of Christ's first or spiritual resurrection (20:
1—9); a conflict to end with the final judgment (20: 11—15).[1]   A picture of the pros-
perity, comfort and delights which will
attend Christ's spiritual reign on earth and
its consummation in heaven closes the picture of what John declares is "shortly to
come to pass" (1: 1, 3; 22: 6, 10); the first
book of the Old and the last of the New Testament presenting the same personal and present Redeemer, unchanged in character and in
mission, "the same yesterday, to-day and
forever."

The three brief epistles of John, the first
of which seems to have accompanied the
publication of his Gospel, suggest, as does the
Gospel, that false teachers were more and
more perverting the truth of the atonement

---

(1) As Ezekiel and Daniel in their day realized in the in-
cursions of the Medes and Persians the fulfillment of Moses'
permanent prediction that rude Japhetic tribes should invade
the dwellings of Shem (Gen. 9: 27; 10: 2; Ezek. 38: 2, 3;
Dan. 5: 28), so, as the earlier and later Christian historians
relate, Paul saw the Scythians (Col. 3: 11), John the Getæ
(Strabo VII, 3), and later ages the Goths, the Huns, and
finally the Turks overrunning the centres where Christian
civilization had begun to reign. Compare John 5: 25—29.

in some one or more of its comprehensive provisions. John declares that the embodied "word" of God, "manifiested" to all the senses of "man," whose "blood cleanses from all sin" so that God can be "faithful and just to forgive us our sins and cleanse us from all iniquity" (1: 1—10), who is at once our "advocate with the Father" and "the propitiation for the sins of the whole world" (*kosmos*) (2: 1, 2), is denied by some to have "come in the flesh" (4: 3). Such make God a liar by virtually denying these connected facts, that every man is and has been sinful in nature and in life (1: 8, 10); that the fulfillment of God's law is to be "true" because real in the redeemed as in Christ himself (2: 3—8); that the sins of even little children are forgiven for Jesus' sake, and that they may know the Father as revealed in him (2: 12, 13); that the distinction must be made between "lust" that comes from the world (2: 15—19) and conformity to God's law which the Holy Spirit's anointing and Christ's atonement secures (2: 20 to 3: 10); that this truth was revealed at the beginning and illustrated in Cain and Abel (3: 11—24); that the open "confession" of Jesus as our "propitiation" begets controlling

"love" to God and man (4: 1—21); that
true "faith" in him overcomes the power of
the world, as the Spirit's work and as the two
ordinances of baptism and the supper attest
(5: 1—8); and that the witness within the
believer begets an assured hope of eternal life
(5: 9—12). The Christian's love, faith and
hope are testimonies, thus, stronger than the
senses, so that the redeemed "knows" the
whole range of essential truth (1: 3; 2: 27;
4: 2; 5: 13—20). Closing his first and chief
epistle with a warning against the love of the
world, which is "idolatry," John's second
epistle presents the same denial of Christ's
true nature (v. 7); and his third indicates
that this spirit of Antichrist arises from
worldly ambition (v. 9, 10); while both urge
that Gospel "truth" is always attested by
Gospel "love." The last voice of the Gospel
is the "echo" of Christ's mission; to "fulfill
the law" by "the truth" as to His atonement.

KNOWLEDGE OF THE ATONEMENT WHEN THE NEW TESTAMENT WAS COMPLETED.

The survey thus far taken has shown that
ideas of propitiation, sacrifices for expiation
and reasonings as to their efficacy, preceded
revelation and gave language in which to

embody its successive statements as to the
atonement; and that two tendencies of
thought as to the nature of the atonement
prevailed among men both with and without
revelation. One class, like the Chinese and
Romans, satisfied that human reason could
not fathom the design of their immemorial
customs and the cause of their instinctive
convictions, trusting to the *form* of sacrifices,
became ritualists. The other class, including
especially Brahminic and Grecian sages,
adhered indeed to "immemorial custom," yet
sought, often superficially and fancifully, the
reason of the custom; and so became rationalists. It might be anticipated that the same
tendencies that from man's creation pervaded
human thought, and were specially called out
by the teachings of Christ and of his apostles,
would form a guide in tracing the intricate
developements of human reasoning as to the
atonement in subsequent Christian history.
The tests of revelation and the proofs of inspiration accord with the fact thus referred to;
and aid to a just consideration of its results.
The only conceivable test of a claim to supernatural knowledge of spiritual truth is the
possession of supernatural power over material laws; a power not claimed by Confucius,

Socrates, Mohammed and like religious
teachers, even in degenerate ages; a claim,
however, sustained by Moses and Daniel, by
Jesus and Paul, in the climactic eras of
Asiatic and European science. The necessity
of Christian faith, testing first the proof of
revelation, has led human reason to its
designed office of classifying revealed statements as to the atonement.

In this classification, the facts as to its
material, formal, instrumental, efficient and
final causes, have led thoughtful minds to
dwell successively, on the nature of man to be
redeemed by the atonement; on the influences
acting in him by which its work is effected;
on the human sufferings, especially the sacrificial death, of Christ as its means; on the
united Divine and human person of Christ
as its author; and on the ultimate end of
the atonement which was to make known to
His intelligent Universe His perfect character
and government; to which ultimate end the
redemption of so insignificant a being as
man was subordinate.

Three important facts, brought out in every
age of investigation, are therefore guiding
clues in threading the mazes of Christian
history. First, no man has ever been brought

into position to see the harmony of spiritual truth in the atonement until his own spirit has, by personal experience, realized. that truth; as Jesus and Paul so plainly taught (John 3: 2; 1st Cor. 2: 8—14). Second, as the only possible point of view from which to comprehend the harmony of the material Universe is the centre of physical force and the Being who wields it, so the only permanently satisfactory view of the nature and ground of the atonement is simple trust in the character of its Divine author and in the fact of his assumed responsibility; to which assumption, recognized as a fact, the little of universal moral truth which a finite being, human or angelic, can know, is like a child's view and thought on the ocean shore; a consideration which explains the perfect absorption of Paul, Peter and John in their extreme old age in this one fundamental truth in the teaching of Jesus (2 Tim. 1: 12; 1st Pet. 4: 19; John 10: 28; 17: 11, 24). Third, the comprehension of each separate department in this field of truth, is progressively attained at each new stage of advancing personal experience; every great leader in Christian thought, as Luther, finding, like Paul, new phases of truth in the

central prophetic declaration, "The just by
faith shall live" (Hab. 2: 4), according as he
ponders it in his early (Gal. 3: 11), his
matured (Rom. 1: 17) or his latest (Heb. 10:
38) Christian experience.

PRINCIPLES OF BIBLICAL INTERPRETATION INFLUENCING VIEWS OF THE ATONEMENT.

As the records of revelation are in human
language, prose and poetry, didactic and
imaginative, so the laws for the interpretation of these varied classes of literature must
be observed in ascertaining the meaning of
their statements. In law codes, whose statements are at once the most simple and the
most important, the following five rules have
been recognized in ancient and modern
times. The meaning of words is determined,
first, by their common use; second, by their
connection; third, by their subject-matter;
fourth, by the consequences of any meaning
given them; and fifth, by the history indicating the design of the statute. In the interpretation of history, poetry and general literature, in which words are used figuratively
as well as literally, regard must be had, first
to the design, second to the circumstances,

third to the cast of mind, and fourth to the culture of the writer. In Bible interpretation three added special principles must guide in applying the rules already noted; first, that the inspired Hebrew and Greek originals alone are free from human errors; second, that to the words of those originals the imperfect conceptions of the Hebrew and Greek nations, from whose languages they are drawn, are not to be attributed; and third, that only personal experience of the spiritual truth revealed can enable any mind to apprehend the inspired statements.

From the necessary laws of human thought several classes of interpreters, taking their names from their distinctive tendencies, have in all ages of the Christian Church appeared. There is first the *historical* school; tending to literal interpretation and ritualistic conceptions; whose extreme is illustrated in the Roman view of Christ's statement as to the bread used at the supper, "This is my body." There is, second, the *allegorical* school; tending to regard even history as symbols, making each individual mind the judge for itself of their import, and thus leading to rationalistic conceptions; as illustrated in the second century by Origen, culminating in

Swedenborg, and ruling among Unitarian interpreters. There is, third, the *theological* school; tending to conform all Bible statements to a system of religious truth already established; illustrated in the revival of logical methods in the twelfth century, and specially marked in the distinctive Protestant Churches. A fourth is the *philological* school; who insist on the classic signification of words in the Semitic and Greek languages as the ground work of all true Biblical science; overlooking the fact that in the selection of words from the Hebrew and Greek the inspired writers were subject to the same necessity as translators of the Scriptures into the Chinese or any other language; the words of classic authors being applied to a new subject, the terms most nearly expressing the new conception being chosen, while the context and subject-matter must explain the new meaning implied. There is, finally, the *experimental* school; who are controlled by the fact that only the mind personally acquainted by experience with the new spiritual truth can successfully apply to Divine revelation the rules of interpretation belonging to all written records. At every step in tracing the history of opinions, as to the atonement, the influence of these differing schools of interpretation will appear.

The Atonement in Christian Writers Prior to the Union of the Church and State under Constantine.

In every age different classes of writers, preachers like Chrysostom, allegorists like Origen, advocates like Augustine, and Bible interpreters like Jerome, have set forth the atonement in simple or adorned forms of thought; while historians like Eusebius have sought to draw from all these differing utterances the common principles belonging to the connected system of truth. In modern times such general ecclesiastical histories as those of Gieseler and Neander, and such specific histories of Christian opinion as those of Dorner, Ritschl and Shedd are invaluable in tracing the expressed thought of the earlier as well as of the later Christian ages; while in each age the fresh personal conviction as to common experience attained from Bible study, will be heightened by an independent review of the writers of that age.

All historians accord in the observation that the Apostolic Fathers, who in the close of the first century were either pupils or hearers of the apostles, merely quote the words of the New Testament. Their quotations, however, indicate that they recognized Christ's sacrificial sufferings as the instrument and Christ's Divine assumption of personal responsibility as the essential ground of atonement. Thus Clement says (c. 18, 32), "We are saved by that through which God from the beginning hath justified all men." * * "By the will of God he gave his body for our body and his soul for our soul." They were called also to meet indirectly the errors rife in the days of the apostles; especially the denial of Christ's true humanity as well as his Divinity;[1] the rejection of the real renewal of man's spirit and of the body's resurrection;[2] and even the introduction of material and ideal Oriental and Grecian philosophic theories of evolution and its denial of true moral accountability.[3]

---

(1) 3d Thes. 2: 4; Coll. 2: 19; Heb. 10: 29; 2d Pet. 1: 16; Jude 4; 1st John 2: 22; 4: 3.

(2) 1 Cor. 2: 14; 15: 12; 2d Cor. 5: 12, 17; 11: 13, 18; 2d Tim. 2: 18.

(3) Eph. 4: 14, 19; Coll. 2: 8, 18, 23; Heb. 13: 9; 1 Tim. 1: 4; 4: 1—4; 6: 20; 2d Tim. 3: 8; Tit. 1: 14, 16; 3: 9; James 3: 15; 2d Pet. 2: 1; Jude 11; Rev. 2: 6, 14, 15. The words *genealogia*, united with *mythos*, led many early Christian writers, also Grotius in modern times, to suppose the doctrines of imaginative writers like Empedocles and Lucretius, whose doctrines of "evolution" are only poetic "myths," to be the errors opposed by Paul and John; as they were exposed by the Greek historian Polybius (9. 2. 1) about B. C. 170.

The Patristic Fathers, or pupils of the Apostolic Fathers, were in the second century called more directly to correct the errors of former generations; hence they resorted more to *theories* of Christian truth; and hence, also, their constant allusion to the central and essential truths of the atonement as unquestionable is the most emphatic testimony. The philosophic perversions of Christian doctrine set forth by Celsus were offset by the clear statements of contemporaries in the latter half of the second century. Origen, presenting often the actual personal conflict of Satan and of Christ in Bunyan's style of allegory, like Bunyan also presents the comprehensive truth as to the atonement; making Christ's assumed responsibility, culminating in his personal "offering," the essential truth in redemption. Irenæus, again, (ad. Diog.) says that Christ "redeemed what was originally his own * * in such a way that neither should justice be infringed nor the original creation of God perish," and he asks, "In whom was it possible that we, unholy and ungodly, should be justified, except in the Son of God alone?"

In this age, as all historians allow, the con-

flict between good and evil, as personified in
the prevailing Egyptian and Persian philosophy, led Christian teachers to the extreme
in picturing the personal conflict between
Satan and Jehovah, or Christ, as presented
in the Old Testament, in the life of Jesus
and in the apostolic writings; a philosophy
which led Origen to his conception that
Christ as the Son was generated by the
Father, and the Holy Spirit created by the
Son; and which also suggested the Gnostic
theory of Manes, that the Son and the Holy
Spirit are two emanations from the Father of
light struggling against the kingdom of darkness. Ritschl suggests that it was the lack
of theological science which prompted this
personification; whereas it is only the necessary form of language presenting the fact
maintained by Christ and his apostles, employed by all successful Christian preachers
in every age, and realized in the maturest
convictions of the profoundest Christian rea-
soners as the ultimate truth in the science of
the atonement. This conclusion is sustained
in Justin, the truly philosophic writer of
this age; who, after exhausting all systems of
Oriental and Grecian philosophy then rife,
and finding no satisfaction till an aged

Christian led him to the New Testament view
of Christ as the personal Redeemer, wrote
those masterly treatises which, like Paul's
epistles in a former age, met Jewish and
Gentile objections by the complete harmony
of truth revealed in experimental knowledge
of Gospel redemption. To Trypho, the Jew,
Justin shows that the "Jehovah" who met
Adam, Enoch, Noah, Abraham, Jacob and
Moses, was the very Christ crucified at Jerusalem; his *personal* assumption being the
reply to all objections as to the atonement.
To the Gentiles, himself a Greek, Justin
shows how the truths in the conflicting systems of Plato and Aristotle and of their successors are harmonized and realized in the
life and death of Jesus.

The most important event of this era was
the establishment of the Canon of the New
Testament. The writings of all men are collected after their death; those of inspired
writers of the Old and New Testament necessarily being included in this law. Jesus
wrote nothing, but left to his disciples not
only to recall his words but to add all necessary truth (John 14: 26). Paul and Peter
employed amanuenses, and hence left few or
no autograph writings. Paul, and also John,

wrote uninspired, as well as inspired, letters
to some Churches; and these were after their
decease to be discriminated (1 Cor. 5 : 9; 2
Cor. 10: 10; 3 John : 9); Peter intimated
that this discrimination would be the responsible duty of future generations (2d Pet. 1:
15; 2: 1; 3: 1, 2); and Luke, John and
Paul intimate that Christ's followers after
their day must make this their care lest
unfaithful men add to or take from the
records God himself approved (Luke 1: 1—4;
John 21: 24; Rev. 22: 19; Heb. 2: 3, 4).

For three reasons this duty could not be
performed until two or three generations of
instructed Christians had lived. First, the
writings of John were not all completed till
the reign of Trajan, nearly in the second century. Second, some of the inspired apostolic
writings, as the Epistle to the Hebrews, the
Epistles of James and Peter, and the Apocalypse, not being addressed to a particular
person or Church, had no specially appointed
guardian of their authenticity and authority.
Third, as in the progress of Christianity in
modern times, for instance in India, a succession of generations trained to Christian ideas
must grow up before all minds can come to
distinguish between the incomplete views of

able men converted from other religions and
the complete truth coming from the lips and
pens of instructed European Christian teachers, so in the age after the apostles two or
three generations must pass before the perfect
word of inspired penmen could be separated
from their own uninspired letters and from
the imperfect reasonings and precepts of
their uninspired successors.

Under Nero, A. D. 67, Paul's Epistles were
partially collected (2d Pet. 3 : 16). During
the second century the collection was so
complete that Marcion, the rationalist, could
make his own imagination his guide in select-
ing what to admit; Irenæus (adv. Haer. 4:
32) and Origen (in Mat. 29 : 9) had indicated
the principles on which the inspired volume
was made up; and Tertullian had unfolded the
proof that they were "authentic" (de Praescr.
36). In the next century Eusebius (Eccl.
Hist. B iii & iv) reviewed the lists made in
the former age and cited the proofs of their
completeness; while at the Council of Nice,
called by Constantine A. D. 325, the recognition of the entire volume was almost universal.

In the generation following arose the first
acceptance of an error, opposed by Origen

when first suggested, which lingers yet in the partial reasonings of many Christian leaders. Praxeas at Rome had contended that Christ, as Divine, was generated by the Father; but his view had little influence till its revival by Arius nearly two centuries later. Sabellius, however, following others who had suggested it, elaborated about A. D. 255, the view that Christ was but a man, in whom the Divine Being manifested himself; a view which in his own, as in later ages, was shown to be founded on a very partial grouping of Scripture statements; one indeed, excluding from its survey the plainest declarations.

THE ATONEMENT IN THE WESTERN OR ROMAN CHURCH AT CONSTANTINE'S CONVERSION.

The practical Christian statesman, who reads in connection Eusebius' " Ecclesiastical History" and his " Life of Constantine," finds a clue to the essential Gospel truth maintained when State patronage first tested spiritual Christianity. Constantine's first religious convictions were formed when at the Court of his father some official corruption was brought out, and the enraged Emperor sternly demanded of the head of the national religion, " Who among Romans could be trusted "; in response to which challenge the trembling augur was forced to respond, " The Christians can be trusted." Led to study the Bible, embracing from personal conviction the Christian faith, maintaining it though allowing perfect freedom to other religions on his accession to empire A. D. 306, making it his life-employ in his military campaigns and imperial visits extending from Britain to India to distribute copies of the Sacred Scriptures and to preach personally to crowds in theatres and in his large audience-tent, all Constantine's words and acts showed his practical wisdom in making the simple words of revelation and the experience founded on faith in the personal Redeemer the end of all controversies as to doctrine; since he found them to be but bids of political aspirants for ecclesiastical preferment. He founded Con·stantinople as a second Rome that he might mediate between the Eastern and Western Churches; he gathered a general Council at Nicæa, East of his new city in Asia; he presided over its stormy debates; and by his personal influence secured the simple scriptural statement of Gospel doctrine since called the

Nicene creed, embodying that essential and
universal truth, as to which in that age the
Greek could affirm "*pisteuo*," while the
Roman, too, declared "credo;" to which,
also, every Christian can now respond "I
believe." As Neander intimates, however,
the age of "Church" instead of "Christian"
history was now inaugurated; the former
of which the records of councils make
conspicuous, while the latter is "a treasure hid in the field" wherever the true
word, sown in successive ages, found root.
Happy the man who by searching finds this
true history!

Three great eras are marked in the history
of the Roman, or Western Church, beginning
with the era when political aspirants could
pervert or subvert this Christian faith; first,
the age from Constantine, A. D. 306, to the
fall of Rome and its subjection to Gothic
sway A. D. 475; second, from the Druidical
supremacy given to Roman Bishops to the
first recognized Pope A. D. 604; third, the
long age of Papal supremacy till the Reformation. In each of these the alternation of
rationalistic and ritualistic partial views is to
be found contending against the comprehensive "truth," not as it is embodied in any

limited human system, but "as it *is* in Jesus," the personal Redeemer.

THE ATONEMENT UNDER THE TOLERANT CHRISTIAN EMPIRE.

Constantine proclaimed religious freedom A. D. 313, his moral support only giving Christianity predominance. The practice of old Roman religious rites was first forbidden under Theodosius I A. D. 376, and the code of Theodosius II, giving civil power to religious teachers was proclaimed A. D. 423; the reaction against which in the Eastern Empire and Church triumphed A. D. 529 at the proclamation of the Code of Justinian. In this age, when all the accumulated religious wisdom of the world was met and mastered by "the truth as it is in Jesus," the atonement appeared in a light unsurpassed in clearness and fulness by that of any subsequent age.

The central focus of that light is hinted in the clear conception and apt illustration of of Augustine (De Trinit. 8. 4.): "What was his personal appearance we are entirely ignorant; consequently the features of our Lord's fleshly nature are varied and sculptured according to the innumerable diversity

of individual conceptions; which nevertheless were one whatever they were." Greek
sculpture and painting sought to embody
ideal excellence as superior to any copy found
in nature; it brought out intellectual cast
in the profile, emotional character in the
front face, and moral and executive energy
in the quarter view; one class of minds was
absorbed by one partial view and another by
another; hence, *truth* in art, though partial,
was attained by each; while *all* views combined secured comprehensive truth and
beauty. The personal Redeemer is the central light in the religious Universe; infinite
distance and innumerable observers are around
him; each is naturally absorbed in his own
point of view; that point of view only one
finite being can possibly occupy; all views
are necessarily distinct as well as partial;
and each is therefore true though not the
infinite truth.

As Shedd in the earlier, so Dorner in this
succeeding age has noted, that the question
" What think ye of Christ?" is the essential
inquiry; and views of the " Person of Jesus"
control all subordinate conceptions as to his
work. Arius contended that Christ was
Divine, not in essence but as a representative

of the Father, not eternally begotten but the "first born of every creature." Athanasius, on the other hand, insisted that three personalities, in all respects distinct, existed in the one God; thus *defining* what no apostle of Christ was inspired to define. Yet, amid the heat of controversy, as to the personally assumed Divine responsibility—the ultimate ground of atonement—both used kindred expressions. Athanasius said, "He who created men from nothing could suffer for all and thus be their substitute." Arius, in view of his work, often declared (e. g. ad Euseb.) that Christ by the Divine "will and counsel, before time and the Universe, was made full God (*pleres theos*) only-begotten, unchangeable;" and as such He was Creator of all things, as well as of man, in order that by atonement for man He might reconcile the Universe to God.

In the next age, the question as to the Person of Christ, the author of the atonement, being at rest, discussion turned on the Work of Christ in giving individual efficacy to the atonement; the controversy of Augustine and Pelagius virtually hinging on the inquiry "Which gives origin to redemption in man; man's acceptance of it as an act of free will,

or the Divine Spirit's influence?" . Pelagius
insisted, as did Arminus ten centuries later,
that his view did not at all affect the general
doctrine of atonement; and in this age
the most complete conceptions prevailed of
Christ's comprehensive scheme.

Jerome became the Bible Student of the
ages; spending more than thirty years in
Palestine to perfect his scholarship; establishing the principles on which the inspired,
as distinct from uninspired writings, were
selected; elaborating a Latin translation of
the Scriptures which is now the foundation
of the Vulgate; working out a full and ana-
lytical commentary which to this day is of
standard value; giving due place to each of
the principles of true interpretation established in the distinct Schools of succeeding
ages; and insisting that the practical meaning of inspired statements recognized by all
experimental Christians is the essential truth
of the Sacred Scriptures. He recognized
Christ as the Creator and Mediator known to
Adam; and calls attention to the parallel
between the opening records of Moses and of
John. He sees the double meaning of
"faith" in Habakkuk's prophecy which Paul
developes. He distinguishes between the

"soul" (*anima*) (Matt. 26: 36) of Christ, which slept with his body, and his "spirit" (*spiritus*) which went to Paradise. Christ is the "Mediator of the Law" (Gal. 3: 19, 20); "natural law" as opposed to a "revealed command" is alone known to mankind "from Adam to Moses" (Rom. 5: 14); and he adds the comment, "all men have sinned after the similitude of Adam's transgression." In the expression "whole creation" (Rom. 8: 22) he shows that only "intelligent beings" can be included, and in general accords with the interpretations followed in the survey taken in this treatise.

Augustine, the logical thinker of his age, replies to the partial theories of his time, as in the passage above quoted; and as Ritschl says, presented "the elements of many theories" of the atonement. In his "Confessions," which gives the history of his own growing conceptions gained in his progressing Christian experience, there can be traced, as in the history of Paul and of Luther, the successive partial views of the atonement which make up the entire "truth as it is in Jesus." In his "City of God," to which treatise Ritschl specially refers, Augustine combines into a system those truths as to the

material, formal, instrumental, efficient and
final causes, which together make up the
comprehensive theory of the Atonement. He
especially sets forth in all his writings the
personal Redeemer, assuming at man's origin
the entire responsibility which his creation,
fall and recovery imply.

THE ATONEMENT IN THE SYSTEM OF MOHAMMED.

The inherent error of the Roman political
constitution, and the corrupting influence of
the promotion of political aspirants to leadership in the Christian Church, which brought
on the decay of Roman military power and the
successful conquests of the Persians in Western Asia, of the Huns in Eastern Europe and
of the Goths at Rome itself, till the Empire
finally fell A. D. 475,—these causes prepared
the way for the triumph of the military prophet
Mohammed. While faithful missionaries were
spreading gospel truth through India, Persia
and Armenia in Asia, and through Britain,
Germany and along the Alps in Europe, the
first Pope succeeded the last Roman Bishop
A. D. 602; and despite the lingering influence of the great and good men of the former
generations, the errors of partial systems,

urged by aspirants for place, outweighed the power of truth at controlling centres.

Born A. D. 571 in Arabia, awakened to new religious thought by a Greek monk on a visit to Jerusalem as a merchant-clerk, marrying the rich Jewess whom he served, guided in study by Jewish and Christian scholars, Mohammed resolved to proclaim himself the prophet of "Islam," the "true faith of Abraham, who was neither a Jew nor a Christian," yet the spiritual "father" of both. In the "Koran," or "Reading," are embodied his professed visions; each filling a "Sura" or chapter, one hundred and fourteen in all; successively promulgated as he rose to power, but collected by his followers after his death. Admitting the Divine authority of the Old and New Testament records,[1] he claims that they are parts of successive revelations given through Enoch, Noah, Shem, Abraham, Ishmael and later prophets;[2] that he was the one foretold by by Christ as his successor;[3] that the Jews

---

(1) Referred to s. 2 ; declared s. 35 and 43.

(2) Declared s. 4 ; designed to " preserve safe " former " scriptures " s. 5 ; " every age hath its book " s. 13 ; the Koran confirming Moses' law s. 46 ; " the books of Moses and of Abraham " s. 53, and of " the posterity " of Noah and Abraham s. 57.

(3) " Remember Jesus the Son of Mary said * * I am the apostle of God * * bringing good tidings of an apostle who shall come after me, whose name shall be Ahmed " s. 61. The

had corrupted the Old and the Christians
the New Testament, though attested by miracles;[1] and that his testimonials were the
perfections of his writings and his success
with the sword.[2] His special mission was
to restore the doctrine of the "unity" of
God; and thus the unity of religion which
existed before idolatry and polytheism; and
he resists the Christian claim that there were
"three gods," God, Jesus and Mary (s. 3, 4,
5, 9, 42). Hence he cites and confirms the
entire Old Testament history, from the fall
of man to the last prophet; and he claims to
have received new revelations explaining its
teachings (s. 2, 7, 11, 20, 28). He especially
confirms the New Testament history of
Christ; dwelling on his miraculous birth, on
his miracles of healing, on his perfect life
and teachings, and on his ascension; and
rebuking the calumny of his time that the

word "Ahmed," the same, without the prefix, as Mohammed,
means "renowned;" the reference being to John 14: 16, and
the Greek *parakletos* being changed to *perikletos*.

(1) The Jews at Sinai "demanded that Moses show them
God" s. 2 and 4; they misinterpreted their scriptures "through
envy among themselves;" and "concealed many things in the
scriptures" s. 5. The Christians' "doubt concerning Jesus,
the word of truth," s. 19; "have made schisms in the matter
of their religion" s. 21, and make Mary a god, and "their
priests and monks lords, besides God" s. 9.

(2) Though Satan sometimes suggests errors, s. 22, and though
its revelations are fragmentary s. 17, 25, since "signs were
abused" he gave none s. 7; but he demands of objectors "let
them bring six chapters, even one, like it" s. 10 and 11.

father of Jesus was a human or angelic being,
and he not a direct creation of God's Spirit
(s. 2, 19).

Mohammed's main effort is to present the
person and work of Christ in such a light as
not to exclude, but rather render necessary
his own professed mission. To this end he
avails himself of the partial statements and
philosophic errors which had become rife
through Christian teachers.[1] In the second
century the Platonic philosophy had been
quoted by the most intelligent Christian
writers as illustrating the union of Father,
Son and Spirit in the Divine nature; Justin
saying in his appeal to the Roman mind
(Apol. 2, 13) "Not unlike are the teachings
of Plato and of Christ." Plato had represented the infinite God as manifested in the
"Logos" or Word, as man's spirit is manifested by speech; and he had spoken of the
exerted energy of God as his Spirit. The
Greek Old Testament translators had used
the word "logos" in such passages as Ps. 33:
6; and John had employed it in his Gospel
(1: 1, 14), in his epistle (1: 1) and in the
Revelation (19: 13). That the allusions of

<hr/>

[1] In which he is followed by Rev. John Miller in his
"Questions awakened by the Bible;" See Part III, pp. 35, 89.

Christian writers to Plato were not designed to suggest an analogy, but only an illustration, is manifest from the earnest remonstrance of Irenæus (adv. Haer. 2. 48, 49) to those who ask, "In what manner then does the Son proceed from the Father?" He declares that the figure "Word of God" is an "indefinable" conception; like Paul's figure (1 Cor. 15: 37) illustrating the resurrection. Availing himself, however, of this usage, and laying stress on the preposition *pros* (rendered "with" John 1: 1, 2; 1st John 1: 2; 2: 1) properly meaning "near," Mohammed wrote (s. 2), "The angel said: O Mary, verily God sendeth thee good tidings, the Word proceeding from himself * * one of those who approach near God." He declares "infidels" (s. 5) those who say, "God was Christ the Son of Mary;" that "it was not meet that God should have a Son;" that "the sectaries differ among themselves" as to Jesus (s. 19); and that "Jesus is no other than a servant" (s. 43). So difficult, however, was it to establish this idea in face of New Testament declarations, that one entire vision (s. 110), entitled "The Declaration of God's unity," a vision which some Mohammedan doctors have declared is "equal in value to a third

part of the Koran," is made up of this single
sentence: "Say; God is one God; the eternal God; he begetteth not, neither is he
begotten; and there is not any like unto
him." It is easy to perceive that Mohammed
gained influence over the minds of his followers, familiar with Christian truth, by his
opposing a partial view, and especially because
the attempt to define what Irenæus had
declared "indefinable" had exposed the truth
to assault through this admixture of error.
Mohammed, however, often confirms the
Gospel truth as to Jesus by revealing the
error which had truth as its counterpart; for
example making "Adam," not Christ, to be
"the Son of God in human form," whom the
angels were called upon to worship, when
Satan refused.[1] Yet he expressly says, (s. 3)
"verily the likeness of Jesus in the sight of
God is as the likeness of Adam; he created
him out of the dust, and then said, Be, and he
was."

While admitting that Jesus was the great
moral teacher who reconciled man to God,
Mohammed in three ways seeks to do away

[1] This refusal of "Eblis," Satan, to worship with the angels
the first who wore human nature is five times repeated (s. 3,
7, 15, 17, 20); indicating the Christian belief that Christ, not
Adam, was the object of angelic worship at the origin of
Satan's fall.

with Christ's expiatory redemption; first, by
substituting "forgiveness" for justification,
as the *end* needed; second, by ignoring the
universal offering of sacrifices as the memorial
of its *ground;* and, third, by denying the
death of Jesus as its accomplished *source.*
All readers of the Koran have noticed that
each *Sura,* except one, and that the last written, s. 9, begins, "In the name of the most
merciful God." Everywhere God is declared
ready to forgive sin to those who pray for it.
Occasionally the word "expiate" is used; as
(s. 3) in the prayer, "O Lord forgive us our
sins, and expiate our evil deeds from us."
Offerings are commended; but no distinction,
such as Moses intimated, is made by Mohammed in his statement (s. 5) as to the offerings
of Cain and Abel; and the sacrifices required
of Moses are but alluded to (c. 2). And yet
sacrifices in all ages and nations are declared
to have been appointed; Mohammed representing God as saying to him (c. 22), "Unto
the professors of every religion have we
appointed certain rites, that they commemo-
rate the name of God in slaying the brute
cattle which he hath provided for them."
No hint, however, as to the *meaning* of sacrifices is given by Mohammed.

Most of all, the death of Christ is studiously and repeatedly explained away. In his leading vision (s. 3) he says, " The Jews devised a stratagem against Jesus; but God devised a stratagem against them; and God is the best deviser of stratagems. God said, " O Jesus, verily I will cause thee to die and I will take thee unto me." Again (c. 4) he more definitely states that his enemies said, " Verily we have slain Christ Jesus the Son of Mary, the apostle of God; yet they slew him not, neither did they crucify him, but he was represented by one in his likeness;" tradition affirming that on Simon of Cyrene, a bad man made to bear his cross, God stamped Jesus' image so that he was crucified in his place. Mohammed adds, " They did not really kill him; but God took him up unto himself;" Christ being translated as was Enoch. No testimony to Christ's personal exaltation was withheld by Mohammed that did not preclude the confirmation of his own special mission. But, to admit the death of Christ, who was sinless, required the admission that he died not for himself but for others; an admission fatal to Mohammed's claim as a prophet on a footing with Jesus as well as with all who went before him. The failure of Mohammed

to prove by the gift of Divine material power
that he had Divine Spiritual vision,—the
early resting of his claim to inspiration on
the literary merit and scientific accuracy of
his statements which are now disproved,—
his later staking of his authority on his
success in arms, which like the crescent on
his followers' banner once waxed but now is
waning,—and above all his effort to attach
his faith to that of Jesus whose Divine mission he everywhere affirms,—all these palpable
testimonies make real his own adopted emblem; for as the waxing and waning moon
borrows all the light it reflects directly from
the sun, so Mohammed was but a dark
satellite of our dark earth, while Jesus is
"the Sun of righteousness," giving light not
only to the earth and its satellites, but also
to the whole Universe.

THE ATONEMENT IN THE PAPAL ROMAN CHURCH.

The near association of early Arabian followers of Mohammed with Christian scholars,
which, after the brief conflict of arms, became
like that of Mohammed himself to the
Christian teachers of his youth, had a special
influence on views of the atonement. This

influence deepened from the eighth to the tenth centuries, while the Mohammedan Universities of Bagdad on the Tigris and of Cordova in Spain were rivaling those of Alfred in England and of Charlemagne in France; during which period the interchange of thought modified both the opinions and the spirit of religious leaders.

The Mohammedan denial of Christ's Divinity seems to have cemented Christian scholars in maintaining it. In the eighth century, indeed, the theory was earnestly urged that Christ was, as are his followers, but an "adopted" Son of God; a doctrine met by Alcuinus the comprehensive scholar of the time, who urged, A. D. 794, that Christ was "as truly the Son of God as he was the Son of Mary." Shortly after this, A. D. 807, an effort to give a supposed exaltation to Christ as Divine led to the doctrine that the Holy Spirit proceeds from the Son as well as the Father; whose persistent urging at last led to the insertion in the Nicene creed of the phrase "filioque;" to which the Greek Church have from the first dissented. A yet more objectionable tendency was the materialistic spirit of ritualism which insisted on the literal interpretation of Christ's words as to the bread of the supper, "This is my body." It was not strange that an age which could accept the claim that even Christ's material body was perpetuated and Divine would demand a view of the atonement specially material.

It was in the eleventh century that Anselm wrought out the elaborate theory of the atonement as a material substitution; which, as we have seen, became allied·to the doctrine of bodily penance, of priestly absolution, of physical purgatory, and finally to that corruption which startled Luther and the Reformers, the barter of papal indulgences. That these were not inherent in the system as developed by Anselm, and that his own view was superior to his theory, is manifest from his own words, as well as from the hold Anselm's theory maintained on Calvin and his less comprehensive successors. That Anselm's view did not limit the merit of Christ's sacrifice in the flesh appears in his declaration, that it "suffices for satisfying what is due to justice for the sins of the whole world, and infinitely more."

That the spirit of even this age allowed dissent from the prevailing doctrine is indicated in the counterpart view presented by

Abelard; whose romantic passion was in keeping with his theological suggestion. Seizing upon the figure of wedded love, everywhere in the Old and New Testament employed to set forth the moral influence of Christ over his redeemed, Abelard goes so far as to contend that "without any expiatory sacrifice" men might have secured to them "the *katallage*, or reconciliation" which is the atonement of the Gospel. It is plain that the suggestion of the modern "Moral Influence Theory" is in the mind of Abelard.

The current of thought in the Roman Church, however, was fixed. With the keenest of philosophical acumen the theory of material substitution was successively set forth. In the thirteenth century Thomas Aquinas urged the figure of a debt paid and of a ransom offered. And yet, as proof that the higher conception of Divine assumed responsibility is natural and undying in every Christian mind, Aquinas says, "If God sees fit to remit that penalty which he has affixed to law only for his own glory, no injustice is done."

The more significant fact is found outside of the writings of the men who in all ages only seem—and that by their own self-assertion—to be exponents of the prevailing Christian thought. From the days of Ambrose, who flourished only fifty years after Constantine, all through Northern Italy, and in the Alpine valleys along the French, Swiss and German borders, as the Sabbath worship of the Church of St. Ambrose is to this day a monument, the clear-thinking rural people, living aside from the superficial thought of the crowded city, took the Word of God. alone for their guide; and in the personal Redeemer to whom it leads, whose history from Eden's intervention they traced, that truth lived which gleamed forth at the Reformation. As Ritschl intimates, that light of Christ's own appointment should have been ever afterwards the pillar of fire to guide and control all future Christian leaders. For, the Reformation was but the breaking forth of the smothered fire of Christ's grace, and the hidden light of his truth, which is always clear and pure in the *renewed* mind.

THE ATONEMENT IN THE GREEK CHURCH.

The history of opinions in the Greek Church, made too subordinate in German authorities, demands for many reasons special study. The copies of the Old and New Testament, prepared under Constantine with great care and distributed to every section of the Empire, were made up of the Greek translation of the Old Testament quoted by Christ and his apostles and of the original Greek New Testament Scriptures. While in all the Western Church, throughout Europe, uninspired translations were necessarily made to take the place of the inspired originals, from the first the language of common worship and of Bible study in the Greek Church has been the unchanged words used by Christ's apostles.

The essential doctrine, on which from the age of Constantine to the present day the Greek and Latin Churches never could agree, has related to the Person of Christ. The Greeks have from the first insisted on the express statement of Christ himself (John 14: 26; 15: 26; 16: 7), that the Holy Spirit in his *essence* "proceeds from the Father" only; and is "sent" by both the Father and the Son. They have so exalted the three natures in the Divine Being as to make baptism a triple immersion; first into the name of the Father, second of the Son, and third of the Holy Spirit. In opposition to both the Sabellian and Arian views they have

insisted on the Divine existence of the Son
originally with the Father; and on the distinction between the human body and soul
as distinct from the human spirit of Christ.
There has followed from this fundamental
doctrine, logically as well as Scripturally, a
rejection of these several doctrines of Rome;
image worship of the bodily Christ; adoration
of the host as worship of his body; transubstantiation, or conversion of the bread and
wine into the body and blood of Christ;
change in the form of baptism from supposed
bodily necessity; the celibacy of the priest-
hood as a bodily virtue; and bodily compul-
sion to conformity in religious faith and
practice. Though not unwaveringly, nor
always consistently held, the connection of
all these divergences of the Grecian from the
Roman faith is seen clearly in the proposed
articles of alliance between the two Churches;
articles penned by skilful lawyers when in
1339, and again in 1439, the progress of the
Turks made the Greek emperors anxious to
explain many differences that forbade union.
Most important of all is the fact that the
Greek theologians so adhere to scripture language that even Ritschl regards them as
lacking "in science;" whereas their philo-

sophic synthesis often hides scientific analysis.

Basil, to this day the highest authority in
the Greek Church, bishop of Cæsarea in Asia
Minor from A. D. 370 to 379, wrote just
after Constantine and amid the Arian controversy. Among his numerous treatises
those on the Holy Spirit, Baptism, the Lord's
Supper and Penitence reveal his view of the
Atonement. He insists that the scriptures
alone are the source of doctrine, referring to
Eph. 2: 20; he makes the New Testament
the guide to Christian truth in the Old
Testament, saying, "I would indeed, first of
all, that those things drawn from the Old
Testament should respond to those correspondingly stated in the New Testament;" and he
urges that when we affirm what "we believe"
(pisteuomen) we use Scripture language. As
to the relation of Father, Son and Spirit he
alludes to the fact that the Latins had but
one word (substantia), for essence (ousia) and
substance (hypostasis); that in former controversies as to the person of Christ, Sabellius
had contended there were in the Divine Being
three aspects (prosopa) though but one substance (hypostasis); and he urges as vital
that we recognize three substances (hyposta-

seis), a word not identical with the Latin phrase three persons (personas).[1]   As to the distinct relation of the Father and Son to the Universe he notes that Christ himself (John 5: 20) says all things are "shown" to him by the Father; and that while all things are said (1 Cor. 8: 6) to come "through" (dia) Christ, all things are said (Rom. 11: 36) to come both "through" (dia) and "from" (ek) God; and he then calls attention to the specific prepositions (John 15: 26) "from" (ek) and "with" (para) used in describing the procession of the Spirit.   He alludes, again, to the fact that God sends the Son, and Christ the Spirit; and that in the commission (Mat. 28: 19, 20) the three are recognized in distinct worship and work.   In presenting the results on man of Christ's spiritual influence he quotes 1st Thess. 5: 23, 24; as to the spiritual meaning of baptism he refers to Rom. 6: 4; and in speaking of the Supper he quotes Phil. 2: 6—8.   In presenting the comprehensive idea of the reconciliation (katallage) or atonement, he pictures Christ as assuming from the beginning the responsibility of Creator (ktistes); this assumption implying that all man's spiritual necessity is

---

(1) Basil's Epists. 38, 69, 125, 210, 214, 258, 263.

met; and that, as God, Christ will be faithful (pistos) to man. Basil finds both the merit and efficacy of Christ's sacrifice in Phill. 2: 6—8; on which passage he remarks: "When, therefore, the soul, trusting in these and such like words, has learned the majesty of the glory and the extreme (hyperbole) of Christ's humiliation and obedience, that *such an one* was obedient unto death for our life, I think that it must be so moved that it would be set right (katorthoi) in disposition and be won to love towards God the Father."

In Theodoret, bishop in Syria A. D. 420, the grandeur of Greek theology is set forth in ten sublime orations on "*Pronoia*" or Providence. The whole sweep of revealed truth as to Christ is made the climactic exhibition of God's Providence. The tenth, entitled the Incarnation (Enanthropesis), traces Christ's history as Divine and human from the origin of the Universe to its consummation. He is the infinite God, Maker of the Universe, of angels and of men. His one aim is, by uniting himself to his lowest spiritual creature—linked as no other spirit is to an animal nature—to raise his whole spiritual creation to the loftiest possible conception of His moral glory. His incarnation

before angels, Satan's pride, Adam's fall, his
walking in Eden, and his meeting Enoch,
Abraham, Moses and Daniel, pass in review·
His birth, life, death, resurrection and ascension, making up his sacrifice, are interwoven
with appeals indicating the moral impression
on all intelligent beings made by such a
sacrifice of such a being. Among them are
these: "If the physician does not contract
the disease he heals, much less did the perfect God suffer stain by taking our nature.
We adore him because he did not entrust our
cure to angels, but took on himself (anade-
chomai) the healing." "He subdued Satan
the tempter in Eden." "So great was the
care of God, the Lord of all, towards man! So
great was the providence which the Creator
showed toward his ungrateful creature! So
great was the considerateness (prometheia) of
that great exemplar towards his own image!
He assumed it from the beginning; he made
it worthy by his own likeness." Theodoret
closes thus: "Taught by His providence
penetrating through all his works, beholding
his unparalleled love towards men, and viewing his immeasurable pity, cease, O man, to
struggle against thy Creator; learn to extol
his beneficence; and reciprocate his benefac-

tions by grateful acknowledgments. Adore the Divine works which are apparent; but inquire not too curiously into those which are hidden. Do not in this imitate Adam. Offer, rather, praise to the Creator, the Provider and the Redeemer, Christ our true God."

Besides these, many other names might be quoted who, like their artist ancestors, exalted science, by embodying its essential truths into one living form. Thus Cyril, who wrote in Egypt about A. D. 430, in his " Catachetics," in the book on Penitence, describes Christ as making man in his own image, speaking to Moses at Sinai, inspiring David and ruling by his providence in all man's history. He illustrates (II. 11) Christ's atonement by referring to David's forgiveness of Shimei when he cursed him; citing the peculiar word of the Greek translation (parabibase) in 2d Sam. 12: 13, " The Lord hath *put away* thy sin," and remarking: " David knew that he who remits, to him it is remitted." As to the efficacy of the atonement for other beings than man Cyril uses (II. 10) this peculiar language: " How far he condoned (Gr. sun-echorese, Lat. condonaverit) for angels we are ignorant." In the " Ekdosis tes Orthodoxou Pisteos " of John of Damascus, written about A. D. 745, a kindred comprehensiveness of views as to the atonement might be traced.

In their earlier controversies with the Latin, or Roman Church, the Greeks were the maintainers of religious liberty in opposition to the Gothic priestly rule introduced at Rome. Basil, in the fifth century, alluding to the image-worship forced on them, says, (Epist. 257) "Our ancestors were persecuted by worshipers of images; now we are persecuted by those who bear the image of Christ;" the latter clause being specially suggestive. A century later, Evagrius, the historian of the Greek Church up to the end of the sixth century, cites (c. 11) the fact that the Emperor Justinian only fifty years before had superseded the Theodosian code by his own; thus restoring religious freedom. In the ninth century, when Photius wrote, the controversy hinged on Church independence, rather than individual liberty. In the eleventh century the error of the Roman Church as to transubstantiation was urged by Michael; who arraigned the sophistry which admitted that Christ's expression, "ye are the salt of the earth" is figurative, but would not admit the same as to the expression "This is my body;" while he, also, censured the adoration of the body of Christ, who laid down his soul (animam) for us. As noted above, the discussions of 1339 and of 1439 turned on the perverted practices of the Roman Church as growing out of their sensual view both of Christ's person and of his sacrifice.

Ritschl, while recognizing little of science proper in the Greek Church of the Middle Ages, yet cites with commendation these words of Nicolaus, in the fourteenth century, on " Life in Christ ": " We are declared righteous, in the first place, because free from accusation, he who had done wrong vindicating us by his death; and in the second place, because we are represented as righteous persons because of that death." The Greek conception is manifestly the comprehensive view of assumed responsibility presented Rom. 8 : 20, 33, 34.

THE ATONEMENT AMONG THE REFORMERS.

The spirit of free thought, as well as of Christian grace, which called out the leading Reformers, did not change the intellectual or emotional cast of mind which leads to an absorption in one or another preferred field in the Universe of Spiritual truth. To this both Dorner of Berlin and Ritschl of Gottingen, in their comprehensive historical survey of theories of the Atonement, agree; as also the general scholarship of our day attests.

As their special national mission the English reformers called back the human mind to the Bible as the only source of truth; the German to redemption by justifying faith in Christ as the essential doctrine of Redemption by Christ; the Swiss to the ordinances of the Christian Church as the essential signs of spiritual grace; and the Dutch to the comprehensive harmony of partial views in "the truth as it is in Jesus." Yet more, as Dorner suggests, while fulfilling their mission the Greek Church held up Christ as a Prophet and the Roman Church as a King, the Reformers, from the need of the times, dwelt on Christ as a Priest; to which must be added that Christ as "all and in all" is the comprehensive view of the Redeemer of all. Dorner farther suggests that in the progress of an age, or of an individual mind, there is a tendency to be absorbed now in the *objective*, *i. e.* the Divine in Christ and his works, and in justification his essential gift; and now in the *subjective*, *i. e.* the human in Christ and his work, and in salvation as the work of

man co-working with God. Both Dorner
and Ritschl insist that the inspired Scriptures were adopted as the only source of
truth, by the Reformers; to which Dorner
thinks they adhered, while Ritschl thinks
they held still to traditional partial views.

On the fundamental point, the making of
the word of God their sole guide, Dorner
thinks there has been a progress towards
entire conformity, realized at last in Schleiermacher. Ritschl regards it the great mistake of the Reformers, that instead of
attempting to reform old and partial theories,
they did not resort to a new and independent
analysis of the inspired records. Dorner
points to the new era in the science of interpretation as applied to the Scriptures revived
by Erasmus and Reuchlin; a science begun by
Origen (Hom. V in Lev.), when he suggested
three fields in the work of interpretation,
the historical presenting the body, the moral
the soul, and the mystic or hidden the spirit
of revelation; and while commending the
Anabaptist principle of strict adherence to
the letter of the inspired word, Dorner indicates the error of so insisting on the literal
meaning of language as to make the expression "Word of God" always refer to Christ,

and never to the Scriptures. Ritschl dis-
criminates between Anabaptists and Baptists;
the former of whom, numerous in former
ages all along the Alps, maintained that the
Scriptures are the rule of faith, and, without
regard to the *mode* of baptism, insisted that
only those renewed by Christ's spirit were fit
subjects for baptism, and that therefore those
consecrated in infancy should be re-baptized;
while the latter, as Menno, maintained that
there should be a return to the spiritual significance of the ordinance both as to its
mode and subjects. Ritschl avows that the
Baptists of the Alpine regions of Germany,
Holland and England, though, as a class,
" guiltless of theology," and often " mystic "
in their interpretations, yet led the way to
Scriptural and thus to comprehensive views
of the atonement.

Applying their principles to past theories,
Dorner and Ritschl indicate their differing,
though only slightly diverging, and sometimes parallel views. Dorner thinks Anselm's " Cur Deus homo," why God became
man, " the harbinger of the Reformation ; "
yet admits there was in Anselm himself a
reaction from his advanced conception.
Ritschl thinks " too high a place " is given

to Anselm; that he "only gives weight to
the suffering of Christ," a vital element in
the Atonement; and that he developed the
fact of "substitution" from Rom. 3: 22—26.
Both agree that he had wonderfully clear
apprehension. Dorner thinks that Aquinas
took "a step" beyond Anselm, showing that
the "incarnation was only indispensable
because of sin" in *man;* that while Aquinas
presented this important *intellectual* view,
Duns Scotus developed the *emotional*
aspect which determines the will; and he
concludes that while Anselm saw God, Abelard man, Aquinas satisfaction and Duns
Scotus merit in the Atonement, "all the way
from Augustine through the Middle Ages to
the Reformation, a common consciousness of
the exclusive merit of God's grace" appears.
Ritschl gives a like place to Aquinas, Duns
Scotus and even to Abelard as presenting,
each, distinct and essential elements of the
one truth; Abelard showing that Christ
"awakens love by His act of love, and that
this love constitutes the ground of forgiveness;" saying, "Aquinas not only as Anselm
makes Christ's sacrifice of infinite value
because of his infinite Divine nature, but
because he is the head of the human race that

is to be redeemed"; that Duns Scotus thinks
"only Christ's human nature suffered, and
hence its merit is not infinite;" and Ritschl
explains this limited range of "objective"
view which each writer takes by the "subjective philosophy" which in each restricts
his view.

The Reformers did not break loose from
the partial views compelled by medieval
philosophy; and hence the cluster of ruling
minds holding partial truth. Luther in the
convent of Erfurt conceived the first element
of redemption, the gift of justification for
past sin; dwelling on the first word of the
declaration "The *just* shall live by *faith;*"
in toiling up the "Scala Sancta" on his
knees at Rome long afterwards, the word
"live" gave him the view of the second element of redemption, the work of salvation;
and this combined view gained from the word
of Christ led him to write: "Then I felt
myself a new man." "From that hour I
saw the precious holy Scriptures with new
eyes. I went through the whole Bible. I
collected a multitude of passages which
taught what the word of God is."

Calvin, closely following Anselm, dwelt on
Christ as a priest; he "exalted" justification

the first part of redemption, as Luther salvation the second part. His office as a political, as well as religoius Reformer, led him to forget that as the word of God is each man's guide, so each man's mind, equally God's gift, is made to be for him its interpreter; and hence not only adherents of the Roman and Greek Churches but his own fellow-townsmen of Geneva were prejudiced against the truth presented by him and his successors; and a reaction followed. Zwingle, going beyond Luther, showed not only that penance, but reliance on the merit of saints, is opposed to Christ's redemption; and that the emblems of bread and wine in the Lord's Supper are but signs of spiritual grace bestowed directly by Christ. Dorner thinks that all the leaders in the Reformation agreed that there are two elements in the atonement; Christ's sacrifice as its ground and man's obedience as its realized fulfilment; all believers being assured of this that "Christ is our righteousness." In reviewing the whole field in the history of doctrines Ritschl says: "I think I may venture to reaffirm, that neither Zwingli nor Luther, either discovered the thought which was the leading one with them as reformers, or rediscovered it, merely by study of the Bible; but

that they imbibed it from a tradition current
within the Church."

Socinus, led from what seemed extreme in
Calvin, denied the Divine in Christ's nature
and the priestly sacrifice in his work; urging
that if the substitution were actual there was
no gain, and no mercy in it; that the character of God and his relation to man are such
that no sacrifice is demanded; and that the
doctrine of the innocent suffering for the
guilty is denied Ex. 18: 20.

Grotius, to meet this extreme of Socinus,
wrought out that theory which his studies as
the founder of the Science of International
Law suggested; that Christ, though a man,
was the representative of the Divine Government; and his sacrifice a condoning, a satisfaction rather than an equivalent for the
demands of violated law. He cites Hebrew,
Grecian, Persian, Gothic, English and Dacian
precedents, showing that in all lands and
ages men have recognized the justice as also
the necessity that one suffer for another in
family, social and national relations; as is
indicated Ex. 20: 5 and 2d Sam. 21: 1—9,
and in attainder for treason. He quotes
Roman moralists and lawyers, Seneca, Cicero
and Ulpian, also modern, in proof that the

fine paid by a friend may condone for the
crime of another; the suffering of the substitute being both an "expiation" (2d Sam.
21: 3) for past violation and a "security"
(Heb. 7: 22) for future obedience; both of
which also are indicated by Paul in his
reasoning addressed to Gentiles as indicating
how human and Divine justice seek this double
element in atonement (Deut. 21: 23; Gal.
3: 10). The defects of his theory are in our
day apparent; first, because attainder, or the
forfeit by children of the property of a father
because of his crime, is in keeping with the
medieval law of primogeniture, but is rightly
denied in the American Republican Constitution; and second because Grotius' view of
the spiritual nature, office, and especially of the
purely moral reign of Christ, is made analogous
to that of governments ruling by force.

Arminius, going beyond both Grotius
and Socinus, and at the same time seeking to guard against what he regarded the
opposite extreme of Calvin, while admitting
the Divine nature and expiatory sacrifice of
Christ, failed to regard the harmony of the
Divine and human in the second part of
redemption; and hence in the first part also.
The points of Calvin's view to which he

objected were, *first*, the absolute election of some to be redeemed; *second*, the limit, even in the Divine intention, of the efficacy of Christ's expiatory sacrifice; and, *third*, the resistless control of the Divine spirit in the work of salvation. In this third and main objection, linked directly to the first and indirectly to the second, Arminius certainly fails to realize the harmony Paul discovers in the *controlling* yet *cooperative* work of Divine power in human salvation (Rom. 8: 14; 9: 16; 2d Cor. 5: 18, 19; Phill. 1 : 6; 2: 12, 13). As a consequence of this failure, in the second objection, the terms merit and efficacy are confounded. Man's control over the mind of his fellow-men by argument is real in its foreknowledge and purpose, yet limited; while God's foreknowledge and purpose are unlimited, since He both works upon man by His truth, and in man by His Spirit. Man's devotion in moral effort is correspondingly limited both in merit and efficacy; while Christ's cannot be limited in *merit*, since it is infinite in value, nor in *efficacy* since it is commensurate with His purpose. Dorner says that Arminius, seeking to remedy Grotius' partial view by making Christ's sacrifice protect God as well as the Universe, makes that sacrifice a substitute, not *as* but *for* the penalty demanded by justice. Hence Ritschl intimates that while the view of Arminius only tended *toward* the truth as to the work of salvation, so his view only tended toward the truth as to the gift of justification.

The Anabaptist and Baptist view, drawn from the writings of Schweckenfeld, Osiander, Menno and others, though differing in minor details, was drawn from direct statements of the Scriptures. Osiander, in advance of Luther, taught, referring to 2d Cor. 4 : 4, and Coll. 1 : 15, that Christ, as God-man, had, in effect, before Adam or angels were created, finished redemption and justification ; and that He imparts to us His Divine nature, whence we are justified, our redemption being in effect accomplished when we are justified. Christ when he came to suffer was truly a man in body, soul and spirit ; growing in stature, wisdom and favor with God and man. His human soul was descended from man ; but God was his spirit's father ; and hence his nature was sinless. God did not *assume* humanity but "*became* flesh," or man. "Christ suffered entirely and unitedly in both natures ; and entirely as to both

natures He makes us righteous and blessed."
" The body of Christ was only the instrument
by which he suffered." "Redemption," including justification and salvation, "must be
sought by faith· in the spiritual reigning
Christ; in whom everything is to be found;
and from Him it must be really derived and
conveyed "into the redeemed." After this
general statement Ritschl remarks: "Rightly
considered this amounts merely to a completion of the fundamental view of the Reformation which has been accomplished by
theology." His statement as to the Church
organization of the Baptists is this: "Instead
of aiming at a community of persons set apart
by God, by His word and by His sacraments,
they aimed at the formation of a sect, consisting of actively holy and sinless persons."

ADVANCING VIEWS OF THE ATONEMENT SINCE THE REFORMATION.

The reality of this advance is indicated in
the character of the historical surveys, traced
with such care and frankness by Dorner and
Ritschl in Germany and by Shedd in our
own country. The title of Ritschl's treatise,
" Justification and Reconciliation" is significant. The sincere effort has been not to

controvert the error always inherent in and enhanced by a polemic defense of any partial truth; but to seek out and combine in harmony the minute observations in the narrow field of the Spiritual Universe to which every explorer must be restricted if his research be thorough. In Germany, historians, critics and theologians have sought a combination of results, as well as minuteness of observation. Neander wished to trace the history of Christianity rather than of the Church; Tholuck, Hengstenberg, Lange, and other interpreters, have sought light from the past as well as from their own convictions; and Dorner and Ritschl have appreciated truth in ancient systems as well as in modern reasonings.

The measure of advance in completeness of view has been differently estimated. Dorner, John-like in charity, thinks that the objective element, love of God's word, irrespective of traditional prejudices, has preponderated over the subjective element, pride of preconceived opinions and practices; while Ritschl, with Pauline logical acumen, recognizes more fully the unconscious influence of a favorite philosophy and of ancestral committal. The marked fact that at the very dawn of the

Reformation, Wickliffe and Luther attained in their translations such clear views of the words *pneuma* and *psyche*, of *kattalage* and *aphesis*, and of *dikaios* and its compounds (see pp. 10-13), surpassing the range of vision which many of their successors have attained, is a most instructive hint to guide in tracing subsequent history. The "single eye," so important in Ritschl's esteem, and the "exceeding broad command" opening to Dorner's vision, when combined, are together the measure of the progress made in a *comprehensive* view of the atonement. The kindred double aim in Shedd's invaluable history, supplementing German histories, though not precluding the necessity of independent review of older writers and especially of personal analysis of Scripture statements, aids greatly the effort of Bible students to attain to *harmony* in the view of the atonement. [1]

During the first century after the Reformation till the early part of the seventeenth

(1) See Doctrine of the Person of Christ by Dr. J. A. Dorner, at Göttingen, transl. in 4 vols. Edinboro 1861 ; History of Protestant Theology by Dr. J. A. Dorner, at Berlin, transl. in 2 vols. Edinboro 1871 ; Justification and Reconciliation by Dr. Albrecht Ritschl, Göttingen, transl. in 1 vol. Edinboro, 1872 ; History of Christian Doctrine, Wm G. T. Shedd, D.D. New York, 1864.

century the views of Calvin and Luther prevailed in their special fields. Dorner thinks that about A. D. 1600 the objective tendency, or the ruling power of Scripture statement, began; that it extended to about 1750; that it was then again succeeded by the subjective rule of reason and personal bias in Bible students; and that since 1800 the power of Scripture truth has held more control over the intellect and heart of Christian scholars. Ritschl thinks he discerns in the progress of thought ever since the Reformation, as also ever before, the controlling influence in Christian students of traditional prejudice and of individual predilection, which has prevented comprehensiveness.

In France the spirit of the Reformation was soon overpowered by the worldly domination; and ritualism prevailed. In Switzerland, after Turretine's masterly restatement of Calvin's views, a reaction to the opposite extreme as to the person and work of Christ succeeded; and rationalism began a reign which has lasted till the present century. In Holland, from A. D. 1600, where Arminian, tending more and more to Calvinistic views, prevailed, three of the five leading theories of the Atonement took shape;

the Dutch Republic permitting the views of
Socinus, Arminius and Grotius to meet in
earnest yet scholarly conflict.

About A. D. 1630 Cocceius called back
thought to the two-fold element in the atonement taught in Scripture; the Old Testament leading to faith in the Redeemer yet
unrevealed, though its special mission was to
secure the fulfilment of law in his redeemed;
while the New Testament revealed and made
prominent the plan of redemption for the
past, yet maintained that fulfilment of law in
the future is also redemption; the Law making men appreciate the Gospel, while the
Gospel makes them appreciate the Law. At
this juncture the philosophy of Des Cartes,
followed by Leibnitz, gave a new aspect to
the harmony of Gospel faith. The doctrine,
now rife, of the harmonious co-operation or
correlation of forces in nature, seen in the
development of plants and animals from
their germs, was extended to a harmony
between Divine and natural agency in creation, in miracles, in human redemption and
even in the Divine nature; man having an
animal soul directly tainted by inheritance
from Adam but a spirit directly created, only
indirectly subject to sin and directly subject

to the Divine Spirit's influence; and God the Father, Son and Spirit operating as distinctly and yet as harmoniously in creation, Providence and Redemption as do the physical, animal and rational natures of man in every human act. At this same era the English Baptist Pilgrim Robinson, driven to Holland, being invited to aid in the discussions between the two theological professors of Leyden, Episcopius the Calvinist and Polyander the Arminian, gave such strength to the former by his knowledge of the Hebrew and Greek Scriptures as also of the Latin Fathers, that, as the Chronicler of the day [1] states, " not only once but a second and a third time he so put to a *non-plus* the adversaries of the truth in this great and public audience, that, as it causes many to give praise to God that the truth had so famous a victory, so it procures Mr. Robinson much respect and honor from those learnéd men and others." In England the extreme view of the "Friends" appeared somewhat later in the "Apology of Barclay," addressed, like those of the early Fathers, to the ruling sovereign, then Charles II; Barclay contending for propositions sub-

---

(1) Prince's Chronology; and also Backus' History of the Baptists.

stantially these: that the foundation of
spiritual knowledge is Christ in man; that
the Scriptures as a guide are subordinate to
the light thus in man; that not only those
who had the Old Testament but devout
Greeks and Romans were saved by Christ
though unknown to them; that justification
is the work of Christ in men who accept his
light; and that a perfection in which there is
growth and liability to sin is the result of
justification.

At this era, as Dorner states, North America began to lead thought as to the work of
Christ. The Puritan theologians, carrying
their aspiration for a new social and civil
life into their religion, sought by fresh study
of the Scriptures and of the Fathers, new
analyses of revealed truth. The confession
of faith of Dunster, selected as the first Presi-
dent of Harvard University because of his
thorough mastery of the Hebrew, Greek and
Latin and his extended range of Christian
scholarship, reveals the comprehensive as
well as harmonious views then attained.

In the eighteenth century religious thought
was occupied in showing the necessity as well
as consistency of Christ's character and work,
and its harmony with the rapid advance in

material and moral science, and consequently in popular elevation and self-government. In England the tendency to materialism from a partial view of Bacon's philosophy, was met by the demonstrative arguments of Clark the friend of Newton, and by the answer to objections in the Analogy of Butler; and these led to new and valuable views of Christ's person and work. In Germany the philosophy of Leibnitz led to Lessing's "Education of the Human Race"; to Swedenborg's view of the Divine in Christ's human nature, in the Scriptures, and in the mere animal or physical being of man as an inhabitant of the present and future worlds; and to Wolff's harmony of the Divine and human in a reign of Heavenly love.

FINAL PROGRESS TOWARDS HARMONY IN THEORIES OF THE ATONEMENT.

In the nineteenth century, as Dorner says, "the regeneration of Protestant theology was realized." Among the numbers who contributed to this in Germany, Dorner thinks Schleiermacher preemiment; the partial truth brought out by many becoming in his works Scriptural and comprehensive. Giving evangelical completeness to Schelling's view

of nature and man as but the manifestation
of God the indwelling and ruling spirit, and
to Hegel's add d assumption that man's
spiritual conception of God and of nature is
fundamentally true to the reality, Schleiermacher sought to establish an inner, organic
and vital relation between the Divine and
human both in Christ and in the Christian;
thus establishing an essential unity not only
in the Divine and human natures separately
existing, but in the union of the two in
Christ and in the Christian. While, however,
Dorner thinks this view an advanced comprehension of Scripture statement, Ritschl
regards it only the theory of Abelard in a
less sensuous form. He recognizes the
" ethical theory" of Atonement as the product of this age ; and he gives this analysis
of its features : " By reconciliation the human
spirit is transported back into fellowship with
God ; by redemption individual appropriation
of the results of reconciliation is secured ;
and justification is subjective realization of
reconciliation." It is an illustration of the
present earnest seeking after revealed light
on the atonement, that Neander, in his
" History of the Planting and Training of
the Christian Church," not only gives an

analysis of each of the epistles, but adds an exhaustive statement of doctrines brought out in their distinctive yet harmonious parts by Paul, Peter, James and John. In the epistle to the Romans he finds the clear distinction between sin in the animal intelligence and impulses, and in the spirit of man; and the reconciliation, or atonement, he finds to be subjective in 2d Cor. 5 : 20 but objective in Rom. 5 : 10.

In England the effort at harmony on the ground of Bible statements was illustrated, early in the century, in Watts the Independent; whom Dorner notices. His sermons and tracts urge that in statements as to the person of Christ "in Arian and Socinian controversies," as well as in Pelagian and Arminian discussions as to the work of Christ, a true study and statement of Scripture truth be followed; saying "I should be very glad if a man might be permitted to imitate the blessed work of angels; and might desire to look into the glorious things of Christ without being suspected of a profane curiosity or a violation of faith." In his youth Watts, with others of his class, had caught the spirit of Andrew Fuller the Baptist; whose "Fundamental Principles of the

Gospel," developed in several treatises, gave
cast, as Prof. Stuart remarked, to modern
New England theology. The Methodist
movement again, uniting at first Whitefield
the Calvinist and Wesley the Arminian,
brought into such close fellowship the Arminian energy in the Methodist and the
Calvinistic stability in the Episcopal Churches
that the best men wished the separation had
never occurred. In Scotland·the movement
of the Free Church called men back to the
Bible, always the Scottish text book; which
has led gradually on, not only to a union of
Old and New Schools in America but to a
Pan-Presbyterian conference fraught with a
future of new development. It is amid
this movement that the note in his last
diary of the world-renowned missionary
explorer Livingstone has been quoted with
enthusiasm even by American Unitarians:
" What is the atonement of Christ, but Christ
himself! "

In Switzerland and France, through the
influence of the "regeneration of Protestant
thought" in Scotland, Gaussen and D'Au-
bigné have awakened a new life and light;
Malan has wedded Arminian convictions of
responsibility with Calvinistic conceptions of

dependence; and the Haldanes, leaving the command of British frigates to herald a comprehensive view of redemption and its author, have led even a Professor of Mathematics in the Univerity of Montauban in South-eastern France to exclaim of the atonement: "It seems too *great* to be true! I have a great *Surety!*"

In New England, where Emmons and Edwards had carried the partial view of the " reign of law" in the Spiritual Universe to an extreme which had fostered the doctrine of Deism in the material universe, the points of departure and return in the dissentients of two schools have led to a study which has made Shedd's history in some respects more valuable than those of German Protestant writers; guiding and increasing the tendency of modern thought to view the atonement as "Moral Substitution." Channing, while opposing the hyper-Calvinistic views, in his discourse on Unitarian Christianity, says: "A difference of opinion exists among us as to * * the precise influence of Christ's death on our forgiveness. Many suppose that the event contributes to our pardon, as it was a principal means of confirming his religion and of giving it a power

over the mind; in other words, that it
procures forgiveness by leading to that
repentance and virtue which is the great and
only condition on which forgiveness is
bestowed. Many of us are dissatisfied with
this explanation; and I think that the
Scriptures ascribe the remission of sins to
Christ's death with an emphasis so peculiar
that we ought to consider this event as
having a special influence in removing punishment, though the Scriptures may not
reveal the way in which it contributed to
this event." Having thus avowed the in-
adequacy of at least three out of the five
theories above grouped, namely the first,
second and fourth, the mind of this great
leader certainly seemed opened to a view in
which each of these might find its appropriate
place. Among like utterances from successors of Channing, every Christian will echo
statements like these in the discourses of Dr.
Bellows. On Rom. 8 : 28, 29, he says: "It is
glorious to know that God has an eternal
interest in our souls and an eternal desire
and purpose to have them conformed to the
image of Christ;" and again on Hag. 2 : 7:
"The moment Christ should be the Desire of
all Nations, he would come. This with-

holding was the *education* of the world.
Christ *promised* did for the Israelites what
Christ *given* has done for us." A very different conviction and feeling is awakened however by the discourse on "The Sufferings of
Christ and the Law of Vicariousness" from
Coll. 1 : 24; in which he says: "If Paul
could do anything to fill up that which is
behind in the afflictions of Christ, it is very
clear that however great and transcendant his
sufferings, were it was nothing peculiar in the
nature of the sufferer which gave efficacy to
his pangs." This certainly makes Paul
superior to Christ, if there was a "lack," as
this interpretation implies, which Paul could
supply. Dr. Bellows certainly corrects his
own statement when he adds : "Sustaining
supernatural and extraordinary relations to
the race * * however much greater and
more efficacious than any, or were it possible,
than all other sufferings of apostles, martyrs
and saints, Christ's afflictions may have been,
the sufferings were the same in kind, design
and effect with theirs ; namely by the law of
sympathy, the example of disinterestedness,
and the influence of costly service to remove
obstacles either in the circumstances, the
wills or the affections of others to the prac-

tice of obedience or the pursuit of holiness."
Channing's deeper conviction, partaken by a
large class of the membership as well as of
the ministry of the Unitarian Church,[1] saw
deeper meaning in the connection of this
text, Coll. 1: 14—24, and also in such passages as Heb. 10: 14; 12: 24.

The indeterminate position of Unitarians
has developed two tendencies in their own
body; that of " Liberal Religionists " as distinct from " Liberal Christians," and that of
the " Universalists." The former, of whom
Theodore Parker is a type, are the severest of
critics on the inconsistency of admitting the
supernatural in Christ's nature and work,
and in the Lord's Supper implying a recognition of an expiatory character in his death,
while nevertheless all which these admissions
compel is not accepted. Liberal Religionists, however, are more inconsistent, in
extolling the moral system of Confucius, of

(1) The writer's father, when in advanced life invited to min-
ister for about a year and a half to a Unitarian congregation in
Massachusetts, found a large portion of the people led to the
view that Christ's sufferings are expiatory; and after he and
his Church retired several united with them. The writer himself had in Washington D. C. many Unitarians as hearers, several of whom he was invited to visit in extreme sickness; and,
when oppressed with doubt they were urged to divest themselves of all views personally cherished or heard from others
as to Christ and his sufferings, and to ask God as they read the
New Testament to guide them to the "truth as it is in Jesus,"
they soon found "rest."

Zoroaster, of Socrates and of Cicero, while yet
they ignore their reasonings as to the expiatory nature and efficacy of sacrifices, and
have little sympathy with men of views like
to those of these sages, who, in the first
century after Christ, became the most intelli-
gent of Christians.	The Universalists, on
the other hand, who a century ago left the
Church of the Puritans mainly from political
reasons, have come now to accept the Scripture statement as to the Divinity and the
expiatory sacrifice of Christ; contending
specially that his sacrifice so avails that all
men are finally redeemed by its efficacy.

The position of Dr. Bushnell, the recognized modern exponent of the " Moral Influence " theory of the Atonement, is a most
instructive closing illustration of the tendency of modern theology as to this central
Gospel truth.	In the ardor of youth, hoping
to be a bond of union between the divided
New England Church, he delivered two
discourses on 1st John 1: 2 ; the first before
the Harvard Divinity School July 9th, and
the second at Yale College Aug. 15th, 1848.
Their point is found in the sentiment, that,
since God " had no pleasure in sacrifice,"
when Christ came, he met the pledge, " Lo I

come to do thy will," by "*his obedience ;*"
and the atonement was "the loving life, the
guiding experience of Christ himself." In
his work published 1866, "The Vicarious
Sacrifice grounded in principles of universal
obligation," he premises: "No doctrine of
the atonement, or reconciling work of Christ,
has ever yet been developed that can be said
to have received the consent of the Christian
world." His own doctrine is.that the self-
sacrifice of the mother, the nurse, the patriot-
soldier, is the type of Christ's vicarious sacrifice ; and he dwells on the vicarious sacrifice
of good angels, of redeemed men, of the Father
and of the Spirit. Christ's vicarious sacrifice
is of like nature; for, "he is not here to die,
but he dies because he is here." His atonement, however, is not mere example as a
moral power, but the accumulated influence
of vicarious sacrifice in sharing disease,
sorrow, and every human ill; his propitiation
is the reconciled sentiment of spiritual beings
when law and government are restored ;
while expiation is an idea wholly classical,
and nowhere taught in the New Testament.
A few years brought an advanced thought;
the error of his former position as to propitiation was recognized ; and in "Forgiveness and

Law," published in 1874, he recalls the latter
half of his former work. His advanced
thought is, that God, as well as created
spiritual beings, is propitiated; the germ of
his conception being found in Edwards' idea
that "God's love and pity fixed the idea"
of man's sin and its penalty "in His mind as
if He had been really they." A hint as to
the Divine influence, is found, he thinks, in
Plato's statement on virtue; that it is "neither by nature nor instruction" we are made
virtuous, but "by the inspiration of the
gods." Expiation, he again insists, is not an
idea in the Hebrew *kaphar* to cover; and
though the idea is found in the Greek *ilaskomai*, the Gospel idea in "justification" is,
as the word implies, to "make righteous;" and
Christ but "reconsecrates the law by his
sufferings in the flesh." The result of such
a theory is that the universal demand of the
human mind for an expiatory sacrifice cancelling past sin, so felt by the Greeks that
they had several words to express it, is *not
met* in Christ's redemption; the "making
righteous" is only present reformation, and
in no sense clearing from past guilt; and the
redeemed man must ever remain unjustified
though pardoned.

The two elements of redemption must be, what all thoughtful minds have recognized in all ages; first justification, not simple pardon for the past; second salvation, beginning in regeneration and progressing in future growing reformation. Theories that omit the former, and Christ's expiation as its source, never have satisfied advanced Christian thought or ripening religious experience. Theories that overshadow the second by the first, are powerless to redeem the world to Christ. Both appear in harmony when the assumed Divine responsibility of Christ as Creator, Sufferer and Surety is recognized.

The growing progress towards harmony in the combining of these two elements is the secret of the "regeneration" of evangelical theology so apparent in every Christian country in the present age. It is the hidden spring of the American effort to make theology "*Biblical;*" "systematic" theology implying a previously accepted general scheme of truth into which all Scripture must be brought; "dogmatic" theology averring that these schemes have taken fixed form in propositions which are, not Scripture statements, but, supposed abstracts of those statements; and "polemic" theology avowing a purpose to disprove supposed error rather than to present manifest truth. Dwight of Yale, Woods of Andover, Miller and Hodge of Princeton, Storr and Flatt transferred to Gettysburg, the Baptist circular letters called forth at Philadelphia in the midst of the American war,—all alike have been calling back universal Christendom to the simple words of inspired Scripture with a voice that Germany as well as England now everywhere echoes. The theory of the atonement wrought out in Biblical theology must be that which is found on the very surface of all Bible statements; the assumed Divine responsibility.

A vital fact tending to this ever approximating harmony of views has been developed in the New World. Leading minds from every nation and national Church of Europe have here met with leaders in every form of dissent; and all Christian scholars have been obliged to re-examine traditional views and see what among past opinions has the character of essential truth. The European conception of Christ's kingdom as made up of nations and of families, naturally drawn from Christ's commission (Matt. 28 : 19) and

from Paul's reasoning (1 Cor. 7 : 14), has come
to be regarded as unattained and as unattain-
able in this as in the apostolic age. There
can be no national Church organization
here; children pass from one denomination
to another; the Churches become necessarily
independent associations of believers in
a certain form of doctrine and of Church
organization; and thus the Churches of all
denominations come to be made up more and
more of positively renewed and avowed
believers. This tendency the works of Dr.
Philip Schaff [1] strikingly illustrate; and its
reflex influence is felt in Europe. National
Churches in every nation of Europe, even to
Russia, have come to recognize as evangelical
dissenting bodies. By intercourse the essential doctrines of the " Creeds of Christendom "
have been found to harmonize; the differences being far less in vital principles than
in external ordinances. In the great confer-
ences of the Evangelical Alliance, and of
national Churches essentially Presbyterian,
the " Communion," *koinonia*, or what is
common in all Christians, has been found to
consist in inward experience and not in

---

(1) Church History, Creeds of Christendom and Harmony of
Reformed Confessions as related to the present state of Evangelical Theology.

outward forms and ordinances.[1] Going farther, the union of denominations in securing common translations of the inspired Scriptures has led to oneness of views; in France, Jewish Rabbis, Old Catholics and Protestants uniting in the Associations of which Guizot was a member and Dr. E. Petavel the Secretary; in England and America denominational demands leading to a harmonious cooperation initiated by the British Parliament. The vital result in this movement is a common recognition of the nature of inspiration as in accordance with evangelical Christian experience; both alike resulting, not on the one hand from the mind's own inherent and self-sufficient energy; nor on the other hand alone from a Divine infused influence exerted on the mind; but both Christian experience and Divine inspiration consisting in the cooperating act of a mind moved by direct Divine influence not mechanically but through its own self-acting energies. When Christian experience such as this is the recognized bond of Church union, and Revelation given through such inspiration makes the Sacred

(1) See twelve papers read at New York, Oct. 1873; especially that of Rev. Mr. Marston of London.

Scriptures the Divine guide of Divinely
renewed minds, approximating harmony in
views of the Atonement must be the result.

APPROXIMATE HARMONY AS TO THE ATONE-MENT IN GOSPEL PREACHING.

The best Theological text-books distinguish between systems of Bible truth for the
school, and practical views to be presented by
preachers. The distinction between teaching
and preaching is marked in the ministry of
Christ (Matt. 4: 23: 11: 1) and of his apostles (Acts 5: 42; 15: 35); and the work of
the school to meet "false philosophy," and
of popular address to win men "to the
acknowledging of the truth," is fixed for all
time in Paul's pastoral instructions (Coll. 2:
8; 1st Tim. 1: 4; 2d Tim. 2: 2, 23, 25; 4: 2).
This distinction, however, relates not to the
"matter" but to the "manner" of Gospel
presentation; for Jesus had no private doctrines not fitted for every hearer (Luke 12: 3).

The word *kerusso*, to herald or preach,
calls attention to the fact that the very words
of the commander must be those of his
mouth-piece; while added explanations must
be distinguished as his illustrations. Catch-
ing this idea, early preachers in the Greek

and Latin tongues spoke in "familiar discourses" called "homilies" or "sermons;" in which, as the discourses of Jesus and of Paul indicate, man's daily observations in nature and among men, and above all his personal experiences, appealing alike to the judgment and to the sensibility of hearers, are made to give reality and moving power to revealed spiritual truth.

Preaching is thus associated with plastic art, as sculpture and painting; which through the eye present truth to the mind. The scenes which the preacher portrays in words, embodied by the artist's pencil, brush and chisel, have in all ages brought home the truths of the Old and New Testament to the minds of children and of people having but childhood's mental development; and these embodiments by art were approved in early Christian times as truly as are illustrated Bibles in our day. The early conversion of the Greeks to Christ brought many artists into the Christian Church. Irenæus in the second century states that statues and pictures of Christ were in his day common among a sect who specially extolled the humility of Christ. In the third century, when heathen converts were thus misled, the Council of Illiberis, in the Pyrenees, passed this decree : " that pictures ought not to be introduced into the Churches, lest that be worshipped and adored which is painted on the walls." In more enlightened regions, however, this abuse was corrected ; Eusebius in the fourth century mentioning that statues of Christ were treasured as works of art in the houses of Greeks and Romans not converted to the Gospel faith ; while Augustine in the fifth century alludes to ideal likenesses of Christ as accomplishing the double end; first, of aiding, ·like a vivid description in words, the effort of each mind to form a conception of Jesus as the perfection of human nature; and second, of presenting, through the varied aspects which different minds frame of the human in Christ, a suggested harmony in the varied conceptions of his Divine union with the Father and Spirit.[1] The representations of art addressing the eye, however, can only aid to elevated conceptions of the " man " Christ Jesus ; while preaching must present the Person of Christ in his united Divine and human character. Most of all plastic art may tend to a perversion of the

---

(1) Iren. cont. Haer. L. I, c. 25 ; Canon Illib. 36 ; Euseb. Hist. Eccles. I. viii, c. 18 : August. de Trin. VIII. 4.

Work of Christ; making an admiration of
the sensuous image to be mistaken for a
devotion to the Spiritual Redeemer. The
infinite wisdom which ordained that "by the
preaching of the Gospel" men "should be
saved" also ordained that the completeness of
Christ's truth, as well as the fullness of His
grace, should thus be perpetuated in all
subsequent ages.

Dorner hints that the purity of the Gospel
doctrines among the Alpine Churches was
specially guarded by the fact, that, without
schools of the prophets the simple and sole
study of the Bible gave at once light and fire
to their unbroken succession of Gospel her-
alds. An added and accordant fact is this:
that the embodiment so largely in "homilies" of the Christian thought of the Greeks,
not only of Chrysostom but of Theodoret and
Basil, made Christ's personal assumption of
Divine responsibility in the combined office
of Creator and Redeemer, the essence of His
atonement. The necessity of giving a palpable and effective presentation of the whole
Gospel made Huss, Luther, Wickliffe and
other Christian leaders to become, like Paul,
specially preachers of the word. As perfect
absorption in the one comprehensive and over-

mastering truth, known from experience
to be true, made Paul, before Hebrew,
Grecian or Roman auditors, to be superior to
all known orators, and to be so recognized a
century after his day by Longinus the Greek
rhetorician,[1] so has it been in every age and
land of Christian history; the tide of Gospel
eloquence rolling northward and westward
till its sublime reverberation echoed from
the Welsh mountains to the American shores.

The approximating harmony of views as to
the atonement in preaching is seen in the
fact, that a stranger casually entering almost
any evangelical Church in Europe, and
especially in America, can rarely judge what
denomination of Christians are assembled.
The comprehensive view of the atonement
which Gospel preachers attain finds an eminent, though not an exceptional illustration
in McLaurin's sermon on "Glorying in the
Cross;" in which, under the headings "the
design, the preparation, the spectators,"
Christ's agony on the Cross is made, indeed
the central and culminating, but only the
instrumental cause, through which the Divine
Agent accomplishes the eternal yet gradually

---

(1) See preserved fragments of Longinus quoted by Hug.
Introd. to New Test. Part II, Sect. 80.

developing design of reconciling His acts
with His character in the view of all His
intelligent creatures. Again, the nice bal-
ancing of apparently conflicting, yet only
reciprocally acting elements in the atonement, which the preacher conceives, has a
masterly if not unrivalled exhibition in these
sentences from Richard Fuller's sermon on
" The Attraction of the Cross: " " What if I
were unable to account for this energy!
What if I should just say that there is an
electric chain which binds our ruined race to
the wonderful Being who hangs there in our
likeness; that as two lutes, of the same form
and tuned exactly in unison, when in the
same room one is struck, the other, though
untouched by mortal minstrelsy, will own a
kindred sympathy and give out soft and
gentle murmers! What if I should only tell
you that something like this takes place;
that when Jesus assumed our form and
entered this world, and was smitten for us,
there was a mystery in his pangs which should
forever cause the sensibilities of human
hearts to vibrate, and waken the play of
feelings tender and unearthly! What if I
should use the idea of an Apostle; and say,
that, in becoming man, Jesus Christ took

not on him the *individual* but the *nature ;* and that, as by this assumption he finished an atonement sufficient for the whole world, and became in this sense 'the Savior of all men,' and the sins of all thronged, and crowded, and gathered, and pressed, in crushing and excruciating weight upon the sufferer, so by the same union there goes forth, there is sent back and abroad and into men's souls, wherever a crucified · Redeemer is preached among them, an *effluence,* a sensation, a sympathy thrilling and irresistible ! What if I should only say this—and the Scriptures would bear me out—it is enough !" " That the atonement affects us so feebly, is owing, not to that atonement's being now too common a topic, but to our contemplating it too little.   How intense, still and soft, yet severely, sublimely intense, is the efficacy of the cross of Christ, where its entire, unmutilated influence is permitted !"

ESSENTIAL AGREEMENT AS TO THE ATONE-MENT IN PRAYER AND PRAISE.

Besides preaching, Christian religious services include worship in prayer and praise. Prayer looks past all acts of the Creator to His personal assumption of responsibility in his creation. Its common character is indicated in the Lord's Prayer; which mankind universally, heathen or Jew, Mohammedan or Christian, child or philosopher, alike recognize as fitting and full in all its ascriptions and petitions. That all true prayer is essentially an appeal to the assumed responsibility and pledged fidelity of the Divine Being as the real Father and Provider of His petitioner is seen in the recorded petitions of Abraham and Job, of Moses and Samuel, of David and Daniel, of Peter and Paul. How perfectly one in their views of the person and work of Christ as our Redeemer the prayers of all Christians are, is seen in the oneness of Romanists and Protestants, of Calvinists and Arminians, of Unitarians and Trinitarians, when in prayer sincerity of spirit and truth to essential convictions is called out.

Again, the hymnology of the Old and New Testament Churches is an approach to harmony of views as to the person and work of Christ. The Old Testament Psalms, and the New Testament hymns beginning with Christ's own song of praise after his interceding prayer at His last supper, are expressions of the mind's actual view and of the heart's real feeling in the utterance of praise for the character, and of thanks for the acts of the Divine Being. In one branch of the Christian Church the Psalms of David meet all the demands of praise; so complete are they in their expression of truth. In the three matin-songs at the dawn of Christ's appearing, those of Mary, Zacharias and Simeon (Luke 1: 46 to 2: 35), the great design, and the greater author of that design, overshadow even his sacrifice. The recorded songs of heaven, "the song of Moses and of the Lamb" (Rev. 15: 3), which extols the victory of Christ over the accuser of angels and men (Deut. 32: 43 as quoted Heb. 1: 6; Rev. 12: 7, 10), and the general chorus of praise to the "Lamb slain," (Rev. 5: 9, 12), ascribe all "authority," as well as "glory," to the "Redeemer" of men, who is also the "reconciler" of angels. (Coll. 1: 20.)

Pliny's mention in the first century (Epist. X, 96) that the Christians sang "a hymn to Christ as God" hints the essential character of all Christian hymnology. In the hymns of the Grecian, Roman and Reformed Churches the character and work of Christ, the Atonement, is substantially the same. In the third century Clement of Alexandria

sings of Christ as a shepherd; in the fourth
century Ephraem of Syria as the sun and a
bridegroom, Gregory as the world's light yet
the light of each household, and Synesius of
Cyrene as the true wisdom; in the fifth
century Anatolius of Constantinople as the
deliverer from sin; in the seventh century
Andrew of Crete as a forgiving Lord; yet
later Cosmas of Jerusalem as radiant with
the glory of Transfiguration, Theophanes as
the restorer of Paradise and the guide to its
bliss, Theoclistus as winning by His love,
John of Damascus as the hearer of prayer
and the Lord of the resurrection, Stephen of
St. Sabas as inviting the sinful to trust and
to rest; and finally, in the fourteenth century, Phile as all in all to His redeemed.

In the Latin hymnology the strain of
praise to Christ is sterner in the character
ascribed to the Redeemer, yet possessed at
times of a deeper plaintiveness. Ambrose of
Milan in the fourth century, introduced that
form of congregational song which not only
has lived in his native city to this day but
has prevailed everywhere in the Reformed
and evangelical Churches. His own sublime
"Te Deum laudamus," Thee we praise, O
God, called forth by Augustine's baptism,

and his numerous hymns extolled by Augustine, present Christ as Creator and Lord, and picture Him as assuming from Creation the ordering of every event in man's future history that He might secure His redemption. On Him "the sins of all are laid;" while yet, ascended after his suffering, He sits on His "ancient throne." With hymns like these the common people in those early Christian ages beguiled their toil by day and their rest at evening; the great congregation, then as now at Milan, chanted them in their Sabbath worship; and hymns, then as always, were the people's theology. In the century following, Hilary sang of Christ as the morning Star, "illuming the inmost chambers of the heart," yet filling the Universe with its beams; and Prudentius pictured Christ as a Gardener watching the bodies of the saints as seed to spring up at the resurrection.

The last of the Roman bishops, at the opening of the Seventh century, originated the sublime Chant called "Gregorian;" and the "Veni Creator Spiritus," Come Creator Spirit, recognized the new birth as the Spirit's permanent work. At the same era, however, at the rise of the "Papal suprem-

acy," the "Pange lingua," the "Salve festa
dies," the "Vexilla Regis" and the "Crux
Fidelis" of Fortunatus, indicate the insensi-
ble steps by which sensuous fiction, betraying
the sincere Christian into trust in forms,
mingles with and finally, like the "leaven of
the Pharisees and Sadducees," corrupts
spiritual devotion. In the eighth century,
again, the English Bede calls back faith in
"the Eternal Word made flesh" by his ver-
sification of the entire Gospel of John;
whose parts, sung as separate hymns, revived
the recognition of Christ's words: "It is the
Spirit that quickeneth; the flesh profiteth
nothing" (John 6: 63). Yet again, in the
eleventh century, Bernard of Clairvaux, who
Luther declared, was "the best monk that
ever lived," in his "Jesu dulcedo cordium,"
his "Jesu dulcis memoria," his "Jesu Rex
admirabilis," and again in his "Salve caput
cruentatum" and his "Ad faciem Christi,"
embodied for the people comprehensive conceptions both of the person and work of
Christ. The corrupting tendency of the age,
however, perverting yet perpetuating true
and inspiring views of the atonement, is
made conspicuous at the same era in the
"Contempt of the World" by Bernard of

Cluny, and in the "Exaltation of the Cross by Adam of St. Victor. A purer as well as a more subduing strain was called forth by the mingled emotions of deep spiritual devotion and of excited animal impulse fostered during the Crusades; a strain successively echoed in the "Come Sacred Spirit" of Robert II of France, in the "Joys of Paradise" of Cardinal Damiani, in the "Sufferings of Christ" of Anselm of Lucca, in the "Broken Gates of Death" of Peter of Cluny, in the "Trinity" of Hildebert, and in the "Praise the Savior" of Thomas Aquinas. The age of Medieval Roman hymnology closes with two chants, the awe-inspiring "Dies Iræ" Day of Wrath, and the sensuous and seductive "Mother dear Jerusalem;" which are types of the double appeal of formal religious service to the æsthetic nature of man; an appeal which may or may not awaken true spiritual devotion.

The spirit of the Reformation added new testimony to the fact that in addresses to God in song human conviction is more simple and sincere, and hence human minds are more in harmony than in the expression of theological opinions addressed to men. In continental Europe, and yet more in English

Sacred Song, this nearness of view is manifest. Critical thought may not, for instance, enter into Watts' sentiment in the line, " When God the mighty Maker died," or into Wesley's statement "A charge to keep I have," "A never dying soul to save;" and certainly clear thought must reject the expression " Freed *from* the law O happy condition" and must adhere to the interpretation "*For* him him shall endless prayer be made." But when in the psalmody of almost every Christian denomination the selections of hymns is made without regard to the theological school of the author, the indication is most manifest that views of the atonement are approximately harmonized in songs of praise to God and to Christ.

UNITY OF VIEWS AS TO THE ATONEMENT
IN RELIGIOUS EXPERIENCE.

The very word "religion," intimating that the spirit of man has been alienated from and must be bound back to His Creator and Ruler, makes every personal inquirer recognize the necessity both of a return to fidelity and of expiation for past fault. Every mind, brought to this thought, is conscious of the distracting inquiry, how far the Author of

his being, and how far he himself as a free
agent, is responsible for his past act. Reason
may hesitate long before solving the doubt;
but when in bodily helplessness and in im-
partial self-examination the decision must be
reached, reason and conscience alike declare
that every one is condemned as guilty in the
past and incapable of personal sinlessness in
the future.

Thus convicted, the suggestion of the
Creator's assumption and implied responsibility arises. No mind can then escape the
conviction that the reciprocal responsibility
of a parent and his child is substantially
analogous to that of the Creator and his
creature. As a mature human being is untrue to nature if not a parent, so the Divine
Being would be untrue to Himself if He
were not the "Father of Spirits." The very
nature of spirit implies self-determination;
that freedom of will makes liability to error,
to wrong and to sin, a consequent necessity;
and, what is more, as men could not
be faithful, compassionate and beneficent
unless some were dependent, erring and
needy, so God could not be faithful, merciful
and righteous unless some among his creatures were sinful. As men become parents

that they may be true to their mission, and
seek to be faithful to their trust though their
children may prove ingrate, so God is true to
His fidelity though some of His creatures
prove unfaithful. In all true religious experience this conviction is reached; that as a
parent's assumed responsibility enhances
instead of diminishing the responsibility of
the child since it calls for fidelity to his
parent as well as to himself, so reason in all
ages has decided as to man's responsibility
for fidelity to his Creator. The desire to
excuse conscious guilt may foster the evasive
inquiry, 'how *far* a parent is responsible for
the character and conduct of a child;' but
this very suggestion in the child's mind is in
itself a perversion of the law of filial responsibility. A like decision, in true religious
experience, is reached by every unbiased
mind; and hence religious experience developes a unity in conviction of responsibility
for personal wrong; personal wrong towards
God being the essential element of sin.

At the same time, everywhere, in His
works as in His word, the Divine Being is
proved to have been seeking, in all His
appointments for man, the highest possible
good of His creature; for good is the *rule* in

His Providence; evil is the exception; and
that exception is the direct result of human
error and depravity. This common conviction of men without revelation is confirmed
by every Greek and Latin writer who describes
the religious experience of thoughtful men.
The fullest confessions as to individual
depravity, guilt and need of Divine expiation
and renovation may be traced in Plato's
Meno, in Aristotle's Ethics (Nic. Eth. iii. 15),
in Cicero's Tusculan Questions (iii. 1) and
Amicitia (c. 24), in Ovid's Metamorphoses
(vii. 18—24) and in Seneca's Ira (ii. 8) and
Clementia (i. 6); all of whom, especially
Cicero and Seneca, indicate that mankind
recognize that the Creator has been true to
His assumed relation, while man has been
untrue to his relation and duty. Still again.
the demands of holiness in God and of justice
in man, as Socrates in Plato's Euthyphron
argues, forbid that the violator of law be
exempted from its penalty; while nevertheless the expressions of submissive trust in
God, frequent in Grecian and Roman writers,
and specially full and explicit in Epictetus
(ii. 16), reveal the confidence of men without
revelation, that in some unknown way,
through man's sincere sacrifices, expiation

acceptable to God and propitiation of His favor is secured. Equally full is the testimony of sages without revelation, that men assume the entire responsibility of their own sin and its penalty when they neglect or offer insincerely such sacrifices. How sacrifices effected that expiation even Confucius and Cicero avowed themselves ignorant; for how the good and holy God could be propitiated when self-inflictions failed to be self-satisfying, and when, too, the infliction of pain on an innocent victim seemed to aggravate instead of allaying self-condemnation, men without revelation never could discover.

Christian religious experience meets this difficulty. The Gospel of Christ is a remedial dispensation; providing in His person and sacrifice a *remedy* for the demands of reason, and a *fulfillment* of the demands of the law. The last utterance of the New Testament, "The testimony of Jesus is the Spirit of prophecy" (Rev. 19: 10), makes the prophecy given to Adam in Eden one with the last record of John the last of the apostles. The Creator himself, having assumed before He made man the nature of His creature, commits himself in promise as well as purpose to all that was essential for the redemption of man. The two elements of that redemption are seen in Abel the first martyr; whose sacrifice of a lamb was a memorial of "the Lamb slain from the foundation of the world to take away the sin of the world" (John 1: 29; Rev. 13. 8); and who, through the faith cherished in his offering, was made as truly "righteous" as if he had always "done good" and never evil (Gen. 4: 7; Heb. 12: 4). This earliest revelation, developed in its meaning throughout the Old and New Testaments, meeting the lack of men still offering sacrifices without revelation,—this accomplishment of what sacrifices only shadowed,—an accomplishment so complete that Hebrews as well as Christians have since Christ's day ceased to offer sacrifices,—makes Christian religious experience to realize, and thus make one, all human conceptions of the atonement.

This experience has displayed alternating as well as advancing stages. It led Abel to sacrifice, Enoch to walk with God and Noah to prepare the ark. It grew in Abraham; when, first, he left his own country, then waited for his heir through whom all nations were to be blest, and finally was ready to offer up that very heir, as God offered His Son, to

fulfil the Divine purpose. Its essential
efficacy appeared, when Job, after long ask-
ing, "How should a man be just with God,"
even declaring, "I know that my Redeemer
liveth," and yet "justifying himself," at
length exclaimed "I have heard of thee by the
hearing of the ear; but now mine eye seeth
thee; wherefore I abhor myself and repent
in dust and ashes" (Job 9: 1; 19: 25; 42:
5, 6). David passed through the first stage
of this common experience when as a child
he recognized the "Lord" as his guiding
shepherd (Ps. 23d); he entered the second
stage when repenting of the "sins of youth"
he realized that the same Shepherd was the
restorer of the wanderer (Ps. 25th); he
reached the third stage, when, startled by
crimes that man could never forgive, he was
assured that His Redeemer would not "impute" his sin to him, but would with his
own sacrifice, fulfilling the mere shadow of
human sacrifices, "blot out" his transgressions; and he ended life in the fourth stage
when his thought of his Redeemer made him
a "present help" in every need, and his
"song in the night" (Ps. 71st). Every
Christian, tracing the experience of Old
Testament believers in the Redeemer to

come, finds views as to the Atonement ever in unison.

When Christ had come, and lived and suffered, and ascended, Christian experience showed that completest of unities, the oneness of "many members" making together "one body." In the Divine enlightment of the twelve chosen of Christ, differing in intellect and impulse, in the three select specimens, the Ethiopian, Saul of Tarsus and Cornelius (Acts 8th to 10th), in the merchant woman, the pythoness and the jailer at Philippi (Acts 16th), the phases of reflected light are numberless, but the orb is one. In Paul, subdued by the person of Christ, preaching of Him first as the "Messiah" to Israelites and proselytes, then as the "Wisdom of God" to Greeks and the "power of God" to Romans, then again as the "hope of Israel" and the desire of all nations" to Hebrew, Greek and Roman rulers, and last, when the hour of his death was nigh, absorbed in the one thought "I know whom I have believed," the different *stages* of Christian experience are as marked as in David. In John, inspired to write in his old age of his Redeemer, absorbed from the commencement to the end of his Gospel and of his Epistles

with the view of Christ as "the Word," that
"was God," was "made flesh," was "the Lamb
to take away the sin of the world," was
"the propitiation for the sins of the whole
world," through whom the little child
receives forgiveness and youth power to
overcome the wicked one, while the aged
fathers think of Him only as He that was
"in the beginning,"—in John the last apostle,
as in Abel the first martyr, Christian experience rests on the personal Redeemer assuming for his dependent and sinful creature, all
that is needed to secure his redemption.

The whole history of Christian experience
after the apostles' day reveals the same full
conception of Christ's complete assumption
in atonement. Justin, a Greek of the second
century, who had fathomed all philosophy
and found no resting place, has all his
longings met in John's teachings. Augustine, a thorough Roman, having exhausted
his lust, his ambition, and then his effort at
self-redemption, lives through the stages of
Paul's experience; developing in that experience, as Ritschl has noted, "the elements
of many theories" of the atonement. Luther,
a type of the spirit of the Reformation,
guided by his experience, sees with an eye so

"single" justification for past sin in that
prophetic embodiment of Gospel truth, "The
just shall live by faith," that he would reject
James' epistle because it seemed at variance
with the first stage of his discovery of the
truth; then again he sees so singly the "life"
of future devotion revealed in that same
declaration, that he magnified the efficacy of
external ordinances, leaving to Zwingle the
completion of the view which a true analysis
of the word "faith," in that same statement,
makes clear; and yet in the *last* stage of his
experience Luther's *theory* was corrected.

Here the connection of Gospel preaching
and of Christian hymnology with religious
experience is suggestive. Any one who
recalls the first stage of his personal Christian experience, fixes on some declaration of
Scripture, or spiritual song, or a self-sug-
gested view of the Redeemer; and these
recalled and suggestive conceptions are
found always to have taken on a comprehensive rather than a partial aspect. The expressions "Come unto me and I will give you
rest," "God be propitious to me a sinner,"
"Lord I believe," "Him hath God exalted to
be a Savior," "I believe that Jesus is the Son
of God," "Believe on the Lord Jesus Christ

and thou shalt be saved," "It is a faithful
saying and worthy of all acceptation that
Christ came into the world to save sinners"
—all guiding stars to the Redeemer—are
comprehensive in their suggested conceptions.
Again the progressive steps, leading to that
first faith inspired by these Scripture declarations, are directed by such strains as these :
the view of Newton, "I saw one hanging on
a tree," awakening conviction ; that of
Watt's, "Till God in human flesh I see,"
kindling hope ; and that of Bowring "All
the light of sacred story, gathers round His
head sublime," inspiring an enduring love.
Yet more, those who observe the final stage
of Christian experience are impressed with
its perfect unity in the single view of the
Redeemer embodied in the last utterances of
inspired Paul. In the strength of manhood
self-confident reason, however sanctified,
cannot but esteem its present conclusions
complete ; though they differ widely not
only from those of other minds but also from
its own earlier judgments. When, however,
as death approaches, the powers of mere
human reason in the "outward man" perish,
while yet the inward man in its spiritual
vision takes on new power, then the pro-

foundest theologian "becomes like a little child." Though his mind be as princely as that of Alexander of Princeton, all his theology is reduced to two simple conceptions; that he is a helpless sinner and Christ a sufficient Savior; and so perfect is his near communion with, and his leaning upon his Lord, that, if any one, adding to Paul's words, quotes, "I know *in* whom I have believed, he will remonstrate· because "a preposition" is allowed to "separate him from his Redeemer."

The universal recognition in Christian experience of this supreme and comprehensive view of all the parts of Christ's work as subordinate to His personal assumption and interposition explains many apparent anomalies in Christian history. It is indicated when a Unitarian echoes Livingtone's latest record, "The Atonement of Christ! What is it but Christ himself!" It explains how an eminently mathematical reasoner, like Comte, having ignored the facts of religious experience because they had never been so presented as to seem worthy consideration, when suddenly assured of their reality by the death-bed utterances of one he tenderly loved, should recast his already published

"Système de Philosophie," making religious truth not only fundamental but the basis of all truth. It explains, moreover, why it is that minds that have attained the greatest eminence as lawyers, jurists and statesmen, when like Guizot and Webster they have experienced an early and transforming religious change, attain not simply by an *a posteriori* induction to all-controlling religious faith, but are held by an *a priori* demonstration, from whose bonds they can never break away though inconsistent in life.

The essential view of the Atonement which alone gives rest to the mind seeking for self-satisfying reconciliation, propitiation and expiation when oppressed with a sense of guilt and sinfulness is combined and harmonized in the record of an experience reported some years since by Dr. Duff the eminent Scotch Presbyterian missionary at Calcutta, India. He was a Brahmin; and had first gone through all the philosophy of the Vedas, which recognize that sacrifices have from time immemorial been offered for expiation; that in the earliest, or Mimansa philosophy, "the death of a victim" was recognized as essential in atonement; while in the Institutes of Menu the last of the Vedas, it is declared (XI. 54) "Penance must invariably be performed for expiation." Unsatisfied with Brahmin philosophy he had turned to Budhism ; which taught that deity was incarnate in Budh ; which preserved this incarnate Deity in two distinct forms, one of Budh seated at rest, the other in the two images of Gaudama, the one worried by a serpent biting his heel and the other with the serpent crushed under his heel ; but, while thus preserving the tradition of Eden, with its subjection for a time to the tempter and its promise of the Redeemer, nevertheless recorded that Budh died like a man, there being no expiation provided in his death. Disappointed in Budh as the incarnate Deity he next turned to Mohammedanism, the religion of the last conquerors of India ; in which he read the Old and New Testament revelations given by Divine testimonials transcending the magic arts of the Brahmins ; and which declared that Jesus, born without an earthly father, was God's special messenger to man, that his disciples claimed that he died as an expiatory sacrifice, but that it would have been unjust in God to have allowed an innocent being so "near to the Divine Being" thus to suffer ; and which, to meet the lack of atonement, declared in every successive vision the mercy of God and forgiveness for those who embraced Islamism. More than disappointed, awakened to a new hope by the Koran, hearing of the men who had brought to India the Old and New Testament, he came to the Christian missionary. For days and even weeks he read the Scriptures and listened to the teacher's expositions and reasonings; but gained no clear and satisfying conception of the atonement offered by Christ. At length, when poring, one day, over the epistle to the Romans, the fullness of Gospel truth broke upon his mind; and, overjoyed, he hastened to tell his discovery to Dr. Duff. "And why," asked the Christian teacher,—"why were you not satisfied with the Koran which declares so fully the mercy of God in forgiving sin?" "Ah," exclaimed the now enraptured Brahmin, who had passed through Budhism and Mohammedanism to reach the Christian faith, "I was not satisfied to be *forgiven* through the *mercy* of God. I wanted to be *justified;* and to see how God was *just* in justifying a sinner!" He had found the solution in the assumed responsibility of Christ for sin and redemption; who, as man's

Creator subjected him to his sinful condition in order that He might show His own glory, and win all His creatures to adoring love, in taking as his own the condemnation of the sinner and in justifying every man who accepts his mediatorial sacrifice.

CONCLUSION.

Atonement in its nature is *reconciliation* between one injured and his injurer; and its producing causes are *expiation* for past injury and *propitiation* because of future pledges. Atonement for sin against God, as the words of every human language and the united sacrifices and vows made by men of all nations attest, is reconciliation of man to God by confession of sin and offered expiation, and also reconciliation of God to man by manifestation of His holiness through proffered propitiation.

Atonement in the relation of a parent to a child, implying assumed moral responsibility in the origin of the relation, makes the parent the first to offer the sacrifice of expiation and proffer the pledge of propitiation; while it enhances the responsibility of the child for his sin if he dishonors his parent's fidelity by trifling with his proffer. Atonement in the relation of God the Creator to man his creature, implying assumed responsibility for the welfare of the being He has formed for His own glory, makes the offer of expiation and the proffer of propitiation to be God's gift to man, not man's to God; in rejecting which offer and proffer man assumes as his own his sin and its guilt.

In the Divine atonement, provided and pledged before man's creation, God united to human nature is the efficient cause; His glory as the source of blessing to His creatures is the final cause; His union, during the entire earthly existence of man, to human nature, culminating* in His death on the cross, is the instrumental cause; the moral influence of this sacrifice on the Universe of intelligent beings is the formal cause; · and the progressing work of redeeming individual men is the material cause. The Atonement, in its comprehensive idea and in its combined conception, is Christ assuming as Divine and human the responsibility of human sin and of man's redemption from it; in himself becoming the expiatory sacrifice for human guilt and the propitiatory surety for human restoration.

The declarations of Scripture from Genesis to Revelation present Christ as the Redeemer

before He was the Creator of man ; from the
first imputing man's sin to His own account
as if belonging to it; and reckoning, His
righteousness as accredited to man's account
whenever His proffer is accepted in faith.
Reason in all ages has found the perfect
balance of this assumed responsibility to be
presented in the imperfectly recognized limit
of parental responsibility; even from the day
of man's first father. Religious experience,
the vital and final test of all harmonized
human convictions, sees the Atonement,
fully and only, in Christ's assumed responsibility.

Writer's Parting with Readers.

During the year of thoughtful revisal of these pages advocates like J. Cook and J. F. Clarke have spoken. A circle of friends have inquired as to the central truth, subordinate issues, statements of Divine and human responsibility, and estimates of individual writers like Calvin and Arminius presented in this volume. Hesitating to criticise and yet more to construct, striving not to find error but truth common to all earnest minds, the inextinguishable conviction of childhood experience, the recognition by men of ripe judgment and removed from controversy, and, above all, the sweet relief expressed by anxious and often dying inquirers, have constantly added new radiance to the light of reason and revelation. These combined influences have compelled the issue of this volume as a *duty;* from which no fear of misconception should allow the writer to shrink.

This view of the Atonement as Assumed Divine Responsibility has involved constant reference to to two other topics of vital present interest, whose consideration may follow this treatise ; " Creation," both of matter and spirit, as it relates to developement from germs and evolution without germs ; and " Immortality," as it respects material and immaterial essences, especially the necessary eternity of the human *spirit* as distinct from *soul*.

INDEX TO ATONEMENT.

INDEX.

INDEX.

INDEX.

INDEX.

INDEX.

INDEX.

INDEX.

INDEX.